NEW WORLDS.
NEW BATTLES.
ASH WILL RETURN...

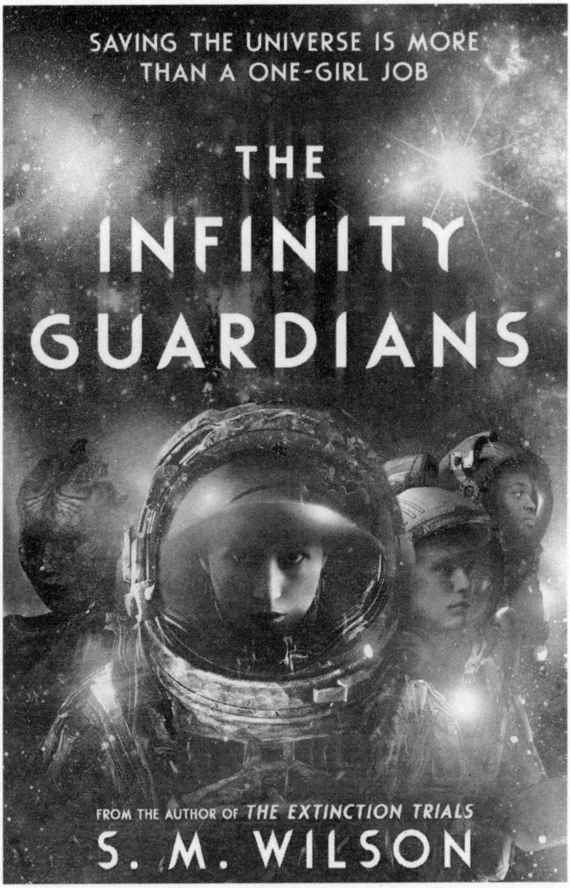

SAVING THE UNIVERSE IS MORE
THAN A ONE-GIRL JOB

THE
INFINITY
GUARDIANS

FROM THE AUTHOR OF *THE EXTINCTION TRIALS*
S. M. WILSON

COMING SOON

For the latest news follow

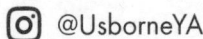 @UsborneYA

ACKNOWLEDGEMENTS

I have always been a huge fan of the original *Star Wars* series and *Star Trek* – mainly *The Next Generation*, but I have a soft spot for all forms of *Star Trek*.

I love the science, and the storylines, and the "what if" factor, in that big wide expanse of space. But YA books only have a few space stories, so I want to send out a huge big, squeezy hug to my fabulous agent Sarah Hornsley from The Bent Agency (and baby Hazel who joined us on this journey!), and to my editor Sarah Stewart at Usborne, for believing that I could write them a mysterious, action-packed space story before it was even entirely created. My own version of Yoda, mixed with a little Captain Picard, made his way into my *Extinction Trials* stories and has managed to sneak into *The Infinity Files* too, so thank you all for allowing me to do that. It makes my little space heart very happy.

There's a great team at Usborne who have all played a part in bringing this book to life. Thank you to my second editor Stephanie King, and to my poor copy-editor Tilda Johnson. Tilda must weep every time she has the job of copy-editing my stories because I know exactly how bad they are. Repeated and overused words, occasional name changes, missing words, random plot points – thank you for making this story readable! For turning my words into beautiful book pages, thank you, Sarah Cronin – I'm always so excited to see them! For Alice Moloney and Gareth Collinson, thanks for proof reading and picking up any of my errors. For PR and marketing, a big shout out to Katarina Jovanovic and Stevie Hopwood for always championing my stories and selling them to the world. For my cover designer Will Steele, and to my cover illustrator Martin Grohs, a huge thank you for your patience and creativity when dealing with a pain-in-the-neck author and giving me a cover that really captures the heart of the story and my main character Ash. Every time I look at it I have the biggest smile on my face.

And finally to my readers. Thank you so much for allowing me to fill your lives with stories. I'm writing these acknowledgements at a strange time. So many people in the UK are in lockdown – a situation none of us could ever have imagined. My day job is nursing, so my days have been longer with virtually no time for writing at all. My partner-in-crime at work is Kathleen Winter, and she's been the one person who's kept me sane through the stress and heavy workload. We say we have a shared brain, and she often knows my words before I say them, just like I know hers! I understand this has been hard on many people, and I want you to know that I'm thinking about you all, and hoping by the time this book comes out, we've all got through the other side happy and healthy.

S. M. Wilson x

In Stormchaser and Lincoln's ruined world, the only way to survive is to risk everything. To face a contest more dangerous than anyone can imagine. And they will do anything to win.

But in a land full of monsters – human and reptilian – they can't afford to trust anyone. Perhaps not even each other...

"This is, at last, the new Hunger Games. *It's perfect."*

Waterstones Bookseller review

This book is for Hector, my accomplice, and Mateo the boycotter.
Also for my mother and my girlfriends, including Veronica.
It obviously belongs to Catalina and her father, who wrote it with me.

Tear This Heart Out

THAT YEAR, MANY things happened in Mexico. For one, Andrés and I were married.

I met him in one of the cafés under the arches. Where else would it have been, since in Puebla everything happened in the arcades, from courtships to assassinations—as if no other place existed.

He was over thirty, and I wasn't yet fifteen. I was sitting with my sisters and their boyfriends when we saw him walking toward us. He told us his name and sat down to talk. I liked him. He had large hands and a mouth that could be frightening, but when he laughed he made you want to trust him. As if he had two mouths. After he talked for a while, his hair sort of shook loose and fell over his forehead as obstinately as he pushed it back, a habit he had all his life. He wasn't what you would call a handsome man. His eyes were too small and his nose too big, but I had never seen eyes so alive, or known someone with such assurance.

Suddenly he put his hand on my shoulder and said, "Isn't it true that they're all assholes?"

I looked around without knowing what to say.

"Who?" I asked.

"Say yes. I can see in your face you agree," he said, laughing.

So I said yes, and again asked who.

One of those green eyes closed in a wink. "All these *poblanos,* you pretty thing. The people here in Puebla. Who else?"

Of course I agreed. I'd always thought that *poblanos* strutted around acting as if they'd held the deed to the city for centuries. Not us, the daughters of a campesino who had stopped milking cows because he'd learned to make cheese. Not him, Andrés Ascencio, who had become a general through luck and every brand of cunning short of having been born into a name with a coat of arms.

He wanted to walk us home, and from that day on he visited us often, to flirt and to lavish attention on me and my family, including my mama and papa, who were as entertained and flattered as I was.

Andrés told them stories in which he always emerged triumphant. There was no battle he hadn't won, no dead man he hadn't killed for having betrayed the Revolution or the Jefe Máximo or whoever.

We all took a liking to him. Even my older sisters—Teresa, who at first thought he was a dirty old man, and Barbara, who was scared stiff of him—ended up having as good a time with him as Pía, our youngest sister. And he bought my brothers' eternal devotion by taking them for rides in his car.

Sometimes the General brought flowers for me and American chewing gum for them. I was never too excited about the flowers, but I felt important arranging them while he smoked a cigar and talked with my father about the hard life of the campesino, or the principal leaders of the Revolution and the favors each of them owed him.

Later I would sit down and listen to them, offering opinions with all the brashness born of my father's presence and my absolute ignorance.

When the General left, I would go to the door with him and let him kiss me, but only for a second, as if someone were watching. Then I would run outside, chasing after my brothers.

We began to hear rumors: Andrés Ascencio had many women, one in Zacatlán and another in Cholula, one in the barrio of La Luz and others in Mexico City. He deceived young girls, he was a criminal, he was a madman, and we'd be sorry.

We were sorry, but years later. Then, my papa made jokes about the circles under my eyes, and I hugged and kissed him.

I liked to kiss my papa and feel that I was eight years old again, with red shoes and a hole in my sock and a bow on both braids on Sundays. I liked to imagine it was Sunday and I could still climb on the burro that never carried milk on that day, and ride to the alfalfa field to hide and shout, "I bet you can't find me, Papa." I waited to hear his steps and his voice coming nearer— "Where is my little girl? Where could my little girl be?"—until he pretended to trip over me. "Here's my girl!" he would say, and throw himself down beside me, holding my legs and laughing.

"Now my girl can't go anywhere, she's caught by a toad who wants her to give him a kiss."

And in fact I had been caught by a toad. I was fifteen and I wanted wonderful things to happen to me. Which is why I agreed when Andrés asked me to go with him to Tecolutla for a few days. I had never seen the ocean. He told me it turned black at night and transparent under the noon sun. I wanted to see it. I left a note saying, *Dear Mama and Papa. Don't worry, I've gone to see the ocean.*

What I really did was give myself the fright of a lifetime. I had seen horses and bulls mount mares and cows, but the erect cock of a grown man was different. I let myself be touched without moving, without opening my mouth, stiff as a paper doll, until Andrés asked me what I was afraid of.

"Nothing," I said.

"Then why are you looking at me like that?"

"It's because I'm not sure that will fit in me," I answered.

"But of course it will, girl, just let yourself go," he said, and swatted me on the bottom. "Look how stiff you are. Of course it won't if you're like that. Relax. No one's going to eat you if you don't want it."

He started again, touching me everywhere, not in a hurry any longer. I liked it.

"Now you see I don't bite," he said, in a tone of voice that made me feel like a goddess. "Look, you're nice and wet." He spoke in the same tone of voice my mother used when she was proud of some stew she had cooked. Then he entered me, moved back and forth, panted, groaned, as if I weren't stiff as a poker beneath him again.

"Don't you *feel* anything? Why don't you *feel* something?" he asked afterward.

"I did feel something, but at the end I didn't get it."

"But it's the end that matters," he said, addressing the heavens. "God, these women! When will they learn?"

And he fell asleep.

I was awake all night, on fire. I paced and paced. A liquid ran down my legs. I touched it. It wasn't mine, it had come from him. At dawn I decided to take all my thoughts back to bed.

When he felt me crawl in beside him, he threw one arm across me. We woke up in each other's arms.

"Why don't you teach me?" I asked him.

"Teach you what?"

"Well, to *feel*."

"That's not something someone can teach you. You learn," he answered.

So I decided to learn. As a start, I worked on being relaxed, so much that at times I seemed half-witted. Andrés talked and talked as we walked along the beach. I swung my arms, let my mouth hang open, as if my jaw was going to fall off, pulled my stomach in and pushed it out, tightened and relaxed my buttocks.

What did the General talk about? I don't exactly remember now, but it was always something about his political plans, and he talked at me as if he were talking to a wall, not waiting for me to answer, not asking my opinion, driven only by the need for an audience. During that period, he was making plans to win the governorship of the state of Puebla from Governor Pallares. He didn't give Pallares credit for having any sense at all, but he worried about him as much as if he did.

"He must not be such an asshole after all," I said to Andrés one evening. We were watching the sunset.

"Of course he's an asshole. And you, why are you butting in? Who asked your opinion?"

"It's all you've talked about for four days. You've given me enough time to form an opinion."

"Listen to our little señorita. She doesn't know how babies are made but now she wants to tell generals what to do. I'm getting to like her," he said.

When the week was over, he took me back home as casually as he had taken me away, and then disappeared for nearly a month.

My parents welcomed me back without question or comment. They were not very secure about their future and they had six children, so they decided to celebrate the fact that the ocean was so beautiful and the General so kind as to have taken me to see it.

"Why don't we see anything of Don Andrés?" my papa began to ask after we hadn't seen the General for nearly two weeks.

"He's busy trying to beat General Pallares," I said. More than thinking about Andrés, I'd become obsessed with this thing about *feeling*.

I wasn't going to school anymore; hardly any girls went to school after the first six years, but I'd gone a few more because the Salesian nuns had given me a scholarship to attend their clandestine school. They were forbidden to teach, so I didn't have a diploma or anything, but it was worthwhile. You were grateful for anything. I learned the names of the tribes of Israel, the names of the leaders and descendants of the tribes, and the names of all the cities and all the men and women who figured in biblical history. I learned that Benito Juárez was a Mason and had returned from the other world to tug at a priest's cassock and tell him not to bother to say masses for him anymore because he had been in hell for quite some time.

In all, I came out with passable handwriting, some knowledge of grammar, a little arithmetic, no history, and several crossstitched tablecloths.

Once I was in the house all day, my mother put her energy into teaching me to be a first-rate housewife, but I would refuse to mend socks and pick out the bad beans. That left me with a lot of time to think, and I began to lose hope.

One evening I went to see the gypsy woman who lived in the

barrio of La Luz and had a reputation for being expert in matters of love. There was a line of people waiting their turn. When finally I went in, she sat down across from me and asked what I wanted to know.

I said to her, very seriously, "I want to know how to *feel*."

She sat looking at me, and I looked back at her. She was a fat, fleshy woman. Half of her very white breasts bulged above the neckline of her blouse. She wore brightly colored bracelets on both arms and gold earrings swayed from her earlobes, brushing her cheeks.

"No one comes here for that," she said. "I don't want your mother to come complaining to me later."

"So you don't *feel*, either?" I asked.

In answer, she began to disrobe. In one second, she had unfastened her skirt, peeled off her blouse, and was standing naked before me without underpants or slip or brassiere.

"We have this little thing here," she said, placing her hand between her legs. "You feel with that. We call it 'the bell' but it must have other names. When you're with someone, think of that place as the center of your body, think how all good things come from there—how you think with it, hear with it, and see with it. Forget you have a head and arms, put yourself there, all of you. And see if you don't feel something."

Then, in another second, she had her clothes back on and was pushing me toward the door.

"Now go. I won't charge you because I only charge for telling lies, and what I told you is the truth. I swear by this," and she kissed the cross she made with two fingers.

I went back home certain that I knew a secret that was impossible to share. I waited until all the lights were out and Teresa and Barbara seemed fast asleep. I put my hand on "the bell" and rubbed it. Everything important was there; that was where I saw, where I heard, where I thought. I had no head or arms or feet or navel. My legs felt stiff, as if they were going to drop off. Oh yes, everything *was* there.

"What's the matter, Cati? What are you huffing about?" Teresa asked, terrified. The next morning, she got up telling everybody that I had woken her up making strange noises, as if I were drowning. My mother was very worried, and even discussed taking me to the doctor because that was how Camille's tuberculosis had begun in the Dumas novel.

Sometimes I still feel nostalgic, wishing I'd had a church wedding with a long red carpet, and that my father had led me to the altar as the organ played and everyone looked at me.

I always laugh at weddings. I know that all that nonsense will end in the boredom that inevitably comes from going to bed and waking up every day with the same potbelly beside you. But the music and the walk down the aisle . . . That moment belongs to the bride, and it still provokes in me feelings more of envy than of amusement.

My wedding wasn't like that. I wish my sisters had been bridesmaids in pink, all silly and sentimental, floating in organdy and lace. My papa in black and my mother in a long dress. For myself I would have liked a dress with full sleeves and a high neck, and a train stretching all the way down the steps from the altar.

That wouldn't have changed my life, but I could have treasured the memory, the way other married women do. I could have remembered myself walking back up the aisle, holding Andrés's arm, and nodding from the heights of my newly acquired nobility, from the status everyone grants a new bride as she returns from the altar.

If I'd had my way, I would have been married in the cathedral, because it had the longest aisle. But I didn't get to choose. Andrés convinced me that it was pure bullshit, and that he couldn't afford to jeopardize his political career. He had fought in Jiménez's anti-Cristero war against the church; he owed loyalty to the Jefe Máximo, and there wasn't a chance in hell he would be married in a church. A civil ceremony, yes, civil law had to be respected, although best of all, he said, would be a military ceremony.

That was just something to say, because in fact we were married like any ordinary soldier and his bride.

One day he stopped by in the early morning.

"Are your mama and papa here?" he asked.

They were, it was Sunday. Where else would they be but home, as they were every Sunday?

"Tell them I've come to get all of you so we can go get married."

"Who?" I asked.

"Me and you," he said. "But we have to take the others."

"You haven't even asked me if I want to marry you," I said. "Who do you think you are?"

"What do you mean, who do I think I am? Well, I think I'm me, Andrés Ascencio. Stop arguing and get in the car."

He went inside, exchanged three words with my papa, and came back out with my family trailing behind.

Mama was crying. I liked that because it added a touch of tradition. Mothers always cry when their daughters get married.

"Why are you crying, Mama?"

"Because I have a feeling, daughter."

My mother spent her entire life having "feelings."

We went to the civil registry. Some friends of Andrés were waiting there: Rodolfo, his closest friend, and Sofía, Rodolfo's wife, who stared at me with contempt. I guess my legs and eyes infuriated her because she had skinny legs and squinty eyes. Even though her husband was the undersecretary of war.

The judge was short, bald, and solemn.

"*Buenas*, Cabañas," said Andrés.

"*Buenos días*, General. What an honor to have you here. Everything is ready."

He pulled out an enormous ledger and took his place behind a desk. I was still trying to console my mama when Andrés yanked me forward to stand beside him, facing the judge. I remember the judge's face, flushed and red-veined, like the face of an alcoholic. He had thick lips and spoke as if he had a fistful of peanuts in his mouth.

"We are gathered here to celebrate the marriage of General Andrés Ascencio to Señorita Catalina Guzmán. In my position as representative of the law, the only law needed to establish a family, I ask you, Catalina: do you take General Andrés Ascencio, here before us, to be your husband?"

"All right," I said.

"You have to say 'yes,'" the judge corrected.

"Yes," I said.

"General Andrés Ascencio, do you take Señorita Catalina Guzmán to be your wife?"

"Yes," said Andrés. "I do. And I promise her the respect the strong owe the weak, and all that, so you can spare us the lecture. Where do we sign? Take the pen, Catalina."

I didn't have a signature, I'd never had to sign anything, so all I did was write my name in the elegant slanting hand the nuns had taught me: *Catalina Guzmán*.

"'De Ascencio,' put that here, señora," said Andrés, who was reading over my shoulder.

Then he added a quick scrawl that with time I came to recognize, and could even forge.

"Did you put 'de Guzmán'?" I asked.

"No, child, that isn't how it's done. I protect you, not you me. You become part of my family, you become mine," he said.

"Yours?"

"What about the witnesses?" called Andrés, who by now had taken over from Cabañas. "You, Yúñez, sign here. And you, Rodolfo. Why else did I bring you, anyway?"

As my mama and papa were signing I asked Andrés where his parents were. Until then, it had never occurred to me that he must have a mother and father.

"Only my mother is still living, but she's not well," he said in a voice I heard for the first time that morning, a voice he used only when speaking of her. "But that's why Rodolfo and Sofía came, my friends. So I wouldn't be without family."

"If Rodolfo signs for your family, then I want my brothers and sisters to sign, too," I said.

"You're crazy, they're only kids."

"But I want them to sign. If Rodolfo signs, I want them to sign. They're my friends," I said.

"Let them sign, then. Cabañas, have the kids sign, too."

I will never forget the sight of my sisters and brothers going up to add their signatures. We had come from Tonanzintla so recently that they still had a country look about them. Barbara was sure I had lost my mind, and stared at me with frightened eyes. Teresa didn't want to play this game. Marcos and Daniel signed, very serious, their hair plastered down in front and standing straight up in the back. They always combed their hair as if someone were going to take their picture from the front. The rest didn't matter. We had pinned a bow in Pía's hair that was almost as big as she was. Her eyes came to the level of the desk, and from the desk up, she was one enormous red bow with white polka dots.

"That's a pretty fancy bow for a little girl," said Andrés. "Don't ever tell me that no one in your family puts on airs." He pinched my waist and spoke loud enough for my papa to hear. I didn't realize then why he said it; today I'm sure it was for my papa's sake. Over the years, I learned that Andrés never said anything that didn't have a point. And that he would have enjoyed the chance to threaten my father. The previous afternoon he had spoken with him. He told my papa he wanted to marry me, and that if Papa didn't like the idea, he, General Ascencio, had ways to convince him—he could make it easy or hard.

"Let's make it easy, General. It will be an honor," my father had said, incapable of opposing him.

Years later, when Andrés's daughter Lilia wanted to get married, Andrés told me:

"Do you think I'm going to give away my daughters the way your father did you? Not on your fucking life. No son-of-a-bitch is going to come along and carry off *my* daughters overnight. The cretins who want to screw my daughters are going to come for them well in advance, and give me time to check them out. I don't give my girls away as a gift. The man who wants them will have to beg me and put out to get them. If there's a deal to be done, we'll do it; if not, he can take a flying leap. And they're getting married by the church, now that Jiménez got fucked in his fight with the priests."

Pía didn't know how to write her name, so she drew a little circle with two eyes. The judge patted her bow and took a deep breath so no one would notice that he was losing patience. Fortunately, that was the end of it. Rodolfo and Chofi signed quickly. Those two fat pigs were dying of hunger.

We went to have breakfast in the arcades. Andrés ordered coffee for everyone, chocolate for everyone, tamales for everyone.

"I want orange juice," I said.

"You'll have coffee and chocolate like everyone else. Don't upset things," Andrés scolded.

"But I can't eat breakfast unless I have juice."

"What you need is a good war. Right here and now you will learn to eat breakfast without juice. Where do you get that business about having to have juice?"

"Papa, tell him that I have juice in the mornings," I asked.

"Bring the girl orange juice," my papa said, with such a tone of defiance that the waiter ran to get it.

"All right. Have your juice. You'd think you were a gringa. What campesino starts the day with juice in this country? Don't get any ideas about always getting what you want. Life with a military man isn't easy. Get that into your head once and for all. And you, Don Marcos, remember that she isn't your little girl anymore, and that at this table, I have the say."

There was a long silence, during which the only sound was that of Chofi's teeth biting into a warm puff pastry.

"Well?" said Andrés. "Why is everyone so quiet if we're having a party? Your sister just got married. No hurrahs? No shouting?"

"Here?" said Teresa, who had a deep-seated dread of looking foolish. "You're nuts."

"What did you say?" thundered Andrés.

"Good luck! Congratulations!" shouted Barbara, throwing rice at us. "Lots of luck, Cati," she said, and threw rice in my hair and rubbed it in, patting and stroking. "Lots of luck," she kept saying, as she hugged and kissed me until we both began to cry.

WE NEVER WERE a couple like other couples. From the time we were married, we went everywhere together. Sometimes no one would be there but men. Andrés and I would arrive, and he would plunge in among them with his arm around my waist. Almost always, his friends came to our house on 9 Norte. It was too big for the two of us. A house in the center of town, near the *zócalo*, my parents' house, and the shops.

I walked everywhere, and was never alone.

In the mornings, we would go horseback riding. We'd drive in Andrés's Ford to the Plaza del Charro, where our horses would be waiting. The day after the wedding, he had bought me a sorrel mare I named Nightmare—though she was a dream. He rode a young stallion he called Al Capone.

Andrés got up as soon as it was light, issuing orders as if I were his regiment. Once he'd opened his eyes, he was out of bed. He would leap up and run around the bed repeating his stock speech about the importance of exercise. I would lie quiet, with the cover over my eyes, thinking about the ocean, or about laughing mouths. Sometimes I lay there so long that when Andrés would come back from the bathroom, where he'd locked himself in with the newspaper, he'd shout:

"All right, lazybones. What are you doing there pretending you can think. I'll be waiting for you downstairs. I'm counting to three hundred, and then I'm leaving."

Like a sleepwalker, I would get out of my gown and into riding pants, comb my hair with my fingers, run by the mirror, button my blouse, and rub the sleep from my eyes. Then I'd run downstairs, carrying my boots in my hand, open the door, and there he would be, counting.

"Two hundred ninety-eight, two hundred ninety-nine. . . . You didn't give yourself time to put your boots on. Again. What a slowpoke." He would already be in the Ford, revving the engine.

I would jump up on the running board, stick my head through the window, kiss him and ruffle his hair, then hop down and race around the car to climb in beside him.

You had to drive outside the city to get to the Plaza del Charro. The sun was already warm by the time the stable boy brought our horses. Andrés mounted without help from anyone, but first he would hand me up onto Nightmare, and pat her neck.

It was open country around there. So we would ride out in any direction as if it were our own ranch. It never occurred to me then that we would have need of all the ranches we had later. This bit of country was enough for me.

Sometimes Al Capone started off like a shot, in any direction that struck him. Andrés would give him his head and let him run. The first few days, I didn't realize that horses imitate each other, and was frightened that Nightmare raced off as if I'd asked her to.

It was all I could do to stay on, and my buttocks came down hard at every stride. I got terrible bruises. Every evening, I showed them to my general, who died laughing.

"You're beating your butt against the saddle. Stand in the stirrups when your horse runs."

I listened to his instructions as if they came from a god.

He always surprised me with something and loved to laugh at my ignorance.

"You don't know how to ride, you don't know how to cook, and you didn't know how to fuck. What were you doing the first fifteen years of your life?" he asked.

He always came home at midday for dinner. I enrolled in cooking classes with the Muñoz sisters and became an expert cook. I beat cakes with long strokes like brushing my hair. I learned to make *mole, chiles en nogada, chalupas, chileatole, pipián,* and *tinga.* A thousand things.

There were twelve of us students in the class, Tuesday and Thursday mornings at ten o'clock. I was the only one who was married.

When Josié Muñoz stopped lecturing, her sister Clarita would already have the ingredients on the table, ready to divide the work among us.

We worked in pairs. On the day we made *mole,* my partner was Pepa Rugarcía, who planned to be married soon. While we were stirring the sesame seeds with wooden spoons, she asked me, "Is it true there comes a moment when you have to close your eyes and pray a Hail Mary?"

I laughed. We kept turning the seeds and made a date to talk later that afternoon. Mónica Espinosa was toasting squash seeds on the gas ring beside us, and invited herself along.

When everything was cooked, we had to grind it.

"Don't depend on someone to help you," the Muñoz sisters said. "Times are hard, so you need to learn how to use the *metate* yourself."

We took turns. One by one, we stood in front of the *metate*, lifted the grinding stone and brought it down, up and down, on chiles, peanuts, almonds, and seeds. But we couldn't do any better than half crush them.

After a few minutes of making us feel like idiots, Clarita began grinding, putting her waist and back into it, slender arms churning, feverishly focused on reducing the ingredients to powder. She was small and strong. As she ground she got redder and redder, but didn't sweat.

"See? Do you see how to do it?" she said when she finished. Mónica began to applaud, and we all joined in. Clarita picked up the towel hanging on a hook beside the sink and wiped her hands.

"I don't know how you're ever going to get married if you're as ignorant about everything else as you are about this."

We finished about three in the afternoon; our aprons were spattered red. We had *mole* in our eyelashes. The turkey was divided into fourteen portions, and each of us left with our portion.

When I got home, Andrés was waiting, ravenous as a stray dog.

I showed him the *mole*, sprinkled sesame seeds over it, brought beer and tortillas, and we sat down to eat. Neither of us said a word. Suddenly in the middle of a mouthful, we nodded our pleasure to each other and kept eating. When Andrés's plate was so clean you could see the blue designs of the Talavera ware, he said he doubted very much I'd cooked it.

"We did it together."

"You mean the Muñoz sisters did it together."

He gave me a kiss and left. I went to look for Pepa and Mónica in the arcades.

They were waiting for me. Mónica was crying, because Pepa had sworn that if someone put his tongue in your mouth when he kissed you, he gave you a baby.

"Adrián did that to me yesterday when my mama wasn't looking," Mónica said between sobs.

What I did was take them to the gypsy in La Luz. They weren't going to believe anything I said. When I asked them if they knew what a man's pecker was for, Pepa said, "Isn't that how they pee?"

The gypsy explained everything to them, rubbed them with an egg, and made them chew a few sprigs of parsley. Then she read our palms. She told Pepa and Mónica they would be happy, that one of them would have six children and the other four, that Mónica's husband would become ill, and that Pepa's would never be as smart as she was.

"But he's rich," said Mónica.

"Very rich, child. No one can take that from him."

When I held out my hand, she stroked the center of my palm and stared at it.

"Ay, child, I see strange things here."

"Tell me," I said.

"Another day. It's late now, and I'm tired. Didn't you come for me to teach your friends? Well, it's done. Go on now."

"Tell her," Pepa and Mónica begged, and I kept my hand out. She took it in hers, again looked at my palm, and smoothed it.

"Ay . . . It's just that you have many men here," she said. "You also have many sorrows. Come another day. Today I must not be seeing clearly. That happens to me sometimes." She dropped my hand, and we went off to get a pastry at Meche's café.

"I wish my hand was as interesting as yours," said Pepa, as we were walking along 3 Oriente on the way to her house.

That night, lying beside my general, I patted his stomach.

I love him now, I thought. Who knows about later? He answered with a snore.

About a week later we asked a friend to come try the honey *muéganos* I'd made in the Muñoz sisters' class. We were drinking our coffee when some soldiers showed up with a warrant for Andrés's arrest. It was for murder, and was signed by the governor.

Andrés read it without making any fuss. I began to cry.

"How can they take you away? Where will they take you? You haven't killed anyone, have you?"

"Don't worry, Catalina, I'll be back in a while," he said, and asked his friend to stay with me. "I'll go ask for an explanation. There must be a mistake."

He ruffled my hair and left.

When the door closed behind him, I started crying again. Their taking him was more humiliating than a kick in the face. How could I face my friends? What would I tell my mother and father? Who would I sleep with? Who would wake me up in the mornings?

I couldn't think of anything to do but run to the church of Santiago. Someone had told me there was a new Virgin there who could work miracles. I regretted all the masses I had missed and all the first Fridays I hadn't taken Communion.

Santiago was a dark church with saints along the walls and a glittering, gilded altar. There, on high, was the Virgin and Child, one of her hands touching his heart.

The rosary was said at six. I knelt forward so the Virgin could see me better. The church was filled and I was afraid my problem would be lost among so many people. At six exactly, the priest arrived at the altar with his enormous rosary in his hands. He was young, he had large eyes, and he was beginning to lose his hair. His voice was so strong you could hear it all through the church.

"The mysteries we are going to consider are the joyful mysteries. The first is the Annunciation. OurFatherWhichArtin-Heaven . . ." he began.

I was answering the Our Fathers, the Hail Marys, and the prayers with a fervor I had never felt, not even in school with the nuns. Inside, I was saying, *Look after him for me, Virgencita, bring him back to me, Virgencita.*

At the end of each mystery, the organ, which was in the choir, played the first chords of a song everyone knew. Then the priest would lift his voice and the audience would join in.

After the litany, two acolytes carried in the censers; they filled them and began to swing them back and forth in the direction of the Virgin. The altar and church filled with a silvery smoke.

"Our Lady of the Sacred Heart, pray for us, pray for us," everyone sang. Down the central aisle came several women crawling on their knees toward the altar, their arms outspread. Two were crying.

I thought that really I should be among them, but I was embarrassed. If I had to go that far to see Andrés free, I was afraid he would never come back.

As the worshipers continued their prayers to Nuestra Señora del Sagrado Corazón, the women neared the altar.

My pleas grew stronger. I spoke very quietly, staring at the Virgin, so tranquil, so secure in her crown and in us looking up at her from below.

But she was not looking at us, her eyelids were closed. She was ageless, without care.

Suddenly the organ stopped and the priest spread his arms; making a cross with each hand, he said, "Remember, Nuestra Señora del Sagrado Corazón, the ineffable power that your divine Son has given you over His precious heart. Filled with faith in your virtues, we come to you to implore your protection, O Heavenly Guardian of the Heart of Jesus!" I don't remember exactly what came next, but soon we were at the point where you had to ask for the favor that had brought you there.

A wave of whispers swept through the church. From every corner came murmurs from a multitude of mouths.

I whispered, too. "Let Andrés come back, don't let them lock him up, don't let him leave me alone."

"No, we shall not leave unrewarded," chorused all the voices when the priest's voice was heard. The church was a sea of outstretched arms.

People were crowding toward the altar, and I was crushed against it. The organ was playing "Adiós, O Madre." . . . We were all singing, "Our hearts beat for you, a thousand times and one. Adiós, adiós." Then from the rear came the sound of yelling.

"*Viva Cristo Rey!* Long Live Christ the King!"

Police poured down the aisle, pushing their way toward the altar. Dizzied by the press of people and the incense, I heard one of them say to the priest, "You must come with us. You know the reason, don't make any trouble."

The organ was still playing.

"Allow me to finish," said the priest. "I am going to give the benediction with the Blessed Sacrament, and then I will go with you wherever you wish."

They allowed the priest to rise from his knees and approach the tabernacle; he seemed to have no fear. I thought it must be his faith in the Virgin. He opened the tabernacle and removed the large host in its crystal container. An acolyte held out the gold monstrance set with red stones. The priest opened it, placed the host inside, and turned toward us. We all made the sign of the cross, and the organ kept playing until the priest walked down the stairs and entered the sacristy. I followed behind. I got only as far as the door, but I watched as he removed his stole and put on his hat. The soldiers did not touch him. He followed them. That was all I needed to lose faith in the Virgen del Sagrado Corazón.

That night I got into bed trembling with fear and cold, but I didn't go to Mama and Papa's house. I had talked awhile with Chema, Andrés's friend, who had been going around asking questions. Andrés was accused of killing a man who falsified diplomas and sold them to army instructors. They said that Andrés had killed him because the idea had been his and he had been head of the whole enterprise, and once the secretary of the army and navy had discovered the false diplomas and located the counterfeiters, Andrés had been frightened and done away with the one who knew him best.

Chema said that was impossible, that my husband wouldn't go around killing for something like that, that he had never been involved in such a stupid business, and that what happened was that Governor Pallares hated him and wanted him out of the way.

I couldn't understand why he hated Andrés, since he had lost. Pallares was the powerful one, why take his anger out on Andrés? Losing was punishment enough.

The next day a picture of Andrés behind bars came out in the newspapers, and I was afraid to leave the house. I was sure that no one in my cooking class would talk to me, but I was supposed to bring the ingredients for stuffing *chiles en nogada* and I couldn't let them down. I got there at ten-thirty, wearing the face of someone who hadn't slept all night and carrying my basket of peaches, apples, bananas, raisins, almonds, pomegranates, and *jitomates*.

The Muñoz sisters' kitchen was enormous. Twenty women could work in it without getting in each other's way. All the others were there by the time I arrived.

"We were waiting for you," said Clarita.

"I just . . ."

"I can't accept any excuses. Women are responsible for seeing that food gets prepared in this world; this is a job, not a game. Start mincing all that fruit. Let's see, girls, who's going to work over here?"

Only Mónica, Pepa, and Lucía Maurer came forward. All the rest looked at me from behind the table. I'd rather they'd come out and said that Andrés was a murderer and they didn't want anything to do with his wife, but in Puebla things weren't done that way. No one offered to shake hands with me, but no one said what they were thinking, either.

Mónica came and stood beside me. She picked up a knife and slowly began to dice bananas as she asked me why they had taken the General away and whether I knew the truth about what had happened. Luci Maurer put her hand on my shoulder, then began to peel the apples she took from my basket. Pepa couldn't stop chewing her fingernails; between nibbles, she scolded Mónica for asking me so many questions, and as soon as she could interrupt, said, "Were you afraid during the night?"

"A little," I said, chopping the peaches.

When we left the Muñoz sisters' house, I stood in the middle of the street with my plate of chilis garnished with parsley and pomegranate. My friends were picked up at two on the dot.

"Don't pay any attention to them," said Mónica, before she climbed into the car where her mother was waiting.

I walked back to our house. I opened the door with the gigantic key I always had in my purse.

"Andrés!" I yelled. No one answered me. I set the plate of chiles on the ground and kept yelling, "Andrés! Andrés!" No one answered. I sank down to cry over the *nogada*.

I had my back to the door, staring through my tears at how green my garden was, when the lock thundered exactly as it did when Andrés opened it.

"So are you sitting there crying for your *charro*?" he said. I got up and ran to touch him. The mid-afternoon sun struck the windows and slanted into the patio. I kicked off my shoes and started unbuttoning my dress. I ran my hands beneath Andrés's shirt and pulled him toward the grass in the garden. There I verified that they had not cut off his cock. Then I remembered the *chiles en nogada* and ran to get them. We gulped them down in large mouthfuls.

"Why did they take you and why did they let you come back?" I asked.

"Because they're shit-asses and stupid bastards," said Andrés.

The next day the newspaper said that the priest of the church of Santiago had been given two years in jail for having organized a protest against the laws relating to worship, and that General Andrés Ascencio had been given his freedom and had received the proper apologies after proving his total innocence in the case of the death of a man who forged diplomas.

I didn't want to go back to cooking class. When Andrés asked why, I told him about the looks and the treatment I'd had to put up with. He pulled me to him and patted me on the bottom.

"What a good girl you are," he said. "Just wait till I run things around here."

I HAD A long wait. Andrés spent four years coming and going without any set routine, seeing me sometimes as a burden, sometimes as a thing you buy and put away in a drawer, and sometimes as the love of his life. I never knew what the next day would bring, whether he would want me to go riding with him, whether he would take me to the bullfights on Sunday, or whether for weeks at a time he'd be gone.

He was possessed by a passion that had nothing to do with me, by a craving for things I didn't understand. I was still a girl. I would suddenly feel dismal, or elated, for the same reasons. I was turning into a woman who went from sorrow to wild laughter without transition, a woman always waiting for something to happen to her, anything, anything except the unbearable sameness. I hated peace; it frightened me.

Often sadness came during my time of the month. And there was no point in telling that to the General, because those things don't matter to men. I wasn't embarrassed by the menstrual blood, not like my mother, who never talked about it and who taught me to wash out the bloody rags discreetly, in private.

Poblanas called the blood "Pepe Flores."

"Oh, I wish Pepe Flores would come," I would say. "Anything to take away the boredom!" When I started feeling sad, I thought about Pepe Flores, about how I wished he belonged to me, how I would like him to take me to the beach those five days a month he visited me.

The house on 9 Norte had a tall ash tree, two jacarandas, and a pepper tree. Behind them, in one corner, was a small adobe room covered with bougainvillea. Through the single window you could see a piece of sky that changed with the weather. I would sit on the floor with my legs drawn up to my chin and think about nothing.

Mónica had told me it helped to drink anisette when you get that funny, tingly feeling in your legs, your waist, and whatever you have under skin that has hair on it. I drank anisette until I broke out in a rash and talked to myself, or anyone I could. A strange courage filled my mouth, and all the complaints I didn't have the nerve to heap upon my general flew into the air.

Andrés was chief of military operations for the state of Puebla, which meant every soldier in that zone was under his command. I think it was then he became a public danger. I know that was when he met Heiss and the rest of his associates and protégés. By then they were earning a lot of money. Heiss was a loud gringo who sold buttons and medicine. He had somehow wangled a post as honorary consul in Mexico City, and during Carranza's time had hatched a plot for his own kidnapping. With the money his government paid for rescuing him from himself, he bought a pin factory on 5 Sur. He was good at cooking up deals. His eyes would gleam as he plotted them. For weeks he never changed out of the same pair of gabardine trousers, and he was getting rich right under the noses of the *poblanos* who had seen him arrive without a centavo and now had to call him Don Miguel. They always talked about how intelligent he was; he dazzled them. But in fact he was a scoundrel.

At first I didn't know anything about him; I didn't know anything about anybody. Andrés kept me tucked away like a toy he talked nonsense with, screwed three times a week, and kept happy by scratching her back and taking her to the *zócalo* on Sundays. But after his arrest that afternoon, I began to ask him more about his business deals and his work. He didn't like to tell me. He always said that he didn't live with me to talk about business and if I needed money to ask him for it. Sometimes I convinced myself that he was right. What did I care where he got the money that paid for the house, the chocolates, all the things I wanted?

I worked at passing the time. I went to see my friends. I spent the afternoons helping them embroider and make cookies. Together we read novels by Pérez y Pérez. I still remember Pepa awash in tears over Anita de Montemar while Mónica and I laughed ourselves silly over her idiotic suffering. We were helping Pepa sew her trousseau. She was going to marry a closemouthed, ugly Spaniard we couldn't imagine anyone wanting for a husband. We said terrible things about him when she wasn't there, but never dared tell her that she would be better off trading him for the tall boy who laughed with her when they came out of mass. She married the Spaniard anyway, and he turned out to be madly jealous. So jealous he ripped out the floors of their balconies so she couldn't go outside.

★　　★　　★

The day of Pepa's wedding, for which I wore a dress of pale green voile and a long pearl necklace Andrés had given me, I woke up exhausted. I didn't want to get out of bed.

Andrés leaped up to do his calisthenics. I lay and watched him start toward the bathroom, going over the list of all the things he had to do. I buried myself under the covers, thinking how much I would like to go to the moon. When I was a little girl, I used to squirm down to the foot of the bed and pretend I was on the moon. That's where I was, on the moon, when Andrés returned.

"Are you going to have one of your days? Why else did you wake up with that face like a dying dog? Let's see, let me take a look," he said. "You have eyes like a cow's. Are you carrying a calf?"

He said it with such pride, with such a satisfied look on his face, that I was embarrassed. I could feel myself blush, so I threw the covers over my head again and scooted down to the foot of the bed.

"What's the matter?" he asked. "Don't you want to have my baby?"

I heard his voice through the covers, and touched my swollen breasts, counting the days I never counted. It had been three months since I'd had a visit from Pepe Flores.

We went to the wedding. The whole time I was thinking how I was going to hate being a mother, and that's why I don't remember much about the festivities. All I remember is Pepa as she left the church, with her clear brow and coronet of flowers holding the veil that fell to the hem of her long dress. She was beautiful. That's what Mónica and I told her as we watched her leave, clutching each other's hands to hold back the tears.

"I'm going to have a baby," I told Mónica, to the sound of the "Wedding March."

"How wonderful," she cried, and kissed me right in the middle of the church.

I WAS SIXTEEN when Verania was born. The nine months I carried her were like a nightmare. I watched my body grow a great bulge in front without ever experiencing maternal tenderness. The first bad thing was having to give up horses and fitted dresses; the second was morning sickness, the bile that rose clear up to my nose. I hated to complain, but I also hated the feeling of being continuously possessed by something alien. When the baby began to move like a fish swimming in the depths of my womb, I was afraid it would suddenly pop out, and all the blood would drain from my body, and I would die. Andrés was the one responsible for my woes, but he wouldn't even let me complain.

"How you women love to feel important about this business of having a baby," he would say. "I thought you were going to be different. You grew up watching animals drop their young without any fuss. Besides, you're young. Don't think about it; you'll see, all your worries will go away."

* * *

Since Andrés had lost his bid to be governor, he had nothing to do. He got a bee in his bonnet to travel, and took me along when he drove to the United States.

I couldn't keep my eyes open. I slept with the sun beating down on my face, even as the car bumped and bucked along the long dirt roads.

"I don't know why I brought you, Catín," he would say. "I should have asked another woman. You haven't looked at the scenery, you haven't sung to me, you haven't even laughed. You're no good as a wife."

I was no good my whole pregnancy. Andrés didn't touch me once—he said he didn't want to hurt the baby—and that made me even jumpier. I couldn't think rationally, I got distracted, I started one conversation and ended with another, and I listened to only half of what I was told. Worst of all was the horror of the birth itself. I was sure it would leave me a permanent idiot. And Andrés was gone more than ever. He didn't take me to Mexico City to the bulls anymore. He left the house alone, and I was sure he was meeting another woman around the corner. Someone presentable, without a melon in her belly and dark circles creeping from her eyes to her cheekbones. He had good reason. I wouldn't have gone anywhere with me. Least of all to the bullfights, where the women were ravishing, with waists like the necks of bottles.

I would sit and mope about being deserted, rubbing my bulge, sleeping. I went out only to eat with my mama and papa.

One noontime, I was walking through the *zócalo* blowing a pinwheel I'd bought for Pía and bumped belly-first into Pablo, a friend from my schooldays. Pablo's people came from Chipilo, and his grandparents from the Piedmont, in Italy. Which explained why he was so blond, with such deep-set eyes.

"How beautiful you look!" he said.

"Come on," I said.

"I mean it. I always knew you would be beautiful when you were expecting a baby."

So I didn't go eat at my parents' house after all.

Pablo delivered milk in a little mule cart. He left Chipilo early in the morning. He invited me to climb in with him, and we drove out into the country. He treated me like a queen. No one had more affection for the baby-to-be than he. Not even me. Although I was no model of overflowing love. That afternoon we played in the field like children. I forgot my swollen belly, I even reached the point of thinking how good it would be to want nothing more than such simple pleasures in life. I looked fondly on the cheap cloth of his pants, his uncombed hair, his hands. Pablo took it upon himself to soothe my anxieties during those last three months of my pregnancy, and I took it upon myself to relieve him of the virginity he hadn't as yet left in some brothel.

That was the only good thing that happened while I was pregnant with Verania. Even the Sunday before she was born, we went to play in the hay. From there, Pablo took me directly to my parents' house, because I was beginning to feel Verania coming out. My general arrived two days later, with twenty bouquets of red roses and some chocolates.

The baby was a month old, and my breasts were covered with stretch marks, when Andrés brought home the two children of his first marriage.

Virginia was a few months older than I. Octavio, who was born in October 1915, was a few months younger. They stopped at the door to my room. Their father introduced me, and the three of us stared at each other, not speaking. I knew nothing about Andrés's life, especially that he had children my age.

"These are my oldest children," he said. "Up till now, they've been living with my mother in Zacatlán. But I don't want them to live in that little town anymore, so I brought them here to go to school. They will live with us."

I managed to nod, and then, showing them the baby, I said, "This is your sister. Her name is Verania."

Octavio came over to look at her, asking why she had such a strange name, and I told him that Verania had been the name of my father's mother.

"Your grandmother?" he asked, and began to stroke Verania's cheek. He was a boy with dark, trustful eyes. He laughed just like Andrés when he wanted to be pleasant, and seemed inclined to be my friend. The same wasn't true of his sister. She stood in the doorway beside her father, reserved, with no affection for me in her eyes. I thought she was ugly; she was overweight, and had sad eyes and thin lips. Her breasts were flat and her hips square, she had no buttocks, and her belly stuck out. I felt sorry for her.

She and Octavio moved into rooms near ours, and suddenly we became a family. I even began to think it would be good to have company when Andrés wasn't around.

That night, I fired a thousand questions at Andrés. Where did those children come from? Did he have more?

For now, those two. He had met their mother early in 1914, when he went to Mexico City with General Macías—an old man who had been governor of Puebla after the constitutional governor resigned when Victoriano Huerta killed Madero. I didn't know very much about what had happened during those years, but Andrés told me all about it on the night of the day his children arrived.

Macías was from Zacatlán, a mule driver, like Andrés's father. He fought in Puebla against the French and joined the troops of

Porfirio Díaz. With Díaz, he became important and rich. When the Revolution began, he returned to the town where he had a ranch and felt protected. Andrés began working for him. He was the overseer of Macías's peons, a bright boy, the son of someone he knew, and gradually he won his confidence. When Huerta offered Macías the governorship, the old man jumped at it, and he took his assistant with him to Puebla. After six months of what might be called governing, he fell ill. He wanted to go to Mexico City for treatment, so he put his affairs into the hands of Andrés, who had become essential to him because Andrés was so orderly and so devoted to his care, and took him along. Andrés knew where Macías left his eyeglasses every time he lost them, and learned to look after Macías's clothes and even pay some of his bills. The general was ill for three weeks before he died—surprising no one—early in January of 1914. Andrés stayed on in Mexico City, woefully ignorant of everything that was going on around him, without a job but with two silver coins, a gift from old Macías.

He liked the city. He found work in a stable in Mixcoac, and stayed on to see what would happen. After all, he was eighteen years old and had no desire to go back to his hometown.

There in Mixcoac, he met Eulalia, a girl who had arrived with the flood of Madero's troops. Her father, Refugio Núñez, was only a foot soldier, but rabid about the cause. Eulalia lived with the memory of the day they entered Mexico City, the thousands cheering as they climbed down from the railroad cars and marched toward the great plaza where the government palace stood; she and her father stayed outside like everyone else to cheer as Señor Madero went in.

Eulalia's father worked in the same stable as Andrés; he was both bitter and hopeful. He had passed on to his daughter the somber smile of defeat and the conviction that soon the Revolution would be back to rescue them from eternal poverty.

Meanwhile, they milked cows and delivered the milk in the cart driven by Andrés and pulled by an ancient horse. Eulalia had no reason to go along on the deliveries, her chores ended with the milking, but she liked to ride with Andrés through the Colonia Juárez and knock at the doors of the big houses, where servants came out in dark uniforms, or occasionally a pale-skinned woman wearing a silk robe and an expression that said the world was about to end. Eulalia showed Andrés the houses that had been damaged the year before by the cannons of the rebellion that had toppled Madero. Andrés still understood very little of it all, but because of the girl said he was a Maderista. Eulalia, Andrés told Catalina, had Octavio's eyes. She was small and strong, and she yielded her virginity one morning on their return from the deliveries.

I wanted to know everything. Strangely, he told me.

They spent their days together, from early morning when they got up to milk, to the evenings that turned into night as they drank coffee and listened to her father tell how Emiliano Zapata had taken Chilpancingo, how the revolutionaries of the north were nearing Torreón, how the traitor Huerta had issued a citation making Don Porfirio a *general de guerra* and sent the decoration to Paris.

Who knows how Eulalia's father was always so well informed. After some gringo marines were arrested in Tampico for looting near the Puente Iturbide, he predicted the landing of the gringo troops in Veracruz. Before Zacatecas was taken by Villa, he foresaw by several days the bloody fight and the more than four thousand killed in that battle.

As he divined everything, he also knew that Eulalia was going to have Andrés's child, and after the inevitable sorrow, he interwove his prophecies about the war with the future of his grandson. Though Eulalia's body was changing, getting larger and larger as the baby grew, she continued to get up early in the morning for the milking, and to ride with Andrés to make the deliveries.

One morning in the middle of July, Don Refugio Núñez woke up predicting the defeat of the traitor. Almost before the words left his lips, the Chamber of Deputies accepted Victoriano Huerta's resignation. After that, he foresaw the fall of Puebla, Querétaro, Saltillo, Tampico, Pachuca, Manzanillo, Jalapa, Chiapas, Tabasco, Campeche, and Yucatán.

"General Obregón arrives today," he said on August 15. And the three of them went to the *zócalo* to welcome him.

Young Ascencio liked Alvaro Obregón. He thought that if one day he had to take sides, he would go with Obregón. He had the look of a winner.

"That's because you haven't seen Zapata," Eulalia told him.

"No, but I know the faces of the Indians from his part of the world," Andrés answered.

They never fought. He spoke of her as an equal. I never heard him speak of another woman that way.

When Venustiano Carranza reached Mexico City and called a convention of governors and commanding generals to be held October 1, Don Refugio told them that Villa and Zapata would not back the aged Carranza. Once again, he was right on target.

The Convention was moved to Aguascalientes, and Villa and Zapata attended its sessions. At the end of October, they approved the Plan de Ayala. Don Refugio began drinking as soon as he imagined it had been passed, and by the time the news was confirmed, he'd been drunk for three days, repeating over and over, "I told you, *Tierra y Libertad*, at last. We've won. Land and Liberty!"

"You can say what you want, but they've made a bad move tangling with General Carranza," said Andrés.

Eulalia patted her stomach and brewed coffee. She liked to listen to her father talking with Andrés.

At the beginning of November, Carranza left Mexico City and from Córdoba disclaimed the actions taken by the Convention. In Aguascalientes, the Convention continued to meet as if nothing had happened. It named a provisional president of the republic and continued to fight the Carranza followers for every village and town.

On the twenty-third, the gringos handed over Veracruz to General Carranza, but on the night of the twenty-fourth, the Army of the South entered Mexico City.

On December 6, Eulalia woke up feeling birth pangs. Despite that, her father decided that before they did anything else, they had to go to the Avenida Reforma and watch the Conventionalist army troops pass by with Villa and Zapata at their head.

A column of more than fifty thousand men marched behind the two leaders. The parade began at ten in the morning and ended at four-thirty in the afternoon. Eulalia gave birth to a baby girl in the middle of the street. Her father received it, cleaned it, and wrapped it in Eulalia's rebozo, while Andrés watched, completely stupefied.

"*Ay, Virgen,*" was the only thing Eulalia could get out between contractions. She said it so often that when they were back home and Don Refugio was bathing the infant, Andrés decided they should name her Virgen. When they went to baptize her, the priest said they couldn't use that name, and recommended Virginia, which sounded almost the same. They agreed.

A week after the birth, Eulalia was back at the stable with the baby at her breast and a smile even brighter than the year before.

She had a baby girl, a husband, and she had seen Emiliano Zapata ride by. That was enough.

Andrés, in contrast, was fed up with poverty and routine. He wanted to be rich, he wanted to be a leader, he wanted to march in a parade, not watch one go by. He was bitter from the time of the milking through the delivering, and he heard Don Refugio's predictions as a series of curses. The Conventionalists and the Constitutionists were fighting all across the country. One day, one group would take the plaza, and the next day the others would take it back; one day, one decree would be in force, and the next day another; for some, the capital was Mexico City, and for others, Veracruz. Andrés's thought was that at least the Constitutionists always kept the same leader, while the Conventionalists had too many and were never going to reach an accord.

"More to the point is that you don't believe in democracy," his father-in-law said to him.

"I've always had a sharp eye, Don Refugio," Andrés told the old man. "How am I going to believe in your democracy? Lieutenant Segovia said it very well: 'A democracy without someone to guide it is not a democracy.' "

January began with the Conventionalists governing in Mexico City, but by the end of that month Alvaro Obregón occupied the city and his Constitutionists were hit by gale winds that took out all the electric street lamps and left the streets of the city dark. Trees lost their branches, and the roof of the shed Andrés, Eulalia, and Don Refugio lived in blew off in the middle of the night, exposing them to the cold. Eulalia laughed at finding herself suddenly without a roof, and Don Refugio began a speech about the injustices of poverty that one day the Revolution would cure. Young Ascencio spent the night cursing and swore to himself he would do anything but continue to live in someone else's house in utter misery.

He started working in the afternoons as assistant to a Spanish priest who served a parish in Mixcoac. To his misfortune, however, that job lasted only a short while because Obregón imposed a contribution of 500,000 pesos on the clergy of the capital, and as they could not pay it, all the priests were taken to military headquarters. Andrés went with Padre José, whom he knew to be very wealthy, and listened as he swore by the Virgen de Covadonga that he didn't have a centavo. Obregón ordered the Mexican priests to be placed under arrest, and released the foreign ones on the condition that they leave the country. Padre José did not waste a single day in bidding his parishioners farewell and left for Veracruz carrying a suitcase filled with gold. At least, that's what Andrés believed, after carrying it to the train station.

Things went from bad to worse. Even the cows were giving less milk; they were thin and half-starved. Eulalia and Andrés scoured the city in search of bread and charcoal. Often they didn't find any, and many times could not pay for the little they found.

In March, feeding the hope of Don Refugio and his daughter, the Army of the South again occupied the city, forcing Obregón to flee. After them came the president of the Convention, and most of the delegates.

No matter how the hopes of Eulalia and her father blossomed, they could not inspire Andrés. To top everything off, Eulalia was pregnant again. They were paid only sporadically at the stable, but docked for any absence. Andrés began to detest his wife's illusions. He wished he were anywhere else. Almost twenty years later, he couldn't explain why he hadn't left.

Eulalia was sure that the men of the Convention could not

know what the masses were suffering, so when she heard that people were organizing to go to one of the sessions with empty baskets, asking for maize, she did not hesitate a minute. Andrés did not want to go with her, but when he saw her at the door, with the baby in her rebozo, looking as if she were going to a celebration, he followed.

"Maize! Bread!" shouted the throng, holding up their empty baskets and hungry children. While his wife shouted with the rest Andrés muttered and cursed himself for a fool, certain they would get nowhere that way.

A representative of the Convention advised the crowd that necessities would be made available, up to a limit of five million pesos.

"I told you, we're going to have more than enough to eat," Eulalia announced the next day as she left with her basket to buy maize at the sale the president had ordered held in the patio of the School of Mining. Andrés did not go with her that day. He watched her leave, carrying the baby and once again large with child. Thin and hollow-eyed, with the brilliant smile she was never without. He thought she must be going mad, and he sat slumped on the ground, smoking a cigarette butt.

When night came and Eulalia still wasn't back, he went to look for her. At the School of Mining he found soldiers picking up abandoned shoes and baskets, and not a grain of maize in the whole courtyard. More than ten thousand people had come for the sale. The struggle for a handful of maize had turned vicious; people milled around in a crush. At least two hundred had fainted: some nearly asphyxiated, others from sunstroke. Ambulances from the Red Cross had taken them away.

Andrés went to the old Red Cross hospital to look for Eulalia.

He found her lying on a cot, her baby scratched and bruised, but with her eternal smile intact as she watched him approach.

She said nothing, merely opened her hand and showed him a handful of maize. As he stared at her, horrified, she opened the other hand.

"I have more," she said.

Soon after, the stable paid them ten pesos. Feeling rich, they went to the San Juan market to buy food. It was about twelve noon when they arrived. The doors of nearly all the shops were closed. A crowd of women stood before one bakery, shouting and pushing.

"Let's go there," said Eulalia. And she began to push with all the might of her thin body.

Suddenly the doors yielded and the women swarmed into the bakery, as much enraged as hungry, swooping down on the bread, fighting over it, and stuffing as much as they could into their baskets. Andrés watched that total bedlam presided over by the Spanish baker who was trying to stop women from taking his buns and rolls without paying for them. He scuffled with the women, struggling to remove from their baskets what they had put in. Andrés watched as the baker moved away from the counter, tugging at the braids of a woman who had emptied a tray of hard rolls into her basket.

There was not a lot of cash in the wooden box the shopkeeper kept on a low shelf, but Andrés grabbed it and looked for Eulalia in the midst of the sea of rebozos and forest of arms; women were still scrambling for crumbs as they wolfed down part of their loot. He went to the door and yelled for Eulalia. She raised an arm to show him the bun she was eating; her smile filled with crumbs. She pushed her way toward him, and he began to run, pulling her along.

"Didn't you get anything at all?" Eulalia asked him, unaware of why he was abandoning the party before it was over. He didn't answer. He let her chew on her anise-flavored bun as they walked back to the stable. She told him she wasn't going to share a single bite since he had been so useless and thickheaded.

Don Refugio had stayed with the baby, and was rocking her in a cradle of burlap sacks suspended from the roof with hemp cord. Eulalia proudly showed her basket of bread to the elderly prophet. Andrés watched as they laughed and hugged each other, and considered keeping the money for a less happy day. But since Eulalia would not stop teasing him, he took out all the money he'd been able to stuff into his pockets.

"Lots of these are pesos!" shouted Eulalia, tossing them in the air.

That same afternoon, she bought herself a rebozo and forced Andrés to spend some of the money on a shirt for himself and another for Don Refugio. For the baby, she found a cap with shiny satin pleated ruffles, and spent the rest on sugar, coffee, and rice. Andrés insisted they keep fifteen pesos.

"Five more than we had this morning," Eulalia said before they went to bed.

When they woke up the next morning, the cannons were so close they considered not going to milk the eight scrawny cows left in the stable. But Eulalia wanted to soak one of her rolls in a bucket of warm milk and left earlier than usual, indifferent to her father's warnings.

They heard cannon fire all day. They took what little milk they had to the Colonia Juárez, but no one opened a door to them. There were no trolleys or cars in the streets, all the businesses were closed, and very few people had dared venture out.

By afternoon, the last Conventionalist troops had left, and the next morning the first Constitutionist forces entered the city. Two days later, more came, and with them, a new military commander, a different chief of police, and a new governor for the Federal District.

Eulalia took a peso bill and went to buy butter, but in the store they told her the paper was worthless. She returned home furious that Andrés had not let her spend everything. She was so angry that she tried to burn all the remaining bills, but her father predicted the Conventionalists would be back, and picked off the bills she had left to burn on the *comal*.

Eulalia was looking pale and sad. Andrés said it was the pregnancy, but Don Refugio contended that she hadn't looked like that the last time.

"They say it's different with every child," Eulalia would say when the subject came up.

Five days later, the Conventionalists retook the city. As soon as Eulalia heard, she took her bills to the store where they had refused them before.

With them, she bought two kilos of rice, one of flour, two of maize, one of sugar, one of coffee, even a pack of cigarettes.

When the Constitutionists returned, and Don Refugio predicted they were back to stay, Eulalia proudly surveyed her precious store of supplies.

Carranza had been in the city a month, and his government recognized by the United States, when Eulalia gave birth to a boy with a precocious and persistent smile like his mother's. Don Refugio was euphoric, he could not imagine a better sign for the prosperity he was determined would come. He named the baby Octavio, before anyone could suggest anything different.

Virginia was barely one, and overnight she was pushed into the background. Her mother and grandfather were occupied with the marvel of a newborn son, and her father barely noticed his daughter's first steps as he brooded about how to make money quickly and never be poor again.

After the milking, he would take the cart and drive around a city that was beginning to take on an orderly, even attractive, appearance.

One day the stable owner asked him to go to a new office called the Department of Price Controls to find out what price had been set for milk, since they didn't want to be charging less.

Behind the information window Andrés saw Rodolfo, his childhood friend from Zacatlán. It was like seeing a ghost. Rodolfo had come to Mexico with the Army of the East; he held the rank of sergeant even though he had never fought in a battle.

He was a paymaster and needed rank to command respect. He was two years older than Andrés, and it had been more than four years since they'd seen each other. Andrés had always thought his friend was a little stupid, but when he saw him in clean clothes, as fat as when they both were in their mothers' care, he questioned his judgment. They greeted each other as if they had said goodbye the afternoon before and made a date to go to dinner.

It was very late when Andrés returned to the shed in Mixcoac. When Eulalia scolded him for not having warned her he would be so late, he told her the story of his friend who was a sergeant, and assured her that soon he would have a well-paying job.

Don Refugio twisted the tips of his mustache and said to his daughter, "Now, you see, I was right. He's been taking the right steps. He gets along well with men from the north. Maybe something will come of all this that doesn't turn my stomach."

"We'll ask him to be Octavio's godfather," said Andrés.

Eulalia smiled her eternal smile and went to lie down beside her son.

"She says she's feeling tired," said Don Refugio. "And for her to say that, she must be about to die."

Unfortunately, Don Refugio was once again correct in his prediction. The typhus epidemic that had been hovering over the city for months found its way into the shed in Mixcoac and laid its hand on Eulalia.

Within a week, her laughter was fading, she could barely speak, her body was burning with fever and emitting a foul odor. Andrés and Don Refugio sat down to watch her die, unable to do anything more than keep cool cloths on her head. No one recovered from typhus. Eulalia knew that and did not want to be a burden in her last days. She merely looked at them with gratitude, and from time to time smiled.

"I hope it goes well with you," she said to Andrés, before she fell into her last day of fever and silence.

OR SEVERAL YEARS, I believed every word of
that dramatic and heartwarming story. I ven-
erated Eulalia's memory, I wanted to have a
laugh like hers, and a hundred different evenings I envied
with all my heart the simple and devoted lover my general
had been to her. Until the day Andrés won the candidacy
for governor of Puebla and the opposition sent a flyer to
our house denouncing him for having been in the service
of Victoriano Huerta when he disclaimed Madero's government.

"So all that about the milk wasn't true," I said, showing
him the broadside as he walked into the house.

"If you're going to believe my enemies before me, we
have nothing to talk about," he answered.

With the paper that accused him in my hands, I sat for
hours staring at the garden, brooding, until he stopped
before my chair, legs at the level of my eyes, his eyes far
above my head, and said, "What, then? You don't want
to be the governor's wife?"

I looked at him, we laughed, I said yes, and forgot

about his attempt to create an honorable past. I did want to be the governor's wife. I had spent five years devoted to the kitchen, nursing, and diapers. I was bored. After Verania had come Sergio. When I heard his first cry, and felt free of the boulder in my middle, I swore that would be the last time. I became an obsessive mother with whom Andrés had little to do. He was head of military operations, despised the governor, and had become partners with Heiss. That was enough to keep him busy, but in addition, he often went to Mexico City to visit his friend Rodolfo, who had climbed to the position of undersecretary. One day, to the jubilation of both, Rodolfo's boss, General Aguirre, became candidate elect for the presidency.

Andrés went with him during his campaign swing around the nation. He spent so much time away from home that Octavio and I could not reach him when Virginia went out one afternoon to buy thread and never came back. We notified the police and looked for her for days, but we never learned what happened to her. When her father returned, he accepted that her disappearance could only mean she was dead.

I didn't learn he had other daughters until he won the governorship. Then he felt an obligation to be a good father and presented me with four more. Marta, fifteen, Marcela, thirteen, and Lilia and Adriana, twelve.

Adriana and Lilia were the twin daughters of a novice in the Capuchin convent, one that Andrés, as a soldier, had helped close during the religious persecutions. Lilia delighted me from the beginning. She had chestnut hair and enormous eyes that revealed a lively curiosity. When she saw me, she asked if I was her father's wife. I told her I was, and from that moment she called me Mama. Adriana, on the other hand, was an introverted girl who had a very difficult time surviving among us.

Verania was four and Sergio three; we called him Checo. Counting Octavio, we had seven children when we moved to the house on Loreto hill. It was high up, but not on the main road; you had to turn off and follow along narrow little streets until you came to a long hedge that ran the length of the block. Behind the hedge and the garden was the house. It had fourteen bedrooms, a center patio, three floors, and a number of reception rooms. I don't even want to think about the work that went into furnishing all that.

I was hanging the last paintings when I heard someone at the door—two hundred workers from CROM, a labor union, who had come to show their support. After them came everyone from campesinos to mariachis, including Heiss and a group of Spanish textile manufacturers. A perpetual fiesta swept into our house with no regard for our privacy. I had to take charge of a team of waiters and flunkies that Andrés's assistants headquartered in my kitchen. From early morning, they were preparing banquets. They set up tables in the garden, and within two weeks I went from being a tranquil mother whose only duty was looking after two babies to commanding forty servants and administering the funds needed to provide food for the fifty to three hundred people we fed every day.

The children were put in the care of nannies from the mountains who were more childlike than they, and I barely had time to see them between one problem and the next. Fortunately, my sister Barbara came to live with me and was elegantly transformed into my private secretary.

That year the legislature of Puebla gave the vote to women, a move celebrated only by Carmen Serdán and four other teachers. Andrés, nonetheless, never began a speech without mentioning the importance of the participation of women in political and revolutionary struggles. One day in Cholula, he began by saying that a number of women had come to him to ask how they could show their support for the Revolution. He answered that in his everyday wisdom General Aguirre had already said that Mexican women should unite to defend the rights of female workers and campesinas, their equality in marital relations, et cetera, et cetera. From that moment, I never believed anything Andrés said in public. Worst of all, three days later I heard him give an impassioned speech about the traditional communal lands of the campesinos while that very afternoon he had drunk a toast with Heiss to celebrate a deal returning property expropriated from him by the nationalization laws. He told so many lies that no one was surprised when people at a rally in the Plaza de Toros grew angry enough to burn down the stands. Many were injured. Only Juan Soriano's newspaper reported it.

That tragedy brought an end to the campaign for support in the city, and we left to tour the state. With the entire household— children, nannies, cooks—we traveled from town to town, listening to campesinos demand land, call for justice, ask for miracles. They asked for everything from sewing machines to a cure for a child with poliomyelitis, roof tiles for their houses, burros, credit, seeds, schools. I enjoyed that tour. I liked driving through dusty towns like San Marcos, but I liked even better going up into the mountains to Coetzalan. I had never seen such vegetation, hill after hill rife with growth that covered even the rocks, ravines whose green walls cascaded to great depths. In Coetzalan, the women wore long white dresses and braided their hair with yarn, which they then wove around their heads. I was amazed that they could walk through the puddles and rocks of the mountainside without soiling even the hem of their skirts. They were small women, no taller than Lilia at twelve, but they carried enormous baskets and several children at the same time. As we drove into the village we didn't see many people. They explained to us that the campesinos around there didn't like the party and feared the elections because there was always shooting and corpses. As a result, they dreaded the arrival of the candidate and didn't want to come out to see him.

Andrés was furious with the organizers of his campaign who preceded us by a few days in every town; he berated them for being so worthless, cracked his horsewhip against the ground, and threatened to kill them all if they didn't drum up a crowd in the plaza.

I got out of the bus with the children; they wanted to walk through the cobbled streets, go into the church, find the market, and buy an orange sprinkled with chili pepper. To get away from Andrés's yelling, I followed the children wherever they wanted to go.

Octavio took the lead; he wanted to impress his sisters. He thought they were beautiful and couldn't get over the idea that someone like Marcela could be related to him. He took her hand at the least excuse, helped her over the cobbles; he was her boyfriend. Seeing them together, it occurred to me that Marcela would look beautiful dressed as the Indian women were. I managed to outfit all of us. Doña Remigia, the wife of the party delegate, helped us get the clothes and do our hair. The skirts belonged to her and her sisters, the yarns, too. I even dressed Verania in a little white *huipil*. We went back to the plaza where Andrés was scheduled to address the few onlookers gathered there. We found it difficult to walk and hold our heads up straight. We looked strange to each other, but people liked us. They began to follow us through the market. By the time we reached the plaza, we brought General Ascencio three times more public than his assistants had rounded up. We went to stand beside him, and he began his speech by saying:

"People of Coetzalan, this is my family, a family like your own, simple, united. Our families are our most important possession, and I promise you that my government will work to give them the future they deserve. . . ." And it went on from there. We listened quietly, only Checo got restless and took off his sombrero and ran around through our legs. Octavio took advantage of the moment to put his hand on his sister Marcela's waist and didn't take it away until the speech about family unity was ended. From Coetzalan, we drove down to Zacatlán, which was Andrés's home country. The Delpuentes and Fernándezes, the people who had owned the town before the Revolution, had watched him leave there poor and bitter and now had to suffer seeing him return to govern them.

The evening we arrived, a man was getting a shave in the barbershop and another customer asked if he was sprucing up to welcome General Ascencio.

"General? General, my foot," the man replied. "He will always be the son of a muleteer. I don't scrape and bow to a ragtag like that."

He didn't attend the dinner the prominent citizens of the town held for us the next day. My general asked about him with interest and lamented that he hadn't joined us. As we left we were told that just that morning he had been killed by a drunk.

As for the rest, Zacatlán had thrown itself into the fiesta. There were fireworks and dancing all night. Andrés wooed me as if it were something that he needed to do, and thanked me for the success in Coetzalan. He was happy.

So was his mother, whom I had seen three times, always in a

thorny mood. She was ecstatic, dancing the night away as if her son had restored dignity and pleasure to her life.

Doña Herminia was a slim woman with sunken eyes and a thrusting jaw. She had thin white hair she pulled back in a severe bun. She was used to poverty, but when her son became important she was quick to become accustomed to the good life, although she never wanted to leave Zacatlán.

Andrés bought her a house facing the *zócalo*. The facade was stone and the balconies had ironwork brought from France by the former owners. There was a room in that house for each of her children and their spouses and every grandchild—who knows why, because as Doña Herminia was not exactly a warm woman, her grandchildren rarely visited her, to say nothing of her sons, who were too busy making themselves important. Andrés, though, liked to make brief visits to Zacatlán. He would go check into the stone house so his mama could spoil him in ways she had been unable to do when he was a boy. It was better that I stayed away, I didn't want to get in the way of that romance. Besides, I never liked Zacatlán, it was always raining, and I found it depressing.

No town was left unvisited. Andrés was the first candidate for governor to undertake such a campaign. He didn't have a choice; Aguirre was the first candidate for president who traveled across the entire country.

I enjoyed it. Despite the fact that the General was already high-handed, he was still approachable then, he still seemed like normal people. By that, I mean he would talk to me without losing the thread of the conversation, or would suddenly kiss one of his daughters, and every night before we went to bed he would ask me whether he had done well, whether I thought the people liked him, whether he had been a success, whether I was prepared to help him in his work as governor.

Once he tried to imitate General Aguirre's custom of spending hours and hours listening to the campesinos. That was in Tezuitlán, another mountain town. They built him a platform, and one by one the Indians climbed up to tell him their problems: they didn't have oxen, some man had taken the land the Revolution had given them, they hadn't got any of the land the Revolution was parceling out to begin with, they didn't want their sons to grow up to be like them. They told him the story of their lives and asked for things as if Andrés were God. He endured that torture only one day. The next morning, I could hear him in the bathroom cursing General Aguirre's idiotic customs, and he asked me if I didn't agree that everyone had his own style. I said yes, of course. The campaign stops became shorter; the one in Tehuacán lasted only an hour. Afterward we went for a swim in the thermal springs at El Riego, a ranch where General Aguirre sometimes vacationed.

Finally the elections were held. I went with Andrés to vote. The next day our picture was in the newspaper, holding hands in front of the ballot box. There was no one else to vote for, so the elections were peaceful, although not marked by a heavy turnout. That Sunday the streets were half-empty; people went to early mass and retreated into their houses, leaving everything quiet. The workers of the CTM, another labor union, voted, and the bureaucrats, and maybe one or two misguided souls, but no one else. That was all that was necessary to allow Andrés to take legal possession of the governor's palace.

Nowadays I hear *poblanos* say they didn't know what lay in store for them, and that was why they didn't lift a finger to prevent it.

I think they wouldn't have done anything much no matter what they'd known.

These were people who lived their lives inside their own houses, their own worlds; a dead body could have fallen out of the sky and as long as it didn't crush them, they wouldn't have made a fuss.

The first days of governing were fun. Everything was new. I had my own retinue: the wives of the men working with Andrés. Checo liked to play he was a little governor, and the girls went to all the balls to lap up attention. Our general watched us having a good time, and I think he enjoyed it. Which may be why he took us to the opening of the San Roque asylum for crazy women. After he cut the ribbon and delivered his speech, he asked them to bring in a marimba and organized a dance right then and there. The poor women looked very elegant in their loose pink dresses, and the music made them happy. Andrés danced with one very pretty woman who had been institutionalized for alcoholism but now that she wasn't drinking had become a lucid abnormality amid a host of women reliving their childhoods, obsessed that someone was following them, or slipping from euphoria to depression. The governor danced with every one of them, and with me, too. I wasn't uncomfortable among the women; it actually occurred to me that San Roque might be a very restful place.

Suddenly Andrés ordered the music to stop and introduced me as the new president of public welfare. San Roque would be under my direction, along with the Casa Hogar orphanage and a number of the public hospitals.

I started trembling. With the children and the household servants, I already felt as if I were besieged by an army that couldn't make a move without my instructions, and now suddenly I had madwomen, orphans, and hospitals besides. I spent the night begging Andrés to remove that burden from me. He said he couldn't. I was his wife and that was what wives were for. "Don't think everything is screwing and singing."

The next day, I went to the Casa Hogar. It might have an elegant name but it was just a miserable orphan asylum, filthy and run-down. The children milled round the patio, half-dressed, with runny noses and the filth of months upon them. They were looked after by women who could barely speak their own names and did not differentiate between misbehaving and mentally incompetent children. They had them all thrown in together. Babies were sleeping in a row of iron cribs with urine-soaked mattresses. There were newborns among them, and for them they had contracted wet nurses who came twice a day to offer the few drops left in their drooping breasts.

I fired them. Them and the four witches who looked after the children. Then a physician who seemed very well-informed took it upon himself to let me know that the children could die if they drank cow's milk.

"They'd be better off dead than here," was my reply.

Who could put an end to my works of mercy? My husband, of course. That evening he said I was exaggerating, and that there was not one centavo to be had for the orphanage or the hospitals, and that the disturbed women already had quite enough with their new building.

"But I went to look, and they don't have any beds," I said.

"Those women have never slept anywhere but on the floor," he replied. "Do you think there are wealthy loonies in there? The rich ones are free to wander through the streets."

"Or be with you."

That morning I had gone by the Nuevo Siglo department store

to pick up a dress for Verania, and the clerk had asked me how I liked the Manila shawl the General had bought for me two days before. I said it was beautiful, watching the look of horror on the face of the owner, who always knew where Andrés Ascencio's purchases went. The shawl had been sent to a woman in Cholula. I had planned not to say anything about it, but I couldn't help myself. Andrés pretended he didn't know what I was talking about, anyway, and the matter was left there.

I called Andrés's daughters together to propose that they help me organize balls and fiestas and raffles to raise money for public welfare. They agreed. They had dozens of ideas, from a premiere starring Fred Astaire to a ball in the Governor's Palace. For a while, I had no idea how the women or the patients or the children were doing, I was too busy organizing events. I think we ended up forgetting whom they were for.

Only because Barbara, my sister, was carrying out her responsibilities as secretary did we finally deliver the underclothing to the children, the beds to the women, the sheets to the hospitals. San Roque was sparkling clean when we arrived, and the women filed by one by one to thank us. Their pink uniforms had faded, and the daylight was not kind to their faces. The young girl who had danced the first dance with Andrés was still there, and another woman told me that her brother had committed her in order to collect her inheritance. I told them to stay close. When the celebration was over, I simply took the two women with us, without any formalities. No one ever asked about them.

That night there was a ceremony at the College of Puebla to celebrate its transformation into a university. That had been one of Andrés's obsessions since the days of the campaign. He had been governor only a few months when he achieved it. He left in place as rector the man who had directed the college, and in return was given an honorary degree. The newspapers were critical, and people said terrible things, but Andrés didn't care. He got himself up in full academic regalia and made us wear our best dresses.

Since we hadn't had time to decide what to do with our former madwomen, we took them with us to the festivities. I lent one of them a dress, and the other wore one of Marta's.

In the course of all the toasts, I introduced the pretty girl to the rector, who hired her as his private secretary, and the disinherited girl to the president of the State Supreme Court, who made it his business to see justice done. I think they disinherited the brother, because about a month later I received a silver tea service bearing a card with the name *Señorita Imelda Basurto*, and, in parentheses, *the disinherited*. Below were the words, *With eternal gratitude for your labor in the cause of justice*.

At first people came to the house to request an audience and to ask me to intercede with Andrés. I listened to everything they said, and Barbara took notes. Every night she would bring me the list of requests and I would hurriedly read them to my general, noting down his instructions: tell that one to see Godínez, that one to come to my office, this one that it can't be done, give that one something from your petty cash box, and so on.

My first great disappointment came when a very cultivated gentleman called to tell me that the city archives were to be sold to a factory that made cardboard. The entire history of the city for three centavos the kilo. It was the first matter I brought to Andrés's attention that night. He didn't even want to discuss it. He simply said that the papers were useless, that what Puebla needed was a future, and that there was no place to keep useless memories. The space that had housed the archive would provide more classrooms for the university. It was too late anyway, Andrés said, because

Díaz Pumarino, his secretary of state, had already sold the archive, and he had earmarked the money for my orphanage.

The next day I had to endure the embarrassment of explaining my failure to Señor Cordero. Of course, the money from the sale never made its way to the orphanage, because members of the Charro Association visited Andrés the morning he had the money on his desk; in addition to his check as governor of the state, he gave them the money from the archive as a personal donation.

That was the beginning of my failures, and things only got worse. One day a lady visited me, obviously distressed. Her husband, a respected physician, owned the house where they were living. A very pretty house on 18 Oriente. According to what she told me, my general liked the house and had called her husband wanting to buy it from him. He had told Andrés that the house wasn't for sale because it was his family's patrimony, and Andrés had replied that he hoped the good doctor would see the light because he wouldn't enjoy buying the house from his widow. With that threat hanging over his head, the doctor agreed to sell it, and gave Andrés a price. Andrés listened as he said so many thousand pesos and then pulled from his desk drawer the assessment stating the value of the house for tax purposes. It was half what the physician was asking. Andrés paid him that amount and then, as the doctor left, gave him three days to clear out. The second day, the wife had come to see me. That night I told Andrés her story.

"So, besides being slow, the woman wants to beat a dead horse. Tell her you know nothing about it."

"But is it true? What do you want the house for?"

"What concern is it of yours?" he asked, and fell asleep.

*   *   *

The next morning, I woke Octavio and told him the story.

"Why don't you stop having those audiences and do something more fun with your time?" he asked.

I kept explaining to him, repeating the story about the house, sure he hadn't taken it in because he was still half-asleep.

"Ay, Cati, don't tell me you don't know that that's how he buys everything," he said, sitting up in bed and stretching. Then he gave a long, noisy yawn.

"Can I come in?" asked Marcela, pushing the door open.

She was wearing pants and a shirt I had sometimes seen on Octavio.

"Aren't you up yet?" she said, walking toward him with her hands behind her back.

"You're a lazybones," she said, emptying over him the glass of water she had hidden behind her.

"Bully!" yelled Octavio, struggling to take the glass from her. They danced around in a scuffle that turned into an embrace and howls of laughter. They were so happy that I was envious of them.

"Well, thanks anyway, Tavo," I said, going to the door.

"Thank you, Cati," he answered, as he watched me close the door behind me.

THE FIRST TIME I saw Andrés furious with Don Juan Soriano, the publisher of the weekly *Avante,* was over the riot at the Plaza de Toros. The second was when he published that antirevolutionaries had slipped into the government of Puebla: that Manuel García, the official mayor, had been the one who denounced the Serdáns; that Ernesto Hernández, a judge in Puebla, had been a member of a questionable organization created by Victoriano Huerta; that Saúl Suárez, collector of revenues for Teziutlán, personally had fired on Venustiano Carranza in Tlaxcalantongo; and that the governor himself had been in La Ciudadela at the time of the coup in which Madero had been assassinated.

"That son-of-a-bitch can consider himself dead," muttered Andrés, folding the newspaper and getting up from the breakfast table.

After that day, I often heard him repeat those words. But Soriano continued to publish his newspaper, drink coffee in the arcades, and walk around the *zócalo* with his wife every Sunday. Everyone knew that he walked from his house to his office, that every night he bought bread in La Flor de Lis, and that he liked to take a solitary stroll after dinner.

I read his newspaper behind Andrés's back. After he threw it down and stomped out cursing, I picked it up and devoured it. There were times I couldn't understand why he was angry.

Maybe it was because often the newspaper failed to cover opening ceremonies Andrés had attended or, when it did, the coverage angered him—like the report of the opening of the Teatro Principal: one photograph of Andrés cutting the ribbon, another of the commemorative plaque saying that the theater had been remodeled during the term of General Andrés Ascencio, and then several lines beneath the photograph asking why there was no credit to the city, since all the work had been done with city funds.

When Aguirre nationalized the oil industry, the only newspaper in Puebla to show any enthusiasm was *Avante*. Andrés was furious; he thought it was crazy to anger powerful countries just to expropriate something he considered of no value. Nonetheless, when Señora Aguirre called on women from all social classes to donate money, jewels, whatever they could, to pay off the petroleum debt, Andrés sent me to be part of the ladies' committee headed by Doña Lupe.

He came home one evening carrying a stack of little boxes.

"Take these to her and tell her you are giving away your children's inheritance," he told me.

There was everything there: bracelets, earrings, diamonds, watches, necklaces, a collection of jewelry as extensive as my own. I went to Mexico City with the girls and the boxes. When we arrived at the Bellas Artes auditorium, it was overflowing. Campesinas had brought chickens, and women with piggy banks filled with five-centavo coins marched up to deposit them on the table in the center of the stage. Even some gringa women spoke against the oil companies and publicly donated thousands of pesos.

The girls and I approached the table with our boxes and, putting on the faces of heroines, handed them to Señora Aguirre. To complete the farce, at the last moment I was truly moved and also gave the pearls I was wearing.

Avante published a photo of me removing my earrings at the table where Señora Aguirre was presiding. I thanked Don Juan Soriano, and Andrés scolded me.

Time seemed to be creeping along. I began to feel as if for centuries I had been wearing my best tender-mother-of-the-people-of-Puebla face as I blew little kids' noses and embraced ancient old men, while at the same time, through my brothers and sisters, or through Pepa and Mónica, I learned that the whole world was talking about the governor's eight hundred crimes and fifty lovers.

Suddenly they would say, "There goes one of them," or, "That's the house he bought for so and so." All I did was keep a list. I didn't count the ones who lasted only a few hours, on a whim, or who yielded briefly in the face of Andrés's threats. I was fascinated by the ones who were fond of him, fond enough to give him children. I envied them, because they knew only the intelligent and sympathetic side of Andrés; they were always at their best when he went to see them, and he never knew their bad humor or their morning bad breath.

I would have enjoyed being Andrés's lover. Enjoyed waiting for him in my silk robe and shiny slippers, using his money for anything I wanted, sleeping late in the mornings, being rid of public welfare and my role as first lady. Besides, everyone feels pity or affection for the lovers, no one thinks of them as accomplices. I, on the other hand, was the official accomplice.

Could anyone have believed that only rumors reached my ears, that for years I never knew whether I was being told fantasies or truths? I couldn't believe that after Andrés killed his enemies he mixed them into the tar and gravel they used to pave the streets. There was a saying, though, that the streets of Puebla were laid out by angels and paved with the governor's chopped-up enemies.

I didn't want to know what Andrés was doing. I was the mother of his children, the mistress of his house, his wife, his servant, his habit, his joke. Who knows what I was, but whatever it was, I had to keep on being it, even if sometimes I wanted to go to a country where he didn't exist, where my name wasn't linked with his, where people hated me or sought me out independent of their affection or scorn for him.

One day I left the house and took a bus to Oaxaca. I wanted to go somewhere far away. I gave brief consideration to working to earn my living, but had thought better of it before I got to the first town. The bus was crammed with campesinos carrying baskets and hens, and children all crying at the same time. An acrid odor, a mixture of stale tortillas and closely packed bodies, filled the air. I didn't like this new life. As soon as I could, I got off to look for the first bus back. I didn't even walk around the town, because I was afraid someone would recognize me.

I got home early, and was happy to be back in my house. Verania and Checo were playing in the garden. I hugged them as if I had just been returned after a kidnapping.

"What's the matter with you?" asked Verania, who didn't like my sporadic bursts of affection.

The next day I felt like crying again, I wanted to crawl into a deep hole, I didn't want to be who I was, I wanted to be anybody whose husband wasn't dedicated to politics, who didn't have seven children with Andrés's name, with his blood, his children much more than mine but my responsibility all day and every day, all for the one moment he might suddenly show up to congratulate himself on how pretty Lilia was becoming, how charming Marcela was, how Adriana was growing, how stylish Marta's hair was, or the Ascencio gleam he could see in Verania's eyes.

I wanted to be anyone else, living in any house other than that fortress with far too many rooms, rooms I couldn't walk through without tripping. Even outdoors, Andrés had had planted a maze of rosebushes, as if someone might chase him in the darkness. He had hundreds of traps set for anyone who wasn't used to threading through them every day.

The house was so far from anywhere that the only way to leave was by car or horseback. No one except Andrés could go out at night; the house was always guarded by a group of tight-lipped men who were forbidden to speak to us except to say, "I'm sorry, you can't go any farther."

I was getting obsessive. I thought it was my duty to guess what people wanted, and before they came to my house I would spend days thinking about their stomachs, about whether they wanted their meat rare or well-done, whether a *tinga* was too much to digest at night or if they hated spaghetti with parsley. And hardest of all to swallow was that when they did come, they ate everything without a word of appreciation or disapproval, and no one was allowed to interrupt their conversation to ask didn't they want to eat before everything got cold?

For many, I was part of the decor, something they paid as much attention to as they would a piece of furniture that suddenly sat down at the table and smiled at them. I found the dinners terribly depressing. Ten minutes before the guests began to arrive, I wanted to cry, but choked back the tears to keep from smearing my mascara and looking like a witch in the bargain. Because that wasn't my thing, Andrés would say. My thing was to be pretty, sweet, impeccable. How would it look if when guests arrived they found the señora wailing with her head stuck under a chair?

It took a lot of effort to disguise my weariness before those men who took their wives by the elbow as if their arms were the handle of a teacup. On the other hand, they were eager, ready to eat a good meal and gauge by the menu how they stood.

Nearly always, I forgot something. No matter how many times Andrés lectured me about how to manage the servants and how to use executive techniques to get everyone to perform their tasks, just as the guests would come in, Matilde, the cook, would remember there weren't any limes, or that there weren't enough tortillas to go around, or that there were too many people for the amount of ice we had in the refrigerator. At such moments, I could easily have hanged a guest, and a good choice one night would have been Marilú Izunza with her mane of blond hair.

That dinner was one of the worst. I woke up that morning hating the color of my hair, the circles under my eyes, my height. I wanted to look different and see if it made me feel like a new person, so I asked my hairdresser to cut my hair any way she wanted.

I ended up nearly bald, with her standing behind me saying that this was the latest style, that even cuts were out of vogue, that with my eternally shoulder-length hair I looked like a village Cristo, that long hair was for girls and I was an important lady. She showed me magazines, made up my eyes and my lips, but failed to convince me. I wept and cursed the hour that my frustration had led me to change my appearance.

I went to my parents' house in search of comfort. My papa was in the kitchen waiting for his coffee machine to spurt a stream of black coffee into the little built-in metal cup. It was an Italian coffeemaker. He stood before it every morning, waiting for his espresso as if he were in a café in Rome. As soon as the black liquid began to pour out and the aroma spread through the house, he would sing the praises of his authentic Italian coffee.

"But that coffee's from Córdoba, Papa," I said every time he launched into his routine.

"From Córdoba, yes, but in all Mexico there is no coffee like mine; here they grind the coffee very coarse and let it boil. It's undrinkable. American coffee, they call it. And only a gringo could think it's good because all gringos have corrupted palates. Their favorite dish is ground meat smothered in sweet tomato sauce. Can you imagine anything more disgusting? Smell this, on the other hand. Smell this and close your ignorant mouth."

When I walked into the kitchen minus my hair and with a face that my hairdresser had painted like a starlet, my papa interrupted his communion with the coffee and whistled, *whiu, whiuuuú!* Then he began to sing: "It was your hair that made me love you, now that it's gone, I can't think of you. . . ."

I hugged him. I stood awhile in his arms, recalling the scent of the country and smelling the aroma of the coffee. It felt good there, and I began to cry.

"Listen, I was just kidding," he said. "I love you anyway, even if you do look like a peeled onion."

"The trouble is that there's going to be a dinner party at my house," I said.

"And what's new about that? In your house there's a party every couple of days. That's no reason to cry. You're a great cook, it's something you inherited. Look at those hands. You have a country woman's hands, the hands of a woman who knows how to work.

My mother did everything herself; you have an army of helpers. It'll work out fine. Who's coming now?"

"What difference does it make? Some men who have factories in Atlixco. But they're going to look at my hair, and their wives are going to laugh at me."

"Since when do you care what people say? With that face you look like your mama. If you're crying, you're never going to please anyone. Not bald, not with hair down to your knees. The trick is to feel happy."

"But I'm not happy," I said, putting my arms around him again.

"What's bothering you? Don't you have everything you want? Don't cry. Look how beautiful the sky is. Think how easy it is to live in a country where there's no winter. Think how the coffee smells. Come, my little girl, come let Papa pour you a cup with a lot of sugar. Come tell your papa all about it."

Of course I didn't tell him anything. He didn't want me to tell him, that's why he began talking to me as if I were a little girl who should never grow up, and we ended up standing arm in arm, gazing at the volcanoes, thankful to have such beauty before us and to be alive to see it. He gave me lots of kisses, and put his hand up the back of my blouse and traced lines on my shoulders until I calmed down and began to laugh.

"Now, like that you look beautiful," he said. "Do you want to be my sweetheart?"

"Of course," I told him. "Your sweetheart, but not your wife. Because if we get married, you'll want me to organize dinner parties for your friends."

Marilú came to the house that night wearing a fur—visible proof that her husband shared his wealth. She was the daughter of one of those Spanish families in which the father is a merchant, the son a gentleman, the grandson a pauper. Her father was the grandson. He didn't have a five-centavo piece, but he was secure in his ancestry and the fact that he could bequeath it to his daughter. With such capital in her pocket, Marilú did Julián Amed the favor of marrying him. Julián Amed was an Arab who got his start selling fabrics in La Victoria market. He would waylay someone on her way to buy vegetables, and with his interminable babble force her to buy at least a meter of his fine cotton. Afterward, at night, when the market closed, he would join his countrymen to play cards, and that was where—after winning several big pots, one of which he collected by killing the loser, who refused to pay him, and ending up with everything he had—Julián put together enough money to start his thread-and-textile factory. He was already very wealthy by the time he convinced Marilú that his money and the Izunza breeding would make splendid children and an exemplary family. Marilú, who, because of undernourishment hidden beneath the massive dining room furniture inherited from her grandfather, was then a pale, transparent-skinned little blonde, accepted after a weak show of hesitation. As soon as she was married, her blue blood gushed to the level of her husband's pocketbook and she became insufferable. As often as she could, she favored me with her opinions.

"How brave you are, living with a politician. You always have to be pretending, and it's *so* difficult not to be frank. I couldn't do it. Julián is always fussing at me because I say just what I think, but I tell him, what does it hurt you? You're a businessman, you don't have to stay on good terms with everyone, what you have is yours because you earned it with your hard work, you're not a politician. Besides, we Izunzas are frank, and you knew that when you married me."

That night I was in no mood to put up with Marilú. Matilde,

the cook, who was sick and tired of all the dinners, fell into a rage because I told her that the meat was too dry. Checo was in his room crying because I hadn't stayed until he fell asleep. Andrés had spent the afternoon praising Heiss, and as the last straw, my hairdresser had left me practically bald. I wasn't in any mood to listen to Marilú, but there she was right in the middle of the *sala* in her fox furs, as if there were no fire in the fireplace, telling all the other women how she'd fired a servant who had been with her ten years because she found out the girl was pregnant and had tried to get rid of the baby with a broomstick.

"Frankly, I was horrified. And all because she didn't listen to me. I told her to be careful around those factory workers, that they weren't to be trusted and did nothing in life but go around trying to find some girl to get into trouble. I told her that when I saw her with her hair combed just so, offering to carry messages to the factory. I told her, don't go thinking about men, you're far better off with me, you have it good here, I treat you well, you can look after my children as if they were your own. Why do you want to get mixed up with some man who can't put bread in your mouth and will only leave you in trouble? But she didn't pay attention. She had to go switching around like a little whore because that's how her kind is, but afterward, oh, yes, the tears flowing, the I'm so sorry, señora, he deceived me, señora. But not with me. I told her very clearly, look, I'm going to be good to you because you've been in this house a long time. I'm going to let you stay until the baby is born. I'm not going to pay you because you won't do half your work, but if you look after the children, I'll be satisfied. But that's it. When your time comes, it's back to your village, because I don't have time to look after you and I don't want my children to know about your situation. What more could she want? Well, she wanted more, all right, she wanted to get rid of the baby. You don't know what I suffered. She seemed like such a good girl, think of all those times I left her with my children. Imagine, in the hands of someone like that; she'd just as soon have murdered them."

"Having a baby is something that can happen to anyone," I said.

"Oh, Catalina, the things you say. You see, you are a politician's wife. But why did you cut your hair?" she asked, swishing her own long mane back and forth. "What did your papa think? You care a lot about what your papa thinks, don't you? The other day he was having dinner at our house and all he did was talk about you."

"My papa had dinner at your house?" I said, startled.

"Of course, he's representing the governor in some business dealings with Julián. Didn't he tell you he was going to be rich?"

I hated the idea that my father was having anything to do with Marilú's husband or acting as Andrés's representative.

"I didn't know that," I said, sounding like a ninny.

"I'm sure he wanted to surprise you. Don't tell him I told you," she said, looking at the other guests, who were pleased to be in on this juicy bit of gossip.

"Oh, I won't," I said. "Have you dyed your hair a little lighter?"

"I don't dye my hair. We were at the beach, and the sun bleached it."

"I can't stand the beach," said Luisita Rivas. "You have to take off your clothes and then get into water that's thick with sand and salt and practically a bathtub for the whole world. It's revolting."

"Oh, no, Luisita. Forgive me, but the sea is divine," said another of the women. I seized the opportunity of this change of subject to get up and look for Andrés.

★   ★   ★

He was in the center of the circle the men made when they stood around talking before dinner, glasses of whiskey in hand, ashes flying any which way. Andrés smoked cigars, and as I approached him he was biting off the tip of one prior to lighting it.

"Will you give me a minute?" I asked him.

"Is it urgent?" he replied, because he had the floor and he hated to yield it.

"Yes, it's a simple matter, but urgent."

"Well, we'll just see what my wife's simple matter is," he said. "Excuse me, señores."

I clung to his arm as if we were going for a long walk. I led him from the sala, through the dining room, and I would have gone farther but he stopped me.

"What is all this?"

"I don't want you to get my papa mixed up in your affairs. Let him get along however he can, he hasn't been starving, so don't mess things up."

"You interrupted me for that? Why don't you go see if dinner is ready yet? And since when do ducks shoot at the shotgun?" he asked, laughing. "And why did you cut my hair?"

I hated it when he acted as if he owned me. But I held my tongue and changed my tone to one that would have better effect.

"Andrés, if you'll do this for me, I'll give you something you want. I'll let you give Mapache to Heiss, but you get my father out of his deal with Amed."

"Mapache to Heiss? Your beloved horse? I'll see what I can do, I promise, little crybaby. Stop now, your mascara is going to run. Come on, let's go back to our guests; they didn't come here to watch us whispering in a corner."

I went back to the women. I would rather have listened to the men's conversation, but that wasn't proper. The dinners always split like that, the men on one side and us on the other, talking about births, servants, and hairdos. The wonderful world of woman is what Andrés called it.

I was always happy to go into the dining room, because at the table the conversation could get interesting. As I was the one who arranged the place cards and seated people wherever I pleased, I put Sergio Cuenca next to me. He was a handsome man and a good conversationalist whom I invited to dinners even when there was no reason, because he was one of the very few of Andrés's friends I found entertaining. He liked to lead the conversation, and when he sat beside me I could whisper things to him I wanted said, without being the one to say them.

"Did you hear that some Indians in Alchichica chased off Heiss and his manager Pérez?" he asked. "They didn't like the tone they used to try to convince them to sow sugarcane in their fields."

"I heard about that," said Don Juan Machuca, a Spaniard who never left his factory in Atlixco yet knew everything that happened before anyone else. "I heard they killed two stable boys. That Heiss doesn't like to waste any time. I think he paid one of their leaders to go talk to the campesinos about renting their communal land. The campesinos didn't want to, and Heiss went out to tell them it was a deal whether they liked it or not. Naturally, the head man was furious, and to show that he hadn't made his own deal, he set out after Heiss as he left. Don Miguel still has a few things to learn."

"Is he all right?" I asked.

"Nothing happened," said Andrés. "Don Mike knows how to handle things. The truth is that the Indian double-crossed him. And now there's some woman going around saying that the land De Velasco sold Heiss belonged to her father. Now, I ask you . . ."

"But, General, those lands belonged to Don Gabriel de Velasco long before the Revolution," said Julia Conde, stirring the air with her green feather fan.

"Doña Julia, always so knowledgeable about what happened before the Revolution. Do you miss those good old days?" Andrés asked her.

"In truth, General, I do. Things aren't the same."

"Right. She was twenty then and now she's fifty," I muttered to Sergio Cuenca, who burst out laughing. "Besides, that land belongs to Lola."

"What are you two laughing about?" asked Andrés.

"Something your wife said, General. She says the land belonged to the father of Lola Campos."

"No wonder you're laughing at her."

"*With* her, General," said Sergio. Then he lifted his glass and entertained us with one joke after another through what was left of the meal.

It was about two in the morning when Marilú slipped into her fox and said good-bye, along with her husband and the other guests. I walked them to the door. Doña Julia Conde was tirelessly fanning herself.

"I don't know, my child," she said to Marilú, "how you can bear to wrap that animal around you. In this country it's hot all year-round. Winter is a fiction. I find I'm always burning up."

"She's never gotten out of menopause," I said under my breath to Andrés, who had his arm around my shoulder.

"You're right, Doña Julia," he said. "Our ladies can't take what they used to. We have to wrap them in furs so they last at least long enough to raise our children. Don't you agree, Julián?"

"Of course he does," said Marilú in farewell.

★　★　★

"Who told you the land in Alchichica belonged to that woman?" asked Andrés after we closed the door.

"She did. She came to see me about a month ago. She wanted me to talk to you and convince you that her father inherited it from his father, and that they grew crops there for many years until De Velasco cheated them out of it, and now that he's bankrupt he finds it easy to sell to Heiss what isn't his. And Heiss buys it for nothing, using the excuse that there's a risk of a takeover. What crooks, Andrés!"

"What did you tell her?" he asked.

"What could I tell her? To find another way, that I couldn't talk to you about it, that you wouldn't listen. What does it matter what I told her? I didn't help her. I was ashamed when she got up to leave without offering to shake hands."

"And if you kept quiet about this for a month, why did you have to be a know-it-all tonight?"

"Because that's how people are. Until it touches you, you don't feel it," I said.

"Catalina, you still don't understand. That land doesn't belong to Lola, you can't believe everything some Indian tells you. And that thread business I got your father into is the most harmless deal you ever came across."

"I don't believe you," I said for the first time in my life. "I don't believe either of those things."

"Do you believe me when I tell you I like you a lot with short hair?" he said.

He began to kiss me right in the middle of the patio, to run his hands over me as we walked toward the stairs to our bedroom. He had large hands. I liked them as much as others feared them. Or maybe that's why I liked them. I don't know.

He kept talking as he took off his clothes.

"What a funny girl we have here; why does she have to know everything that's none of her business?"

After his jacket, he removed his pistol. I wished I had a pistol to wear under my dress. I was slow getting the buttons undone. It was a long dress, cut low in the back and fastened up to the neck in front. A dress that was hard to get into and out of because of the countless buttons.

"You're so slow, Catín," he said. I sat down with my back to him; he was already in bed.

"C'mere," he ordered. I wanted to see the ocean and closed my eyes.

"Why don't you give Lola her land back?" I asked.

"What a silly woman you are! Because I can't," he said, rocking above my body.

"But if you can get my papa out of the web of Amed's thread . . ."

"I hope."

The next morning I was humming some tune to myself as I ran downstairs toward the back patio. Andrés was already on Listón, and the young boy who helped me mount was holding the reins of a sorrel mare.

"Where's Mapache?" I asked.

"He belongs to the man you wanted to give him to," said Andrés. I squeezed my fist until my nails dug into the palm of my hand.

"Then it's a deal," I said as I prepared to get on the mare.

"A done deal," he replied, spurring Listón into a canter.

I started after Andrés, galloping my mare as if she were running away with me. I soon left him behind. I rode through Manzanillo to the Costes woods and straight on to La Malinche, without a thought for Checo's flu or breakfast or the fact that Lilia always looked for me in the morning so I could tell her what the women had worn to dinner. With her, I could sit in the garden and vent my spleen to my heart's content, flattered that she laughed so hard at my gossip.

All I had do was imagine Heiss riding Mapache and I cried and screamed, the wind hard against my face, drying the tears I couldn't stop.

I got home about eleven. Andrés had already left, the children were in school, only Checo was home, grumbling about his flu.

"Only a fool won't go to school," I said, throwing myself down beside him. Then I called Ausencio, the head manservant, and asked him to go look for the maid Señora Amed had just thrown out of her house.

"Tell her we want her to come work for us. That I know about her problem, not to worry."

Lucina arrived the next day carrying her clothes in a cardboard box. She had dark eyes and a ruddy complexion. She didn't talk much, but she told Checo all the stories I didn't know, sewed dresses for Verania's dolls, and gave me back rubs when she thought I looked sad. She became nanny to us all.

The baby she was carrying came out one morning without much to-do. It was a five-month fetus and it was dead. She cried over it for one day. Ausencio, the children, and I went with her to bury it in her village. All of us helped carry the little white wood box she had chosen for it. The tiny cemetery had no walls; it was an open field with simple graves. At the far end, beneath a tree, was the hole for her baby. Ausencio laid the little coffin in it and Lucina hurriedly threw a handful of dirt over the box.

"It was better this way," she said.

Verania wanted to sing "Oh, María, Madre Mía," and we joined in.

On the way back in the car, we were all very quiet until Lucina told us, "Don't be sad. My baby is in heaven now. He's a star. Isn't that true, señora?"

"Yes, Lucina," I said.

After that, Marilú Amed spread the story that I had lured her maid away from her, had forced her to have an abortion, and kept her like a slave looking after my children. She never got over her tantrum.

A few days later, after dinner, I went for a walk with Checo. I took him to the point of Guadalupe hill to watch the evening star come out.

"Listen, Mama," he said. "Do you believe all that about Lucina's baby being a star in the sky?"

"Why do you want to know?"

"Because Verania believes it and I know it isn't true; Lucina's baby is in that hole."

"In the hole?"

"Yes, in the hole. Like Celestino. Papa said yesterday to go look for a hole for Celestino."

"Who did he say that to?"

"Some men who came to see him from Matamoros."

"You didn't hear right. Why would your papa say that?"

"Yes, he did say it, Mama. That's what he always says. Look for a hole for so and so. And that means they have to kill him."

"Oh, Checo, what an imagination," I told him. "Do you think killing is a game?"

"No. Killing is hard work, my papa says."

I heard a rumble in my stomach and the rice, meat, tortillas, cheese, and crêpes all came up as Checo watched without knowing what to do, occasionally asking, "Is that all, Mama?" Finally,

I threw up something yellow and bitter and then there was nothing more.

"Shall we race back down?" I asked my son. And I began to run down the hill as if I wanted to fling myself off.

"You're crazy, Mami. My papa's right. You're a wild mountain goat," the child shouted behind me.

We were exhausted when we got home. Verania was in the doorway holding Lucina's hand. She was a beautiful girl with enormous eyes and delicate lips. Pale like me. Naive like my sisters.

"Why were you so long?" she asked.

"Because Mama was sick," said Checo.

"Sick, how?"

"At her stomach. She threw up all her dinner," said the boy, who was five then. Five insane years old.

Our children couldn't live in the clouds. They were too close to things. When I decided to stay, I also decided for them. There was no way to keep them in a glass bubble.

In that huge house, they lived on one floor and we on another. We could spend our lives without seeing each other. After the night I vomited, I decided to close a chapter on motherly love. I left the children to Lucina. Let her bathe them, dress them, listen to their questions, teach them to pray and to believe in something, even if it was the Virgin of Guadalupe. Overnight, I stopped spending my afternoons with them, I stopped thinking about what they would have for lunch, how to entertain them. At first I missed them. I had spent years closely bound to their lives, they had been my passion, my diversion. They were used to running into my bedroom as if it was their playroom. They woke me at the crack of dawn, even if I had scarcely slept, they played with my necklaces, they dressed up in my shoes and my coats, their lives were interwoven with mine. From that night on, I locked my door. When they came the next morning, I let them knock, without answering. In the afternoon I explained that their papa wanted it to be quiet in the rooms on the first floor, and asked them not to come again.

They got used to it, and so did I.

O N THE OTHER hand, I decided to learn what I could about what Andrés was up to in Atencingo. I began by finding out that the Celestino Checo had heard referred to was Lola's husband, and that his death was the first in a string of deaths. After that, I made friends with Heiss's daughters. Helen, especially. She had two children and was divorced from a gringo who had put her through some terrible times before she found the courage to leave him.

Helen had come back to Puebla looking for help from her father, who, as was to be expected, would not give her five centavos without some return. He put her to work in Atencingo. Her task was to spy on a Señor Gómez, her father's administrator, and to judge how loyal he was in handling business affairs. To do that, she went to live in a desolate, half-empty house with a swimming pool filled with icy water and hundreds of flies in the afternoons.

From time to time I would go visit. I took the children to swim in her dreadful pool while the two of us talked.

"There are almost no men here," she said. And she would tell me her latest experience with one of the local men about town. She was intent on marrying one of them, just as I was sure none of them would fall into that trap. Gringas were fine for a while, but no one wanted one permanently. Helen wanted to marry and have a set of Puebla pottery dishes and a house with a peaked roof. I don't know why she felt it had to be peaked. Every time she spoke about her future, that roof was included as something essential.

One day we were sitting on the patio watching the children swim and drinking one of the daiquiris she prepared and sipped without interruption, when we heard shots. I ran outside in my swimming suit, cutting my feet on the prickly grass and gravel that surrounded the house. Checo came up to me with my sandals.

"Go back in the house," I told him. I put on my shoes and ran toward the sugar mill. A man was dead. A quarrel between two drunks, Gómez, the administrator, reported.

A woman was sitting on the ground, weeping slowly, as if she had a lifetime of crying ahead of her.

When I was near enough to ask who the dead man was, she looked up and said, "He was my husband. Help me, because if I stay here they'll kill me, too, and then who will look after the children?"

Juan, the chauffeur, had followed me. I asked him to collect the corpse. I gave Gómez my best governor's wife look, before informing him, "I'll take the body."

"Whatever you say. The woman stays here, though," he said, when he saw I had my arm around her.

"She's coming with me," I replied.

We walked back to Helen's house. There the woman began to talk as if she had no thought at all for my connection with the governor. I listened without saying a word, my head in my hands. What she told was horrifying. No one could have invented anything like that.

When she was through, Helen, in her silly gringa accent, stopped drinking long enough to say, "I don't doubt it, Cathy. These men are horrible. What great relatives we have."

"I want Heiss to give me back Mapache," I told Andrés, when he came to bed.

"A deal's a deal, Catín. Your papa is out of the woods with Amed."

"But you and your men killed those campesinos in Atencingo."

"What?" said Andrés.

"The one person who survived told me. This afternoon they killed her husband at the sugar mill. I saw him. They murdered him because he came to tell the peons how two days ago Heiss's and your men massacred the people defending the land that bastard gringo bought from De Velasco for three thousand pesos. She said that more than fifty were killed, including children, that you sent the army to disarm them and then ordered in a hundred men with machine guns. Give me back my horse. No one can bring back the dead, but if everyone is going to get something out of this, I want my horse back or I'll tell Don Juan at *Avante* the truth of it."

"You will keep your mouth shut. That's all I need, an enemy in my own bed. The governor's wife spilling her guts to the honest newspaperman. What can you be thinking?"

"I want my horse," I told him, and left to go sleep in the sitting room.

I sank into the large blue chair where once I had spent whole afternoons doing absolutely nothing. Those days seemed so far away. Every time I discovered another of Andrés's atrocities, everything in the past seemed light-years away. For days, I was as if I weren't there, turning things over and over in my mind, wanting to leave, ashamed and frightened, sure there would never be another peaceful afternoon, that I would never be free of my disgust and fear.

That was the worst night I had known. I went to bed trembling. I tried not to close my eyes because I saw the face of the young Indian lying on the floor of the mill, and that of his wife, weeping beneath the folds of her rebozo.

Finally, I fell asleep. I dreamed my children had blood on their faces. I wanted to clean it off, but all I had were handkerchiefs dripping more blood. When I awoke, Lucina was knocking at the door. I opened it and she came in with my tea, cream, sugar, and toast.

"The General says for you to come down in an hour."

"Is it a pretty day?" I asked.

"Yes, señora."

"Have the children gone off to school?"

"They're eating breakfast."

"I feel sorry for the children. Don't you, Luci?"

"Why, señora? They're happy. What shall I get for you to wear?"

I ran down the stairs. I burst into the stables, shouting his name. There he was, elegant body and white star between his eyes.

"Mapache, Mapachito, how did that fucking son-of-a-bitch gringo treat you? Do you forgive me?"

I stroked him, I kissed his face, his nose, his back. Then I got on him and we raced toward the mill at Huexotitla. I was singing, to frighten away the dead. Riding out, I still saw them, but by the time I got home, I had forgotten.

At midday, I went with Andrés to a luncheon. There were

newspapermen there. One who reported for *Avante* asked Andrés about the deaths at Atencingo.

"What happened there was extremely regrettable," he said. "I have charged the public prosecutor to conduct a full investigation and I can assure you that justice will be done. But we cannot allow bands of outlaws disguised as campesinos, demanding their right to the land, to take with violence what others have won with honest work and somber dedication. The Revolution does not err, nor does my regime, which follows its precepts. Good afternoon, señores."

The newspaperman wanted to follow up, but the master of ceremonies took the microphone in time.

"*Señoras y señores, damas y caballeros*, at this time the governor must leave us. We ask you to clear the way to the exit."

People stood up and began to drift toward the door. I watched as four of Andrés's men took his arms and hustled him out; others did the same with me. They shoved us into two different automobiles, and tires squealed as we pulled away.

"What's going on?" I asked the man driving the car I'd drawn.

"Nothing, señora. We're practicing new getaways," he said.

Andrés went to his offices in the Palacio de Gobierno, and I went home.

Andrés's older children were in the game room with some friends. Marta had told me she was going to invite her classmate Cristina, who was the daughter of Patricia Ibarra, the younger sister of José Ibarra, who had been my sweetheart.

We used to say we were sweethearts because we liked to go to La Rosa for ice cream, then walk hand in hand to La Concordia park, where we would kiss each other on the cheek before we said good-bye. One day José was unlucky enough to kiss me just as his sister was coming out of twelve o'clock mass, and saw us. José's family told him that besides being poor, I was a crazy girl who didn't know her place, and his father asked him if he didn't want to go to Europe.

José told me everything, as if I were his mother and it was up to me to save him from his punishment.

"So they're not going to let you be my sweetheart?" I asked.

"You don't know how my family is."

"And I don't want to!" I told him, and ran all the way from the park to our house at 2 Poniente, enraged.

"What's the matter, child?" my mother asked.

"She fought with her little rich boy. Can't you see it in her face?" my father said.

"What did he do to you?" My mother always felt any offense in her own flesh.

"Whatever it is, it's nothing to lose any sleep over," my father answered. And to me: "You should have stuck your tongue out at him."

"I did," I said.

The niece of that blockhead, whose parents later married him to Maru Ponce to form the most boring family of any who strolled through the arcades every Sunday, was Marta's friend, and a beautiful girl.

Cristina's mother came to our house that evening to pick her up just as Andrés was arriving, and he invited them to stay for dinner. All through the meal he flattered them, asked them about the men of their family, and told them stories about bullfighters and politicians.

As José's sister left she said, "Cati, it was delightful to see you again, as elegant as ever."

"You didn't think that ten years ago," I replied.

"I don't know what you mean," she said with a sick smile, and undoubtedly went home with diarrhea, because Andrés had been whispering who knows what to her daughter, who was so flustered she put her hat on backward.

Within three days, he had borne Cristina off to his ranch near Jalapa. He kept her there till the end, and it was from there she came, with her baby daughter, to claim her part of the inheritance. She didn't do too badly. She still lives among her horses and dogs and antiques, doing nothing useful. Even Cristina's son-in-law lives off her take.

But it didn't anger me. Why would I be angry when the whole Ibarra family still feels the shame? And those days, I even found it entertaining. It made me laugh that the General had stolen Marta's classmate, and that it was driving her mother mad. I laughed even harder every time I pictured Señora holier-than-thou dragging herself in and out of church—to no avail. "That one didn't even have time to earn respect," I said to myself, thinking of José, La Concordia park, and the kiss of my dishonor.

It's true that in Puebla everything happened in the arcades. That's where Espinosa was standing when he suffered the knife wound that took him out of the movie theater business. That's where, before she suffered her downfall, Magdalena Maynes came to show off her new clothes. But that girl's life was totally, but totally, changed when her father was murdered. It seems I can see her now; there was never a wrinkle in her linen dress, her clothes fit as perfectly as a mannequin's. They weren't a rich family, but they spent money as if they were. We used to see them frequently because the father had business with Andrés. Everyone seemed to have business with Andrés.

Magdalena was her papa's favorite. On weekends he used to take her to the Casino de la Selva in Cuernavaca. We ran into them there once. Magda was wearing a flower-printed silk dress and her hair was caught back with two combs. She was sipping her lemonade with a coolness that was nearly sultry.

When we arrived, she and her father were sitting at one of the tables in the garden, facing the pool. We had all the children with us. When her father saw us, he got up and led Andrés aside to talk with him. Magdalena chatted with us about how warm it was without missing a flicker of her father's expression. He soon returned to his table but left immediately, accompanied by his daughter, asking him God only knows what and transformed from a frivolous adolescent into a fierce litigant. I thought the change a bit odd, but then so many things were odd we no longer noticed. In the car, on the way home to Puebla, I asked Andrés what had upset them, and he told me it was nothing I needed to know. So I forgot the Maynes.

Months later, the father disappeared. He was kidnapped one night as he walked through the arcades.

Magda came to the house to see me. She looked beautiful in a tailored alpaca suit and gray silk blouse.

"My father went to the movies days ago and hasn't come home," she said.

He probably has a lover, I wanted to tell her, but I held my tongue, staring at my hands as if I were to blame.

"Would you be good enough to ask your husband about him?"

"Gladly, but I doubt it will do any good. If he has your father, he's not going to tell me."

"People say you know how to handle him."

"They also say you sleep with your father. You may find out they're mistaken."

"I hope they are not mistaken, señora." She stood up and left.

Three days later, the father reappeared, chopped into pieces and stuffed into a basket someone left at the door to his house.

I heard about it late that morning when I went to have my hairdresser comb my hair and some scandalized old ladies rushed in to tell everyone about it. My hairdresser, whose name is Ofelia, was arranging a switch in my hair and asking me how it felt, when she saw my tears in the mirror. I sat quietly while she finished putting in the hairpins. The salon was unnaturally silent and the claque of old ladies were staring at me as if I held the knife in my hands. I looked at the fingernails Maura was painting and bit my lips so that not one tear, not even one, would escape as I thought about that gentleman, who was as handsome and as intelligent as everyone said he was.

I went to the Mayneses' house. Many people were there. The widow was sitting between her younger children, her eyes focused on the floor, as quiet as if she, too, had been murdered.

Magdalena was the only one beside the coffin. She saw me come in. I didn't go over to her because I had nothing to say. I only wanted to see her and to find out whether the wreath Andrés sent would fit through the door. Because that was his game. When the dead man was his work, or when he considered the man's disappearance beneficial, he sent enormous flower wreaths, so huge they couldn't get them through the door of the house where the wake was being held.

As I responded to the Hail Marys, I read the ribbons on the bouquets and wreaths. None of them said *General Andrés Ascencio and Family*. When the litany began, I got up and went to see if the wreath was still outside, but before I reached the door I saw two men carrying in one of the arrangements Andrés had ordered from the flower market in La Victoria. It fit through the door.

I left. It occurred to me that Ofelia might know what people were saying; surely one of the women whose hair she had combed that morning had told her something. I went back to see her.

She didn't know any more than I had already imagined. People were saying that Andrés had killed him—no one could think of any other possibility—but there was no proof. I remembered the discussion in Cuernavaca, though, and Magdalena's eyes when she asked me to help her father.

I went home. I locked myself in the small sala, first to chew off my fingernail polish, and then my fingernails. I despised my general. I didn't know whether I most wanted to see him come home so I could ask him about it, or lock myself in this room and never see him again.

He came in laughing. He'd been riding, and his spurs scraped the floor. I listened as he climbed the stairs and walked to the end of the corridor. He stopped at the door to the sala and pushed. When it didn't open, he began to yell.

"No one locks a door on me, Catalina. This is my house and I go anywhere I want. Open up, I'm not in the mood for any of your crap."

Of course, I opened it. I didn't want anyone to hear the racket.

"I know you went," he said. "You saw that I had nothing to do with it. Take off that dress, it makes you look like a crow. I want to see your tits, I hate it when you button up like a nun. Go on, don't go all modest on me, it doesn't become you." He pulled up my dress and I pressed my legs together. The weight of his body made the hooks of my garter belt dig into my flesh.

"Who killed him?" I asked.

"I don't know. Pure souls have many enemies," he said. "Take off that shit. It's getting harder to fuck you than some village virgin. Take all that off," he said, as he rubbed his body against my dress. But I kept my legs tight, tight together, for the first time.

FROM THE MOMENT I saw Fernando Arizmendi, I wanted to go to bed with him. Listening to him talk, I thought how much I
wanted to nibble his ear, touch his tongue with mine, see
the backs of his knees.

My fascination was obvious, because I began talking
more than I usually did, and at lightning speed. I ended
up being the center of attention. Andrés noticed and
broke up the party.

"Catalina is not feeling well," he said.

"But she looks great," someone replied.

"That's the Max Factor, but she's had a headache for
quite a while. I'm going to take her home, and then I'll
be back."

"I feel fine," I said.

"You don't have to put up a good front for these people, they're my friends. They understand."

He took my arm and led me to the car. He put me
into the front seat, sent the chauffeur to the car behind
us, and went around to the driver's side. He slipped be-

hind the wheel, started the car, waved good-bye to the friends who had come to the door to see us off, and slowly drove away. He held his frozen smile until we were a block away.

"How obvious you are, Catalina. You're asking for a slap or two."

"But you, you're always subtle, aren't you?"

"I don't have to be subtle, I'm a man. You're a woman, and when women run around like she-goats in heat, wanting to fuck anyone who makes their belly buttons tremble, they're called whores."

When we reached the house, he got out of the car, moving very deliberately, walked me as far as the door, waited for the servant to open it, and when he was sure that our eternal escorts in the car behind us couldn't see, swatted me on the rear and pushed me inside.

I ran through the house, bounded up the stairs, passed the children's room without stopping as I usually did, and went directly to bed. I crawled under the sheets and thought about Fernando while I touched myself as the gypsy had suggested. Then I went to sleep. I slept for three days. I woke up only to eat a bit of lettuce, a bite of cheese, and a couple of boiled eggs.

"Don't you feel well, señora?"

"I have an illness the General discovered, one I can't even shake with cold showers. But with a week's sleep, I'll get over it."

At the end of a week, I had to leave my room, because that was a long time for a fever. And what was the first thing Andrés told me when I came down to eat breakfast?

That on Tuesday the private secretary to the president was coming to dinner. And who was the private secretary? Fernando. The elegantly pressed and smiling Arizmendi.

From pure shock, I began eating my bread and butter and marmalade and gulping great swallows of black tea with sugar and cream. Andrés was ecstatic about Arizmendi's visit, because it would be followed by a visit from the president of the Republic, and for him Andrés planned a spectacular reception with all the town's schoolchildren waving little flags along the Avenida Reforma and banners hanging from the buildings and all the bureaucrats looking out their office windows, cheering and throwing confetti. I was to arrange for a little girl with a bouquet of flowers to run up to the president in the middle of the street, and an old woman with a letter asking for something simple, so photographers could take her picture five minutes later with her request satisfied. Espinosa and Alarcón had already told Andrés he could hang the largest banners from their movie houses. Puebla was going to give the president the most enthusiastic and splashy welcome he'd ever received. All the things that later became routine for the visit of the most asinine small-town mayor, we invented for the visit of General Aguirre.

I had to do something to cool down, so I began to work as if I were being paid for it. Not one little girl with flowers, but three for every block, and, in the *zócalo*, fifty young girls on horseback dressed in the bright flounced skirts and embroidered blouses of *china poblana* costumes.

I went to the old age home to choose my little old woman and found one worthy of a postcard: hair in a bun, the smile of a gentle virgin, and of course a story we could put in the letter. She was the widow of an old and penniless soldier who had been shot for refusing to take part in the assassination of Aquiles Serdán. She was proud of her husband, and of herself, and found it only fair to ask the president for a sewing machine in exchange for all the sacrifices she had made for her country.

I put all the primary-school teachers to work. I got the idea of having them make paper pom-poms like the ones they used at rallies in the United States. I knew that the president's favorite song was "The Boat of Guaymas" and that the children would not have to exert themselves too much to move pom-poms and feet in time with such a simple ditty. I engaged all the flower sellers in the market to fill La Reforma with flowers, as if the avenue were one long church. In the center of the *zócalo* they were to make a floral carpet with the image of an Indian woman holding out her hand to the president. As soon as that gentleman passed by, all the people along Reforma would take their banners and flowers and run to the *zócalo* so it would be overflowing when the president and Andrés entered in their convertible. Following the presidential address from the balcony, everyone in the crowd would sing Puebla's praises in *"Que chula es puebla,"* followed by the national anthem. I arranged to have bands come from every town in the state. I formed an orchestra of three hundred musicians who would play in exchange for the Santa Ana cotton tunics we gave them so everyone would be in a kind of uniform.

By the time the president's private secretary and Andrés reached an agreement, he was amazed by our plans.

I decided we would eat in the garden and serve the menu we planned to offer the president two weeks later. But that noon, only Andrés, Fernando, and I were eating.

We sat at a formal round table, with Andrés at Fernando's left and me at his right. Right from the consommé, Fernando began to praise my gifts: my talent, my intelligence, my refinement, my delicacy, my interest in the nation and its politics, and, he said, to top it off I cooked like the nuns of Puebla's convents.

"Besides which, if you will allow me, General, your wife has a marvelous laugh. Adults don't laugh like that anymore," said Fernando.

"I'm glad it pleases you, my dear sir. This is your house, and we want you to be happy here," Andrés replied.

"Yes, we do," I added, and put my hand on Fernando's leg.

He neither removed it nor changed expression.

Andrés brought up the subject of the uprising in Jalisco. He lamented the death of an officer and a soldier, and praised the governor, who had given the order to send troops against the rebelling campesinos.

"Some things cannot be allowed," was Fernando's reply.

I, who at that time still said what I thought, objected, "But isn't there some way to stop them besides sending in the army and killing twelve Indians? They gave up six dead for each of the two army men. And no one even knows why they were rebelling."

"That's the woman in you coming out," said Andrés. "You were speaking of her intelligence, Fernando, but now she's the sensitive female."

"Perhaps she's right, General. We should find other methods." With this statement, Fernando put his hand on *my* leg. I felt it through the silk of my dress, and forgot about the twelve campesinos. In a little while, he pulled it away and began to eat as if it were his last meal.

We became friends. Every time I went into Mexico City, I would take some message from Andrés or invent some pretext. What I wanted was to hear his voice, and if possible, see him for a moment. Later, I would say his name the whole three hours of the drive home.

I asked the chauffeur, who had a good voice, to sing "With You in the Distance" and then settled back in the seat of the black

Packard to miss Fernando, and dream. I searched for meaning in Fernando's simplest sentences and almost came to believe that he had declared his love, but discreetly, out of respect for the General. I remembered verbatim every word he spoke to me, and from an "I hope we see each other soon" I drew the certainty that he missed me as much as I him, and that he passed the days counting the minutes until our next chance meeting. I loved to think about his mouth, about the sensation that ran through my body when he kissed my hand in greeting me and in parting. One day I couldn't stand it any longer. He had walked me to the door of his office after an unusual conversation in which we hadn't talked about politics or Andrés or Puebla or the nation, only of the pain of unrequited love—and I thought I could see it in his eyes. When he kissed my hand as he said good-bye, I offered my lips. He didn't kiss me, but held me a long moment in his arms.

That night, my poor chauffeur sang "With You in the Distance" so many times he went on to win the National Amateur Hour. I was glad something good had come of my romance, because the same day it reached its pinnacle, it collapsed. Andrés was waiting for me in the Palacio de Gobierno. I'd gone by the tailor's to pick up the suit he was going to wear for the president's visit. It was very late when I got to his office, but he was still there, defusing a crisis of workers in Atlixco who were threatening to go on strike.

I was radiant as I danced into his office, his suit my dance partner.

"You look beautiful, Catalina. What did you do to yourself?" Andrés asked, staring at me as I came in.

"I bought three dresses, I went to the Palacio de Hierro to get new makeup, and I sang all the way here in the car."

"But you took my message to Fernando, you weren't just wasting your time?"

"Of course, I did all the other things after I'd seen Fernando."

"No question about it, these queers can light a fire," Andrés commented to his personal secretary. "Funny how women love to jabber with them. What is it that women find so attractive? I confess that when we met this one, I was actually jealous, and locked Catalina up. Now he's the only boyfriend I allow her. I love this affair."

The next day, I went to see Pepa to tell her about my disaster. I was sure I would find her at home because she never went out. To my surprise, she wasn't there. Her husband's jealousy—magnified by the fact that they had no children—kept her a prisoner. One afternoon, after she'd been out for two hours, he met her at the door with a crucifix and forced her to kneel and ask his forgiveness and to swear right then and there she had not deceived him.

She found it easier to invent things to do in her house. She turned it into a gilded cage, no corner escaped her attention. The patio was alive with birds, and she crocheted interminable doilies for armchairs, tables, glass-front cabinets, and sideboards. Everything in her kitchen was fried in olive oil, even beans, and everything her husband ate she made herself. You'd think she was in love. She spent hours polishing antiques and watering plants. She acted as if no other world existed, and she never let us question it. Once when Mónica was trying to be blunt and point out that Pepa was living in the 1830s, and that her husband was insufferable and she should leave him and be free to walk down the street anytime she wanted, Pepa gently placed her hand over Mónica's lips and asked if she wouldn't like some tea and cookies.

"You are absolutely mad," said Mónica. "Isn't she, Catalina?"

"No more than I am," I replied.

Mónica had to work because her husband had fallen ill. She started with a store for children's clothing and ended up with a factory.

"Funny, the only one of us with a normal husband is me," she had said that day, laughing.

I sat down on an iron bench in the garden beneath the purple flowers of the jacaranda. The maid, who was wearing a white maid's cap and apron, brought me a lemonade and said that the señora was always back by twelve-thirty. I didn't know what she meant, but since that was only fifteen minutes away I decided to wait.

Precisely as the antique family clock was striking the half hour, Pepa walked through the door, out to the patio, and up to my garden bench.

She was the same woman—no makeup, hair in a braid down her back, the carriage of a little girl—but there was something different about her eyes, something about her mouth when she smiled, as if her lips were somehow new.

"You'd think you had a lover," I said, laughing at the absurdity of it.

"I do," she answered, sitting beside me with a tranquillity I've yet to see matched.

They met in the mornings. Every day, from ten-thirty to twelve-thirty, in a room above La Victoria market rented as a storeroom. Who was he? The only man her husband allowed her to speak three words to. The doctor who attended her every time she lost a baby. Three times in all. A handsome fellow, the doctor most women went to when they were pregnant. Half of them would have welcomed a romance, and many got more dressed up to go to his office than for the Red Cross Ball. Yet he ended up with Pepa, the most difficult of all.

"We fuck like gods," she said, laughing happily, her voice as sweet as if she were saying prayers. She was splendid. Never in my wildest dreams could I have imagined her like that.

"And your husband?"

"He has no idea. He can't imagine that woman can rhyme with human. And you? How are things with you?"

"About the same," I replied.

What could I say? My stupid romance with Arizmendi was a good story to tell some poor creature who never got out of the house. But this new woman with the face of a goddess? I couldn't cloud her paradise with something so prosaic. I kissed her, and went away envying her state of grace.

I NEVER UNDERSTOOD how Fito came to be secretary of defense, but then neither had I understood how he got as far as undersecretary. Even when Andrés had brought him to our wedding as a witness, he was already director of something or other.

Andrés himself was surprised when posters appeared on the walls of houses all over the Federal District, signed by General Juan de la Torre and proposing Rodolfo Campos as candidate for president of the Republic.

And Rodolfo was obviously surprised, because he quickly issued a statement declaring that the signs were a clumsy maneuver, that his only ambition was total cooperation with General Aguirre, and that he had no higher aspirations.

I believed him. What aspirations could the poor man have, when not even his own wife respected him? Dumpy as she was, after one week of marriage to Fito she had run away with the doctor in the regiment for which Fito was paymaster. She simply went off one morning without so much as a note. If someone hadn't quickly passed on the rumor to her husband, no telling when he would have found out. Only recently, an old man who had been in the same regiment told me that when Rodolfo found out, he'd gone to his general and burst into tears as he recounted his calamity.

"Go ahead, Sergeant," the general said. "I authorize you to take a platoon, catch up with them, and deal with them as they deserve."

"Oh, no, General," said Fito. "All I want is for you to send a justice of the peace to force them to come back."

The general did send the justice, and they did come back. When Chofi got off her horse, Rodolfo threw himself at her feet, weeping and asking what he had done to deserve her desertion. He begged her to forgive him and kissed her ankles in front of the whole world, while she, hands on her hips, stared coldly over his head.

Sofía was always a haughty woman. They say she used to be good-looking, but I doubt it. What she did do, though, as her husband rose higher and higher, was substitute piety for promiscuity. If she was screwing some priest or other, you'd never know it, and you never caught a glimpse of it in her face.

I will never forget the day Rodolfo became the candidate for the presidency, because it was the same day Tyrone Power arrived in Mexico City.

I had gone to the airport with Mónica, since by coincidence Andrés wanted me to pay a courtesy call on Chofi. Mónica had a dream that she would be waiting to greet Tyrone Power at the steps to his plane, but when we reached the airport we found that thousands of women had exactly the same plan.

Since her husband had been ill for so long, Mónica had spent years sublimating any hope for an affair into manufacturing dresses. The minute she saw Tyrone Power, however, all those repressed desires came flooding out and she turned into a wild beast. She left me behind at one of the airline counters, and dove, kicking and elbowing, into that seething tangle of women.

In two minutes' time, she was all over the poor man.

"Tyrone!" she screamed. "I've seen all your pictures." As she was the first to reach him, she had time to plant a kiss on him that he answered with his carefully programmed doll's smile. He didn't have a chance to smile a second time; firemen and police had to spirit him out of the airport. His fans tore off his jacket and ripped the buttons from his shirt. I last saw him making his getaway, lifted right off his feet by his rescuers. His hair was standing on end and he had lost one shoe.

Mónica had such a cat-that-just-stole-the-cream smirk on her face that it made me purr just to look at her. I have known few people made so happy by so little.

From the airport, we drove to Chofi's house. We found her all dressed up, something that seemed strange to me because at one in the afternoon she was almost always still in her robe and slippers. That day, her hair was combed in tight curls and she was in black from head to toe. She was not a woman you would ever call elegant, so it seemed a bit superfluous on Mónica's part to point out that the huge diamond brooches Chofi had clipped in her cleavage were not worn during the day.

She was sitting in her Louis XV sala, allowing herself to be photographed by several photographers.

After they left, I assumed it was appropriate to congratulate her, although I didn't know why. I asked the last photographer what all this was about as he left, and he told me that Martín Cienfuegos, the governor of Tabasco, had signed a pact with politicians from several parts of the country to back the candidacy of General Rodolfo Campos for president.

Chofi was as cool as a cucumber. She showed us buttons with the picture of her husband that had just been delivered from a factory in the United States and talked about the pro–General Campos committees springing up all over the country.

I assumed that Andrés had known about this development and had sent me there without explanation so I wouldn't balk at having to call on Chofi as if I were her first lady-in-waiting. I was furious with him, but I listened to Chofi's stories with a saintly smile, and when she was through allowed myself the luxury of expressing my congratulations and of asking her to accept those of Andrés, who had been prevented by pressing local problems from flying to the arms of his best friend and compadre. Then I said good-bye, claiming that I wanted to be back in Puebla before dark.

"So, we'll have six years of this boredom to look forward to," said Mónica at the door. "Revolting. I prefer the Indian movement."

We went to eat at the Tampico. Mónica set about flirting with all the men at nearby tables so effectively that at the end of our meal the waiter brought a bottle of champagne we hadn't ordered, a message that said our bill had been paid, and two roses with a card that read, *Please accept the sincere admiration of Mateo Podán and Francisco Balderas.*

I looked around for Balderas, who was secretary of agriculture and had eaten more than once in my house. He was at a table for two not far away, sitting with a man with deep-set eyes and an aquiline nose, whom I took to be Mateo Podán, a journalist Andrés despised.

"Did you say that the one on the right wants to be president, too?" Mónica inquired. "Forgive me, my dear, but I hope so, and the sooner the better."

The men ended up at our table. Mateo Podán had a quick,

cruel tongue he devoted to describing "our friend" Campos as if I were Dolores del Río, or any woman besides the wife of Campos's best friend, Andrés Ascencio. Balderas was quite taken with Mónica, and asked for her address, among other things.

We left the restaurant about seven. It was so late when we reached Puebla that Mónica's husband was on the verge of overcoming his paralysis to rise out of bed and slap her around. Mine already knew exactly what we'd been up to, including the detail that I had liked Podán's large hands.

"Who gave you permission to go around behaving like a bitch?" he asked when I swept into our bedroom about twelve, singing.

"I did," I said, with such aplomb he had to smother a laugh before starting a shouting match that I ended—after putting on my nightgown—by saying, "Don't get excited. Are you so sure that the Fat Man will be president? You'd better light several candles. And call off your bodyguards. They aren't worth what you're paying them. Anyway, I play on your team and you know it."

By the beginning of the year, Rodolfo's candidacy became inevitable, especially after the assassination of General Narváez, which, according to Andrés, was deserved because the man was such a stupid fuckup. Where on earth had he got the notion to take up arms against the government?

Rodolfo, as secretary of defense, issued orders for the soldiers to be generous with the prisoners and to accept the surrender of the few men who were still armed. Then he resigned, to avoid having anyone say that he used his position to recruit followers.

"That jackass is nuts," said Andrés. "He's going to end up a dog between two bones."

By then, Andrés had realized that he might not want his compadre to be president. He went so far as to thank me for being nice to Balderas and wanted me to invite him to dinner with Mónica. We also invited Flores Pliego, and then, one by one, all the rest of the cabinet. But Rodolfo's bandwagon was already firmly on track. Twenty-four governors who favored him met in Veracruz, and Andrés had to go. With his balls in the meat grinder, as they say, but he went. He came back from there calling his compadre a bastard inside our bedroom door and outside it lauding his successes. The person he could never forgive was Martín Cienfuegos. It drove Andrés crazy that Cienfuegos had beat him to the punch and that he didn't know about Cienfuegos's plans for Rodolfo until it was a *fait accompli*. What really burned him was that Rodolfo had discovered a true friend in Cienfuegos and stopped coming to Andrés with the thousand and one things he always had talked over with him.

Not until the Revolutionary Committee of National Reconstruction was formed to promote the candidacy of General Bravo did Fito remember he had an intelligent compadre and make the effort to come visit us in Puebla.

It was during that time that Colonel Fulgencio Batista, who had just come to power in Cuba, passed through the city. He and Rodolfo had breakfast at our house.

"You know when the hero of Cuban democracy is going to give up his power?" Andrés asked me after they left. "Never. That fucker will be there for forty years if they don't shoot him first."

I jokingly asked if he wished they could get away with the same thing in Mexico.

"I'd like that fine," he said. "Then neither that shit-ass Fito, my compadre, or his bosom buddy Cienfuegos would sit in the chair with the eagle before me. But instead of going through that hassle for six lousy years, I'm better off building my own little center of power and having whoever's president dance to my tune."

He talked that way as a kind of voodoo against the mob of bootlickers swarming around his compadre. One afternoon while they were playing dominoes, Andrés called Fito a son-of-a-bitch and promised him he would never be president. Three days later there was a meeting of governors who, as a statement of loyalty, planned to proclaim their support of Campos for president. Instead of going to the Regis theater to be right in the middle of it, Andrés attended a dinner Balderas had organized for the press, at which Balderas charged that democratic elections would be impossible because he was sure the governors would rig the vote.

A few days later, the members of the CTM, the Mexican Labor Federaration, decided to back Fito, and the convention of the National Federation of Campesinos, the CNC, in the Arena México ended with the campesinos whirling noisemakers and sombreros to cries of "Viva Campos!"

We went back to Puebla. Andrés was as cranky as a wet rooster. I didn't even try to talk to him. I heard nothing but grumbling and cursing. Then one morning as he was reading *Avante,* his mood perked up. When he left the house whistling, I picked up the newspaper with more curiosity than ever. I couldn't see what had pleased him so, because it was filled with accusations against him and his compadre. The article paired them together, claiming that the much praised candidate for president had been the governor's accomplice in crimes in Atencingo and Atlixco, that his house near Heiss's mill had been constructed on lands that once belonged to the campesinos, that Rodolfo and Andrés were in collusion with Heiss to bleed money out of the country, and that it was common knowledge that between them they had more than six million pesos in dollars deposited in gringo banks. The editorial ended by saying that the laws of eligibility for officials should be applied prior to nominating a thief and an accomplice of a governor guilty for so many deaths, no matter how much silence and fear covered them up.

Shortly afterward, *Avante* announced the disappearance of its editor in chief, Juan Soriano, and made a plea for the public to unite and demand that the government bring about his swift return. A few days later, Soriano's body was found on the Hacienda de Poloxtla, near San Martín. Every newspaper in Mexico City published protests and editorials attributing the crime to Governor Ascencio. I happened to be present at the interview with the reporter from *Excelsior;* Andrés used the opportunity to say that he had already requested the intervention of the Senate of the Republic. Let it rest in their hands. He promised that justice would be done.

The next weekend, Rodolfo turned up at our house in Puebla. I was sitting on the patio, facing the door, and could see how he dragged his feet as he came in.

"How's it going, my dear?" he said affectionately, giving me a kiss. "And your husband?"

I walked with him to the back of the garden. Andrés was in the game room, beating Octavio in billiards. Marcela was keeping score with beads strung on a wire, colluding with her brother, who we all knew was letting Andrés win.

"Compadre," said Rodolfo from the doorway, with a firmness I hadn't heard before.

"Compadre," Andrés said, walking to meet him. They embraced.

★   ★   ★

"Now what?" I asked, after we said good-bye to Rodolfo that afternoon.

"Now we'll both be president," Andrés replied.

I still recall the end of that year, and all the next, with the sensation of having fallen into a whirlpool. Andrés named me to be his representative. I spent all my time in juntas, meetings, and civic ceremonies—all the things I found so boring.

I bought a house in Las Lomas. Sometimes it was wholly mine. The children and Andrés were in Puebla from Monday to Friday. On the weekends, only Octavio and Marcela came, to keep me company, they said.

"Catín, can we change the two beds in my room for one big one?" Marcela asked me one day.

Of course I agreed. From then on, and to this day, they have slept in the same bed.

At first, Marcela's father was bent on having her marry. Octavio always begged me to see that the suitors didn't make the grade. I worked at it so hard that one day Andrés asked me, "So you think they make a good couple, too?" and erupted in laughter.

Then came the party convention. Fito became the official candidate and began his campaign. The first place we visited was Guadalajara. There, in a park, Fito took the stage. He defended the family and spoke of the respect children owe their parents. He sounded more like a priest than a candidate. Marcela, Octavio, and I kept elbowing each other, and winking when things became unbearably bombastic. I was truly grateful they were with me. Besides keeping me company, they gave me an excuse to escape the sudden warmth emanating from the Fat Man. Suddenly one midnight he sent a soldier to fetch me, a man lent him by the presidential staff that was already treating him as if he were president. I didn't know what to do, as I wasn't in the least interested in Fito. I wouldn't have wanted to touch him if he were president of the whole world.

Once he sent for me in the middle of the afternoon to show me biographies of him and Andrés that Bravo supporters had published in most of the national newspapers. They began by noting that Fito had been a mail carrier and followed with how he and Andrés both had been in La Ciudadela when Madero was murdered. They continued with a letter from Heiss to the United States government, saying that when it came to the defense of North American interests in Puebla, he could count on the "Ascencio and Campos boys." They ended with a rather incriminating list of well-known crimes.

"Don't let it worry you," I told him. "Andrés never paid attention to articles about him during his campaign. You'll win no matter what, won't you?"

"I want you to come with me to the parade," he answered, hanging his head. The next day, he sent a car to the house. The chauffeur handed me a bouquet of flowers with a card that said, *To bring me luck on this first day of May.*

We watched the May Day parade in honor of Mexico's workers from the balcony of the Calle Madero offices of the CTM. Alvaro Cordera, slim and fine-boned, stood beside Fito, who looked, as he always did, pudgy, with bad posture and that perpetual half smile on his face. Everything went well until the railroad workers marched by, cheering for Bravo and hurling rotten oranges at me on the balcony. I thought Rodolfo was going to pucker up and cry, but instead his boring features hardened into a solemn stare, and without losing his faint smile, he stood firm beside Cordera.

I had worn a pale chiffon dress. Suddenly an orange burst against my skirt. Given Rodolfo's equanimity, I thought the proper thing to do was to smile myself, and not budge. Which is what I did. When the parade ended, Fito asked Cordera if he didn't think my attitude had been comparable to that of a worldly queen. Cordera, with absolute calm, said he did.

"Sofía could never have managed that. God, Andrés chose well!" he said. And on the drive back to my house, he kept repeating, "You are a remarkable and courageous woman." When we arrived, he walked me to the door and as a good-bye kissed my hands and stained skirt.

I wonder if he writes his own speeches, I asked myself as I walked upstairs to my room. He's so banal he could make a career of it.

That afternoon, Andrés called to thank me. He completed the other half of the ode to my virtues.

"You are one fucking bright woman. You learn fast. You're ready for a political career of your own. Keep the Fat Man in line for me," he said.

I could envision Andrés sitting at his desk littered with papers he never read. I could almost see his lips as he laughed with appreciation. There was still something about him I liked.

"When are you coming here?" I asked.

"You come here tomorrow, President Aguirre will be here on the fifth."

I went. The parade went off without a hitch. Thousands of children dressed in regional costumes passed before us in rows of brilliant, well-ordered color. Aguirre expressed his thanks to Andrés; Doña Lupe went with me to the orphanage and donated breakfasts for the next six months. Then we all got into a car and drove up into the mountains. There Andrés had organized a long line of Indians who had favors to ask of the president. We spent the evening listening to them. About eight, I took Doña Lupe to have *café con leche* and an assortment of *pan dulce*. At eleven we returned to find her husband still listening to Indians. Beside him sat Andrés, chewing on his cigar, expressionless and satisfied. Doña Lupe and I went back to Puebla to call it a night. It was four in the morning when my general came into the room we shared.

"The bastard never wears down," he protested, slipping into bed. He put his arms around me. "I keep forgetting what a good woman you are."

"You have too many to keep track of," I answered.

"Don't shoot off your mouth, Catín. If you're so clever, better to say nothing."

"I wonder how presidents feel when their time is up," I said. "Poor General Aguirre."

"Didn't I say you're a good woman?" was his answer.

BIBI IS SLIGHTLY younger than I. When I met her, she was married to a doctor who was always too embarrassed to ask for payment from his patients. When someone asked him about his fee, he said what Indians say, "Whatever you think." He was a good doctor; he cured children of indigestion and colds, and mothers of worry. Once Verania swallowed a caramel and turned purple and I ran straight to him. I thought she was going to die and was terrified that the General would yell at me and call me a negligent murderer.

The minute I stepped inside the consulting room on 3 Norte I felt better. The child was still purple, but the doctor greeted me with absolute calm and then made her drink a cup of hot chamomile tea that melted the candy and let her breathe again. When she coughed and faded from purple back to white, I began to cry. I threw my arms around the doctor and began kissing him. That was when Bibi walked into the office.

"He saved my daughter," I told her, apologizing, although I didn't know who she was.

"That's the way he is," she replied, without changing expression.

"This lady is the wife of General Ascencio," the doctor told Bibi.

"Oh, and how does that feel?"

I shrugged my shoulders, and to the doctor's surprise, we both laughed.

I didn't see much of her after that day. Sometimes we ran into each other in the street, asked about the other's husband (she praised mine and I hers), and inquired about each other's children (she lamented the fragility of hers, I the barbarity of mine). Then we would say good-bye with those kisses that fall on the air as cheek brushes cheek.

Years later, she told me that those meetings made her feel important.

One day her husband just up and died. Without any fanfare—that's the way he was. Without leaving her a centavo—that's the way he was. I went to the wake in gratitude for all the bruises he had "made better" for my children, and because in Puebla you went to all the wakes for the same reason you went to all the weddings and baptisms and first Communions: to fill your day.

There was Bibi, holding her son by the hand. I put some money in an envelope and, after we hugged, gave it to her.

"I owed this to your husband," I said, with the Lady Bountiful air I liked to affect.

"Always so discreet, Catalina," she said.

She wasn't crying. I remember that she looked beautiful in her widow's weeds. She looked younger than ever, and her black eyes were gleaming. She was a pretty woman, so pretty that it would have been a shame for her to have squandered her beauty in Puebla, leading a little boy by the hand who would grow into adolescence as she grew wrinkled from worrying about what to sell to pay for his schooling. She went to Mexico City to live with her brothers, who worked at a newspaper owned by General Gómez Soto.

And it was in Gómez Soto's house that I saw her again. It was an enormous, crazy house, a lot like ours. Bibi was in the garden. She was wearing a blue dress cut low in front and back, and her smile was perfectly in place.

"You look wonderful," I said.

"I'm not as poor as I was," she answered.

"I congratulate you," I said, thinking of my mother, who used that line when she was happy for someone's good fortune but preferred not to know where it came from.

We sat down beside a pool filled with gardenias and floating candles.

"Isn't it divine?" she asked.

"Divine," I replied, and we began talking about divine things in general: about how her stockings came from across the border, about how much she liked the landmark of the Angel de la Independencia, about whether I thought it was proper to accept flowers from a married man. I laughed. What a crazy question. She should go ask any of the women to whom Andrés presented gift-wrapped keys to a car—the car, of course, standing right outside the front door.

"My aunt Nico always said, 'Before marriage, not one flower from a man!' You're not thinking of following her advice?"

That was how we began, and we ended with her confession

that General Gómez Soto had asked her to be the "señora" of this house.

"Just this house?" I asked.

"His wife and children live in his other houses. They haven't yet taken over this one."

General Gómez's wife was pretty much out of the picture. She was about his age, forty-five or so, but from living like a *soldadera*, trooping from camp to camp, and having nine children, the years were rougher on her. The children were grown, some were married. Now she was a little old grandmother who had never expected much from life and whose husband had made her rich. From what I knew about generals, I knew that Gómez Soto would not publicly leave his wife to marry Bibi.

"Tell him yes, but make him put the house in your name," was my advice.

"But that would be impossible, Catalina. I don't dare. He's so good to me; he already gives me so much." She blushed.

"He gives you crumbs," I said. "They give you crumbs. Nothing that costs them anything, sweetheart. They make your pool beautiful, but not legally yours. What a joke! Are you going to be his mistress?"

"At first. But I'll win him over gradually," she said in the voice of a fifteen-year-old at her coming-out party.

About a month after that conversation, Bibi came to visit me in Puebla. She got out of an enormous car, as big as any of mine, looking very happy. She did not have the boy with her, and she was wearing fur in March. Again I belittled General Soto, and even connected him with Soriano's death, which had suited Gómez Soto as much as Andrés, since he'd ended up buying Soriano's newspaper for his chain. She didn't want to hear about it.

We were standing on the terrace, looking at the city below, the dozens of churches crowned by gleaming domes. I loved the view from there. The streets of Puebla were perfectly visible, and you could almost touch the house you liked best.

"I'm tired of looking after myself, Catalina. It's horrible to be a widow and dirt-poor. Every man you know wants to get his hands on you. And almost no one gives you anything. But the general is generous. Look at the car he gave me, look at all the servants. He's promised to take me to Europe and he'll buy me anything I want. We'll go to the theater and see lots of things I'd never see stuck in this hole or bent over a typewriter in the America Studios watching a gussied-up Maria Felix strut by till I'm old and gray while she's as beautiful as ever. No, Catalina, no more advice. Not from you."

"You're right about that," I said. "I'm the world's worst example, and I'm not complaining. So why should you complain? Of course, I've never had anyone to compare Andrés to, I don't think I ever had a choice. I never knew what an ordinary husband was like, someone who didn't have enough to buy me alphabet soup. Sometimes I think I would have enjoyed being the wife of a doctor who knew how to treat the croup. Although you probably suffer the same boredom, only without fur. Why don't you marry your brother-in-law's brother? He's nice and he's good-looking."

"Because he's already married. He's one of the ones I was talking about."

We became good friends. She decided to live with Gómez Soto, who made good on the cars with dark windows and the house with the pool and the flowers, but failed on the promise to travel. He wouldn't let her leave the house even to shop for clothes. Everything was brought to her: dresses, shoes, hats from Paris. As if the poor girl needed a hat with a veil to parade through her corridors. He built her a theater at the back of the garden and brought in artists for private performances. They invited half the town; even puritanical Chofi came one day with her husband. They needed Gómez Soto's newspapers for their campaign, and Fito was prepared to pay him every courtesy.

"Don't worry," Andrés told him as we were on our way to Bibi's house. "Gómez Soto knows who the right people are, and he's grateful. I lent him the money to buy his new presses."

"The state's money?" Rodolfo asked stupidly.

"Of course, compadre, but the 'state' has a first and last name, and a debt is a debt. He knows he owes us. Anyway, it's a good idea to go, and he throws a good party. Right, Catín?"

"Yes," I said, looking at Chofi, who was so furious that her snout seemed longer than ever.

"Well, I don't like having to pay court to his kept woman," she said.

"Pay, what are you paying? Her charm doesn't cost you anything," said Fito. Chofi's nose shrank slightly.

Bibi met us at the door. It had been three months since we'd seen each other. She hadn't been coming to Puebla, and when I saw her I realized why. Inevitably, she was carrying a little present from her general.

She didn't look at all bad pregnant. She looked like a Greek goddess in her long, full dress. Her arms were a little fleshier, but her face looked younger than ever.

"I warned you: a roll in the hay, then comes the *bebé*."

"Don't remind me. I'm terrified the kid will end up with his nose."

"Nose, nothing, how about the personality! How do we have the nerve to reproduce them?"

"Well, they don't have to come out like their fathers," said Bibi, patting her stomach. "You know Beethoven was the son of an alcoholic and a crazy woman."

"Who told you that?"

"I don't remember now, but it's encouraging, isn't it?"

"And your son, how is he?"

"Oh, fine. Odi wanted us to send him to school outside the country for a while, so he's at a wonderful boarding school in Philadelphia."

"At the age of nine?"

"He's very happy. It's a military school, terribly expensive. They have three different uniforms, and beautiful football fields. He needed to be around other boys, he was too close to me."

"Is that what you think, or Gómez Soto?"

"Both of us."

"What a great pair, so in tune when it comes to their values," I said, giving her a hug.

"Well, what do you want me to do?"

"I want you not to treat me as if I were a moron. You can tell Chofi that story about how happy your son is, and if you want, I'll even throw in some details, but with me you can cry. Or don't you feel like it?"

"No, I don't feel like it. Not about that. I cry sometimes, but it's about looking like this, and about being locked up here."

"Getting big is so awful, isn't it?"

"Horrible. I don't know who came up with the idea that women are happy and beautiful when we're pregnant."

"Men, of course. And now and then there's a woman who has that satisfied look."

"What else can they do?"

"Well, get mad. I was furious all through my two pregnancies.

None of that shit about the miracle of life. You should have seen me bawl. God! I hated being six months along with Verania when the tree in the garden was covered with fruit and I couldn't climb up to pick it. I'd been champion every year; I always outdid my brothers by at least three baskets, and then all of a sudden I walk into my parents' house and see my brothers up in the tree, picking away without a rival.

" 'You see, daughter,' said my papa, 'what you lost by being willful.' With that, I began to cry and I haven't stopped yet."

"Fibber. I've never seen you cry."

"Because you aren't in my house at midnight. During the day, it isn't the thing to do, I'm the governor's wife."

We had been slowly walking through the garden. Fito, Andrés, and Chofi were ahead of us, and when they reached the door of the house, Gómez Soto was there to welcome them; the men began to embrace and clap one another on the back. Men are priceless. Since they can't kiss, or say sweet things, or rub one another's swelling bellies, they do all that hugging and thumping, accompanied by loud talk and guffaws. I can't imagine what they see in it. In the process, however, they left Chofi outside, and we had to interrupt our gossip and call her to come talk with us.

"You look very pretty pregnant," said Chofi. "But then, our features look much sweeter."

"It's the extra weight," said Bibi.

"Well, yes, some things you can't help. How can you be expecting and stay slim? Ah, but the nobility of it. I've never known a woman who looked ugly when she was expecting."

"I have, lots," I said, thinking of Chofi, who ever since her first pregnancy has been absolutely square. You can't tell whether she's coming or going; she put on a belly the size of her ass, and tits like an elephant. Poor woman, it was painful. And here she was, about to become the wife of the president and still gobbling everything in sight.

"Lots? Do you? Who have you known who looked ugly expecting a baby?"

"Plenty, Chofi, but you don't want me to name them for you."

"You just like to disagree with me."

"If you want me to, I'll say that all pregnant women are beautiful, but I don't believe it. I never felt so ugly."

"Well, you didn't look bad. You're too thin now. And how have you been feeling, señora?" she asked Bibi.

"Fine," said Bibi. "I'm doing exercises they say are good for you."

"But that's terrible. How can they be good? You'll jolt the little thing loose. You're supposed to rest during pregnancy. You don't want it to come early the way Catalina's second one did."

"Mine didn't come early because I exercised but because my womb rejected it," I said.

"Madness! Since when do wombs reject babies? You went horseback riding."

"The doctor gave me permission."

"Oh, yes, that Dosal is totally mad, he'd tell you anything. When I heard him tell you after you had Checo that you didn't have to drink *atole* and chicken broth for the first forty days, I thought he was insane. Insane and irresponsible. How can you gamble like that with a child's life? It must be that he's queer. Queers despise women and children. Yes, I'm sure that's it."

"How do you like the flowers in my pool, Doña Chofi?" asked Bibi, just in the nick of time.

"Oh, my, aren't they beautiful! I hadn't seen them. Do you grow them here?"

"Odilón has them brought from Fortín every week."

"What a man, so thoughtful," said Chofi. "You won't find many like him. How many hours is Fortín from here?"

"Seven," I said. "We're all crazy."

"Why do you say that, Catalina? Don't be envious."

"I can't afford to be. But it seems crazy to bring flowers from Fortín. It's obvious that the general is madly in love," I said.

"So true," replied Chofi, who when she felt romantic puffed out her bosom and sighed as if she wanted someone, anyone at all, please, to fuck her.

We went inside to sit in a sala that looked a lot like the lobby of a gringo hotel. Carpeted and enormous. It was for good reason we invited so many people to our parties, we had to fill the rooms to keep from feeling like a chickpea in a four-gallon pot.

There were plenty of people at Bibi and her general's party. It was being held to celebrate the anniversary of the newspaper, so all the people who wanted their picture in next day's edition were there. Bibi was not very good at organizing meals, so she had ordered everything from some extravagant young women who said they were French and never prepared enough food. On the other hand, there was imported wine and waiters who filled your glass as soon as it was half-empty. Little food and abundant drink: the party ended in a spectacular bacchanal. First, the men got very red and smiled a lot, then very talkative, and then either stupefied or argumentative. The worst was General Gómez Soto himself. He always drank a lot. As a party began he was nearly pleasant, a little disconnected but seemingly coherent; unfortunately, that stage did not last long. Soon he began insulting people.

"And you, why are your legs so bowed?" he asked the wife of Colonel López Miranda. "You must have been plenty busy to bow your legs like that. This Colonel Miranda's a fucking fool. Look what he's done to his wife's legs."

No one laughed but Gómez Soto, but no one left the party except López Miranda and his bowlegged wife. After that, Gómez Soto began to rant and rave about his father. No one, he said, had done as much for Mexico, and no one got less credit.

"Yes, my father was for Porfirio Díaz. Whaddya expect, you bastards? What else could you be in those days? But thanks to my father, there's a railroad, and thanks to the railroad, there was a revolution. You have any argument with that, you bastards?" he yelled from atop the table.

"How many times a week does he get like that?" I asked Bibi, who was standing beside me, watching with more scorn than horror, as if she had never seen him before.

"Once or twice," she said, without expression. "I'm going to get him down from the table. I don't want him to fall, because he's worse sick than drunk."

"That can't be true."

"You don't know. He gets a cold and thinks he's dying, I can't get an inch away from his bedside, he carries on like a wounded lizard. I don't even want to think about a broken leg."

She went toward the table where Gómez was holding forth. I will never forget her pale figure, holding up her hand to him.

"Come down, Papacito," she said. "It's dangerous. I don't want you to fall and hurt yourself. Come on now, get down."

"Don't talk to me like that!" Gómez screamed at her. "You think I'm an idiot? You think I'm that idiot son of yours? You treat me like I was. I wonder if you don't treat him like me? I bet you do. I've watched you when you put him to bed, how you pet him and coo to him. I bet you've fucked him and liked it better than with me. Filthy whore," he said, leaping down from the table, putting his hands around Bibi's neck, and squeezing.

"Do something," I said to Andrés.

"What do you want me to do? She's his wife, isn't she?"

Chofi began to scream hysterically, and Fito put his arm around her to console her. No one did anything.

Without batting an elegant eye, Bibi struggled to loosen the general's grip.

"Help her," I said, pulling Andrés by the hand to where the general was sweating and puffing.

"Gómez, don't be so dramatic about your love," said Andrés, inserting his hand between Bibi's neck and Gómez's stranglehold. As soon as Gómez let go, I put my arms around Bibi.

"It's nothing," she said to me. "He's just playing, aren't you, my love?" In seconds, Odilón's expression had changed from raging lunatic to playful pup.

"Of course, Catita. Do you think I'd ever hurt this darling girl? I adore her. Sometimes we play a little rough, but it's all a game. I'm sorry if any of you were upset. Music, please, maestro."

The orchestra struck up the chords of "*Estrellita.*"

Bibi smoothed her dress, put one hand on the general's left shoulder, held the other out to him, and rested her head gracefully against his chest, waiting for him to dance.

Soon everyone had forgotten the incident, and Bibi and Odi were once again the perfect couple.

"You're a genius," I told her as we said good-bye.

"Did you like the party, darling?" she asked, as if nothing had happened.

VERY FEW STATES offered women even the stupid right to vote that Carmen Serdán had won for the women of Puebla. For the first time, we were the avant-garde, so on July 7, I began the day looking more elegant than ever and went with Andrés to flaunt my position as his official wife. There weren't many people in the polls, but there were newspapermen, and for them I put on my best smile. I walked up to the ballot box holding the hand of my general, as if I knew nothing about anything, as if I were the dope I seemed to be.

I voted for Bravo, the opposition candidate, not because I thought he was any marvel but because I was sure he would lose, and it was gratifying not to feel even a tiny bit responsible for Fito's coming to power.

In Puebla things were calm. Maybe in my role as the governor's wife that was all I would ever see, but we learned that in Mexico City people had forced President Aguirre to yell "Viva Bravo!" as he was voting, and that the militants of the Party of the Mexican Revolution, the

PRM, had to rescue the Revolution by stealing the ballot boxes where Fito was losing. Organized by sectors, they jumped out of automobiles, pistols in hand, and trumped up reasons to force the polls to close ahead of time.

Bravo was summoned to Venezuela by divine providence. In response to Bravo's plan for armed rebellion, General Campos countered with his plan for Bravo's surrender. Bravo's followers rebelled anyway, and were squashed like bugs. My candidate postponed his return. I had been a disaster as a voter, which was why it seemed appropriate to recognize my error and applaud the Congress when in September it declared that Fito had won by 3,400,000 votes to Bravo's 151,000.

Like me, the government of the United States chose to recognize and support the Fat Man's triumph; they sent notice that they would send Secretary Bryan to the inauguration as their special envoy.

Shortly after, Bravo did return. I never saw Andrés laugh so hard as the day he read the speech my candidate delivered and handed to the press the afternoon he arrived.

"This fucker is a real comic. Listen to this," he said. " 'As neither ambition nor vanity affect my unyielding determination, I come today before the sovereign people of Mexico to offer my resignation from the honorable post of president of the republic to which I was elected on the past seventh of July.' That's rich," Andrés howled, stamping his feet with laughter. "He has 'ardent resolve, deep devotion, unquenchable appreciation, and confidence in a free and happy Mexico.' He has everything but balls."

"What did you want him to do?" I asked. "Get himself killed?"

"Well, yes. At the very least. This is a lot of farting around for no shit in the pot," he said, and didn't stop laughing all morning.

Then he got the idea of sending me to help Chofi look after the wife of Secretary Bryan at the reception in the gringo embassy.

We arrived just as a huge crowd was throwing stones at the statue of Washington. We entered the embassy through a back door and, once inside, heard shots and yelling all the while very sober-faced waiters served toast with caviar and goblets of champagne. Mrs. Bryan was pale, but put on an "everything's fine" air worthy of a great actress. I'm sure she was thinking her government had picked a great time to send her husband to a land of savages, but she smiled from time to time and even asked me about the climate in Puebla.

"*Algido*," I replied. "Chilly."

"*Al-he-dou*, how nice."

After dinner, we learned that a Major Luna had died while attempting to arrest a group of terrorists who planned to assassinate both General Aguirre and General Campos.

"Poor Major Luna, he died serving his country," Chofi said to the lieutenant assigned to protect her who told us the bad news.

It hasn't taken Chofi very long to think of herself as the motherland, I thought to myself as I listened to her babble on about Major Luna's call to service and deep sense of duty. I know it happens to everyone, but I'd thought it would take longer.

Back in Puebla, I thought of Chofi as I was telling Mónica and Pepa about Fito's sleight of hand when it came to listing his assets: two ranches—Las Espuelas and La Mandarina—a house with an orchard in Matamoros, a residence valued at twenty thousand pesos in Las Lomas de Chapultepec, and another close by valued at twenty-seven thousand. No bank accounts.

"They're so tacky," said Mónica. "Begging your pardon, Cati, but who are they trying to fool? You can't tell me they don't have a checking account. Right? Chofi hides their paychecks under the mattress?"

"No account in *Mexico*," said Pepa. "Your compadre is insufferable; we're in for six years of unrelieved boredom. A churchgoer *and* an anticommunist? I thought my husband was the last one alive," she said, laughing with the daring that had developed since her rendezvous in La Victoria market.

"You know why they call Rodolfo 'Tripod'?" asked Mónica. "Because like death and taxes, you can count on him to hold you up."

We laughed. Like all good Puebla women, my friends had tongues as sharp as razors. They said all the things I missed hearing. I loved seeing them. I was so happy I even forgot that Rodolfo's inauguration was the next day and I hadn't yet decided what to wear.

My father saved me from having to make a decision. After I left Pepa's, I went by to see him. He was drinking his coffee and eating cheese and a hard roll he had sliced very thin.

"What do you think about the war?" I asked him. "Won't something worse than a shortage of nylons happen to us?"

"I don't plan to live long enough to find out," he answered.

I made jokes about his habitual pessimism and complained about being the wife of Andrés Ascencio and, as a result, tied to his compadre, Rodolfo Campos, and about how I dreaded having to sit through a long speech read in the moronic tone that Fito affected at climactic moments.

"Poor baby," he said, rubbing the top of my head. "Things will get better. You need to find a good sweetheart."

"I have you," I answered, wrinkling my nose and getting up to kiss him.

We joked around the way we always did. I went with him to put on his pajamas, and I was stretched out beside him on the bed when my mother came with that it's-very-late-for-you-to-be-out look on her face. She never went out after five in the afternoon, especially without her husband. My behavior was scandalous to her. I got up.

"I don't know what to wear tomorrow," I said.

"Wear something black, that's always elegant," said Barbara, as she came into the room.

"I'll see what I have. Take care of my sweetheart for me."

I did have to find something black. When I woke up the next morning, my father was dead.

I don't like to talk about it. I think we all saw it as a betrayal. Even my mother, who was sure they'd meet again in heaven. Barbara took charge of organizing the funeral and all the other details. I don't remember what I did, except cry in public, which the governor's wife is never supposed to do. Nor do I know anything that happened during Andrés's last months as governor. By the time things came back into focus for me, we were already living in Mexico City.

I WANDERED AROUND the house like a sleep-walker, inventing reasons to have someone around. I was so desperate for company that I ended up needing Andrés. When he went away for several days, as he always did, I complained, no longer trying to disguise my feelings as I used to.

"What's the matter with you?" he asked. "Why is your mouth tight like that? Aren't you happy to see me?"

I couldn't find words to tell him how bored I was, how afraid when I woke up without him in the bed, how angry I was having bawled like a fool before the children and having only their quarrels for company.

I became useless, odd. I began to despise the days Andrés didn't come home. I would plan menus for meals and be enraged when by afternoon he hadn't called, hadn't appeared, hadn't done things he had never done but now, who knows why, were so upsetting.

Worst of all, my friends were no longer just around the corner and Barbara was once again my sister who lived in Puebla, not my private secretary or any of that foolishness. Pablo was in Italy, Arizmendi was my own invention; all I had to hold on to was Andrés, and he left me for days in the house in Las Lomas, pacing from the window grille in the living room to the door, looking out for his arrival, reading the newspapers for the sole purpose of learning whether he was with Fito and where.

I kept the house pathologically neat, as if a curtain were going up any minute. Not a speck of dust anywhere, not a painting askew, not an ashtray out of place, not a shoe in the dressing room without its shoe tree and shoe bag. Every day, I curled my eyelashes and put on mascara, tried on dresses, did my exercises, hoping that suddenly Andrés would come home and give everything a reason for being. But he was always so late that by five in the afternoon I wanted to crawl into my pajamas and eat crackers and ice cream, or peanuts sprinkled with *limón* and chili pepper, or all of them together, until my stomach was bursting and I felt a reasonable calm between my legs.

After a week or so of days like that, when I weighed eight pounds more, was crying a little less, even began to get into some novel or other, Andrés would show up wearing his let's-hop-into-bed expression. I wanted to curse at him, throw him out of what was becoming my house, run by my schedule and my wishes, my disorder and my tastes. He would get very talkative and tease me about my fat legs, or tell me some story about a quarrel with someone he couldn't figure out how to screw over.

"Give me ideas," he said. "You're losing interest in my affairs. You're like a zombie."

"You leave me here all alone," I answered.

"Listen, I'm getting tired of this, you always bitching about how I leave you alone. What if I *really* leave you alone? I think I'll move somewhere I'm treated better, where I feel welcome. Because you're not much fun anymore. You need to look for something to do. Your closest ally is dead, your job as governor's wife is over, and you don't know where you fit in the world. Get used to it. Things end. You're not the queen bee here and no one recognizes you when you go out; you can't give parties everyone's grateful to be invited to, you can't organize charity concerts or drive with me up in the mountains. There are lots of women here who aren't cowed by what you have to say, and even some who think what you say is old hat. Poor Cati. Why don't you talk to Gómez Soto's girl Bibi. Or join the National Family Union. There's a lot of work there. They're in the middle of a campaign against communism, and they need volunteers. I'll introduce you to someone tomorrow."

I knew he was railing against communism only because he wanted to annoy the shit out of Cordera, the leader of the CTM. I had heard him talking on the telephone with the governor of San Luis Potosí, a former president now in industry, the day the governor had said that only opportunists and spongers put any stock in communism.

"You were right on target. What a working-over you gave Cordera," Andrés told him. "He deserves it. Count on me if you want to continue down that road. Why don't you come have dinner at my house the next time you're in Mexico City? My wife will be delighted to see you."

"Who will I be delighted to see?" I asked when he hung up so I'd know what kind of dinner to plan and when.

"General Basilio Suárez," he said, and laughed aloud.

"Delighted to see that ass? Liar. And since when are *you* delighted? Didn't you always say he was a fucking counterrevolutionary?"

"Until yesterday, my girl. And until yesterday, you thought he was an ass. But from now on, the whole family thinks of him as a prudent man, even a wise man. Imagine, he actually called Cordera's drivel 'social experiments based on exotic doctrines.' You can't deny he's a find."

"I like Cordera fine," I said.

"You don't know what you're talking about. Cordera is an ambitious troublemaker. He beats that stupid drum about the class struggle and how the workers should be in power. The general put it just right, he's a demagogue. You know Cordero's always been rich. His papa rented me and my brothers the mules we used to haul maize. They had a huge hacienda before the Revolution. What does he know about hunger? I ask you. What does he know about being poor? What does he know about anything? He knows squat and he doesn't care. But he gets a lot of attention. I don't want him screwing around with us. He fucked us when we were poor, I don't want him fucking us now that we're rich."

"I like him fine," I said.

"I suppose you're going to tell me you like that gray suit of his and how you believe that crap about how it's the only one he owns. A pack of goddamn lies. The bastard has three hundred, all alike, but look how he fools everyone. The workers' leader. Run the bastard out, I say. I swear, it's time to relieve him of the job of being savior of the poor. You'll see how it goes for him at the convention. I'm going to make him pay for everything, including that sappy line of yours about 'I like him fine.' "

"Well, I do like him fine," I said, happy to find something that got his goat. The truth was that I'd seen Cordera that time at the parade, liked his high cheekbones and broad forehead, but exchanged only a few words with him.

"That's stupid, Catalina. Why? When have you had anything

to do with him? You don't know what you're talking about." He was livid.

"I know what I see," I said.

"Just shut up. What do you see in him? Tell me, *what*?"

"Just what I said."

"Don't make up stuff, Catalina. You think you can get me mad. You haven't seen any more in him than I have."

"Then you've noticed what a great laugh he has, too?"

"Go to hell," Andrés said. "We'll see how great his laugh is a month from now."

The next morning, Andrés took me to the people at the Family Union. We drove to a large house in the Colonia Santa María, where we found the office of a Señor Virreal. He was seated behind a dark wood desk; he was skin and bones and beginning to go bald. I learned later that he was the husband of a fat woman called Mari Paz, with whom he had had eleven children in quick succession.

"This is my wife, sir," said Andrés. "She's interested in working with all of you." And to me: "I'll send Juan to get you in an hour; you stay to see how you can be of help."

Andrés went out one door as a woman wearing a pearl necklace and a small religious medal of the Virgen del Carmen came in the other. Slim, well dressed, with a devout smile that made me uncomfortable from the moment I saw her.

"Please come with me," she said. "I'll give you a tour of our headquarters and introduce you to some of our coworkers. My name is Alejandra, and it will be my pleasure to be your guide and your sister from now on."

Spare me, I thought, but followed her. The house was old and dark, with a long row of windowless rooms connected by doors.

The rooms were all furnished as classrooms, with tables, chairs, and blackboards. We came to one where several women were working.

"We're filling goodie bags for the prisoners' party," said my guide-and-sister, to explain why fifteen women were silently sitting around tables. The only sound was the murmur of their voices counting: to three, the women putting marshmallow-and-coconut cookies in the bags; to seven, those adding animal crackers; to five, the ladies dropping in handfuls of hard candies; and to two, those responsible for the packets of Tigres cigarettes.

"Hello," they chorused when they saw us.

We were in the midst of hellos and introductions when Mari Paz staggered in with a box in her arms and three children clinging to her skirts.

"I brought the *pombazos*," she said. "I don't know whether there's enough to put in one or two. I made two hundred. How many prisoners are there?"

"A hundred and fifty," said a fat woman with a mustache, never pausing in dispensing her marshmallow cookies. The bags were piling up before the next woman, the one responsible for the animal crackers, who had started talking with the hard-candies woman as if there were no backlog of bags, the product of the mustached lady's industry.

"Well, there are either a hundred too few or fifty too many," said Mari Paz, making a monumental mathematical effort.

"Fifty too many. Shall we divide them among the guards and the wives who come to visit?" asked Alejandra.

"They won't go around. There are always more guards and visitors than prisoners," the mustached lady spoke up again. She had no space left to set her bags, so she turned to the woman next to her and said: "Amalita, I'm sorry to bother you, but if you don't hurry with your animal crackers, and Ceci with the candies, I'm going to have to stop."

"Ay, Irenita, I'm so sorry we're behind, but we'll speed up now, don't worry. After all, we're the ones who need to finish, since we left everything in a mess. We came so early we didn't get anything done at home."

"We're all in that fix," said Alejandra, who, you could see a mile away, was not. Her corps of servants was immediately visible in her hands and her face. Later I learned that her husband held stock in Coca-Cola and the Palacio de Hierro department store and owned a paper mill in Sonora and a textile mill in Tlaxcala. No one believed that she left her house a mess while she devoted herself to pious works, but everyone listened as if she had a patent on truth.

The other women looked poor, at best the wives of men employed by Alejandra's husband, low-grade bureaucrats, even laborers. They started talking about the parish and Padre Falito. I realized that was how they knew each other and that their Padre Falito heard all their confessions.

Alejandra and Mari Paz were the leaders. They set Mari Paz's box of corn cakes on the table, sat me down in front of it with instructions to add one to each bag after it had been filled by the other women, and retreated to a far corner to whisper. By cocking an ear, I could hear what they were saying.

"She's the wife of General Ascencio," said Alejandra.

"We'll have to watch her. Padre Falito says that crowd can't be trusted," Mari Paz replied.

"Falito exaggerates," said Alejandra. "She seems like a nice person, I think she deserves a chance to do good. Besides, we need more people with class, Mari Paz; we need someone who knows society. These women are fine with prisoners, but we can't take them to talk with the snooty mothers at the Cristóbal Colón school."

"I guess you're right, but I don't trust her," said Mari Paz.

I pretended to count. One, one, one, I said, dropping in my cakes like a teacher's pet.

Mari Paz walked toward me with her rippling fat and her three runny-nosed brats.

"Do they smell good? Did they come out all right?" she asked kittenishly.

"Delicious. They'll be a real treat for the prisoners."

"I think they will, you know. All they get is sausage and beans. They asked me please not to bring meat, poor men, one day a year they should have something beside the garbage the government gives them. Oh, forgive me. Your husband is . . ."

"In the government, yes," I said.

"Oh, I'm so sorry, forgive me. I can just imagine what a job it must be to get food for so many, every day. And then to prepare it. They do pretty well, considering they're there as punishment, don't they?"

"I don't know," I said. "But I don't know why you're so concerned about them, either."

"Don't think this is the only thing we do. The treats were Padre Falito's idea. He's a truly good man and very sensitive. One day he went to the jail to hear a dying man's confession, and came back deeply shaken. He told us the building was filthy, and dozens of men were jammed together in cells, alone in the midst of a crowd. He was actually weeping as he recalled it. That's when he had the idea that we could ask permission to go visit the men, to pray with them, and take them some treats. We thought that sounded good, and they gave us permission—you can tell this government isn't against Catholics like the last ones were. So that's why we're going this afternoon. We have the piñatas, the rosaries, the religious cards, the bags of sweets, and ten scapularies Padre Falito wants to raffle off."

"It's all right to raffle scapularies?"

"Well . . . Usually they're sold; people who want them buy them, and then go to the padre and ask him to put them on. But these ten Falito wants to raffle, and he himself will put them on the ones who win."

"And if they don't want it?" I asked, looking toward the door, hoping Juan would appear.

"Not want it?" she said. "Of course they'll want it, it would be unthinkable for them not to want it. It's an honor. Winning a scapulary in the raffle will be like a sign it was sent by God. You don't think anyone's going to say no to God."

"You're right," I said. "There's no way they're going to say no to God."

Juan appeared—truly sent by God—and stopped at the door with a conspiratorial smile.

"What is it, Juan? Are they waiting for us?" He knew he was always to answer that question with, "Yes, señora, it's urgent."

I feigned surprise and hurriedly said my good-byes, promising to be at Lecumberri Prison at five on the dot.

Once outside, I shook my arms and stretched my legs. There was a warm February sun. I took off my jacket. It was colder inside the house than out. Outdoors, suddenly, everything seemed more agreeable. The morning wind had swept the clouds from the sky, and the trees were beautiful.

"Juan, take me to the Alameda," I said.

As always when I needed to recover from a bad experience, I bought ice cream. Juan parked the car, and I got out to walk through the Alameda de Santa María. The kiosk shone in the sun, and mamas and old men and nannies and children and sweethearts filled the benches.

I bought a newspaper. I joined others on a bench and found the news fascinating. The delegates at the preliminary meeting of the congress of the Mexican labor federation, the CTM, were accusing Don Basilio of reaping the harvest from all the hard work done by union members, and of carrying the flag for Rodolfo's opposition. They had declared that this same General Suárez's speech was an attack against former President Aguirre, and demanded that Fito carry out his promise to advance the goals of the Revolution.

"They're at it hot and heavy," I said. "And Andrés is there; I know where he is."

I regretted not having kept up with the news and again itched to be part of all the things Andrés told me were none of my business. Ever since we'd come to Mexico City and I was no longer the governor's wife, Andrés had treated me like his other women. I had let myself be cut off without realizing it, but from then on I intended not to be stuck in the house. I even blessed the stupid Family Union which for a while would serve as my excuse.

"Juan, teach me to drive," I told the chauffeur.

"Señora, the General would kill me," he answered.

"I swear he will never know how I learned. Teach me."

"Well, then," he said.

Juan was twenty-seven years old, ingenuous, and a far better man than most. I moved up to the front seat beside him. He began to tremble.

"If the General catches us, he'll kill me."

"Stop saying that and tell me what to do," I said.

The theoretical lesson lasted the rest of the morning. We drove at least fifty times around the Alameda. Then he took me back to the house and went to look for Andrés, who was at the Palacio Nacional.

"I want to borrow Juan again," I told Andrés at dinnertime. "I'm going to need him a lot at the Union."

"What for?" he said. "He can take you over there and pick you up. I need him."

"And when you're not here?"

"I'm here now."

"I read the manifesto of the delegates to the CTM congress," I said.

"Where did you read that?"

"In *El Universal*. Since I was already out, I bought it. I don't know why I spent all that time cut off from things, but now that I've been out, I feel like a new woman. If you don't want to give me Juan, then give me another driver or let me learn to drive."

"God, what a wheedler you are. I knew you couldn't stay put for more than six months. How did it go at the Union? Can you help them?"

For a minute, I didn't say anything. It was always difficult not to tell Andrés the truth; he was like an invisible spy, always behind the door, knowing everything.

"No, I'm not going to be good at it. If I were cut out for that kind of work, I'd have been a nun and known exactly where I fit in. But get mixed up with those batty women? I'd have to be crazy. I don't need Padre Falito to tell me where to walk, and there's too much I want to do to bury myself in a freezing house, filling bags of candies for a bunch of convicts they're planning to raffle off scapularies to. Besides, the communists haven't done anything to me, and I don't need unnecessary enemies. I think if you're going to get into that charity thing, you have to do it big, be a virtual St. Francis with the poor blessing you and trailing after you. I'd feel like a jackass in Padre Falito's flock, blowing children's noses and praying for prisoners. I'd rather die."

Andrés was laughing, and I was relieved.

"What did you say that priest's name is? Falito? Pretty funny. You're right, it's one thing to get those idiots on my side in order to stick it to Cordera, but something else to get you involved. We should have sent one of the girls. Marta can do it, she'd be a good informant, whatever made me think of you? Did I think you'd lost your mind? That's what you get for not giving me a warm welcome." He laughed again. "So, did you meet little teeny-peeny Falito? How many of those gals do you think have seen his little namesake up close? What a place to take you. You deserve a break. From now on, you're going everywhere with me. No more staying home."

No sooner said than done—because he wanted it and because that's how he was. He came and went like the goddamn tide. And just then the tide was coming in.

"I have to go back to the Palacio. The Fat Man can't do anything by himself," he said. "You come along with me. You can go downtown and see how much you can buy in three hours. After everything closes at eight, come pick me up, and I'll buy you dinner at the Prendes. What do you think of that plan?"

I ran to get my coat and was in the car in three minutes. I didn't want to give him a chance to back out of his invitation. It was cold, one of those rare February afternoons when you can wear a fur coat without burning up two steps outside your door. I wore my fox. It was the most beautiful coat I had. Fur coats can be tacky, but I wore that fox with my boots and felt like a Hollywood star.

When we reached the *zócalo,* we turned right into the Palacio Nacional. Ever since some hero had tried to assassinate Fito, the precautions and searches you had to go through were ridiculous. They checked all the cars, even the Fat Man's, including the trunks, to be sure that when you'd stopped at a corner no one had crawled in. That afternoon the soldiers searched us down to the pockets of my fur coat. Andrés was furious.

"What an asshole Rodolfo is," he said, in front of the soldiers and anyone else who wanted to hear.

When we were finally inside, Andrés jumped out of the car, handed me a wad of money, and told me to buy whatever I wanted. But all I wanted that afternoon was to buy ice cream and walk along licking it without anybody bothering me.

CHAPTER

JUAN GOT THE vanilla ice cream and left me at the door of the Sanborn's on Calle Madero. I felt protected there because the walls are blue Talavera tile from Puebla. The crazy ideas you get. Anywhere there was Talavera, I felt safe, because the first thing I did in any of my houses was unpack my dinnerware. A yellow set with a blue pattern, for fifty people. They say it costs a fortune nowadays; then it was considered common. Everyone wanted Bavarian porcelain, not Puebla pottery, crude and easily chipped.

I stood for a while in the doorway of Sanborn's. Leaning against the wall like a tart, feeling like Andrea Palma in *The Woman of the Port*. Then I crossed the street and walked past the Banco de México; the director at that time was an idiot with thick eyeglasses, whose name I can never remember. Maybe because he was so stupid and ugly. Besides, he had stolen the job from a nice, intelligent man I liked very much because he had been the only one who hadn't laughed at me when once at dinner Andrés told everyone that I cried when they played the national anthem after the news.

I went back across the street and headed toward the Bellas Artes. I loved that building, it always reminded me of a First Communion cake. I went inside. The doors to the theater were closed, but I went up the marble stairs, looking for the source of music that sounded like a long, repeated wail.

I pushed the door and it opened. The auditorium was empty, but an orchestra filled the stage. A man standing before them cut them off and spoke swiftly and with passion, feverishly explaining something as if his life depended on making the musician he was pointing at with his baton understand. He was not very tall; he had broad shoulders and long arms.

I walked toward the front and heard him say, "All right, again, from twenty-four. Everybody. And . . ." He began to sing the melody.

The music sounded sad, strange, more drawn out than before. I had never heard anything like it. I sat down, quiet as a mouse. I gazed at the ceiling, the empty boxes, and let myself drift with the sounds that seemed to issue from the arms of the conductor.

What an amazing profession these men had, so different from any man I'd ever known. The conductor stopped them, spoke, again raised his arms, and the music resumed. Suddenly, with a violent motion, he stopped. He was looking at a young violinist in the third row.

"Where are you, Martínez? You're not following me. You're missing the beat. Is there something more important than what we're doing?"

Martínez, staring at me, didn't answer. The conductor whirled around and saw me in one of the first rows, clutching my fur coat, unable to say a word.

"Who gave you permission to come in here?" he asked angrily.

All I could think of was to present myself as a journalist.

"Good God, what timing you have," he said. He had enormous dark eyes, pale skin. "Wait for me in the back, and don't move, it's distracting."

I got up and slowly walked toward the rear.

"Settled?" he asked from the stage.

"Yes," I answered, and stared at the floor. When the music started again, I got up quietly and tiptoed to the door. I pushed it and ran down the stairs. In a second, I was outside. I found a bench in the Alameda and tried to hum what I had heard but couldn't. Instead, I cried, without knowing why. I felt I was growing old, and had inherited my mother's gift for premonitions.

When Juan found me, it was very late.

"The General's been waiting at the door of the Palacio," he said, and took me to pick him up.

"Where did you go, silly?" Andrés asked, very calm.

"For a walk."

"You must have gone through all the stores. What did you buy?"

"Nothing."

"Nothing? Then what did you do?"

"I listened to some music."

"I bet you found a marimba in the Alameda. Why are you always so common, Catalina?"

"I went to the Bellas Artes. The symphony was rehearsing."

"Then you must have seen Carlos Vives. He's the conductor."

"Do you know him?" I asked.

"Of course I know him. He's the stupidest man I know. His

papa was a general, but he turned out a little odd and took up music. He's just back from London with the idea that this here ranch needs a National Symphony Orchestra—and he convinced Fito. Who *can't* convince the Fat Man?"

"Are we going to dinner?" I said, and my voice sounded as if it didn't belong to me. As if someone else was inside me, walking and talking.

At the Prendes, I left my coat on one of the coatracks. Andrés left his hat and walked in as if he were in his own home.

"Your usual table, General?" asked the maître d'.

"The same, chief," he said.

I never knew why Andrés liked the place, it was horrible. It looked like the dining room of a seminary. The food was good, but it wasn't much fun eating in a place without windows. Especially day after day, as he did.

My oysters arrived at the same time as his tortilla soup, and I started right in while he talked.

"The speech I wrote for Rodolfo is fucking sensational. Cordera won't know how to begin to answer. He goes around holding up democracy to further his own shit, so I've got Fito saying that democracy must be understood as accommodating the class struggle within the bosom of civil liberties and law. And since we're the law, he's royally fucked. Well, look who's here."

I swallowed the last oyster and looked up to see who it was. The conductor was walking toward us wearing a radiant smile and a navy-blue blazer. I wanted to disappear.

"I was waiting for our interview, señora," were his first words. Then he shook Andrés's hand and sat down.

"What's new?" Andrés asked. "Catalina told me she went to hear you this afternoon. Why did you let her in?"

"She let herself in."

"What did she tell you?"

"That she was a journalist and wanted to interview me."

"What a fibber, this girl. Why didn't you tell him, 'I came in because I felt like it'?" Andrés asked me, like an indulgent papa.

"I was afraid," I confessed.

"Afraid of this fellow? But he's just a pup. Probably only a couple of years older than you. He was twelve during the war. His mama and he lived in Morelia, and sometimes his father, who was my superior officer, took me home during some lull in the action. We always found this kid playing a reed flute."

"What a good memory you have, General."

"That isn't the way you used to talk."

"You weren't then who you are now."

"I was just starting out, the way you are now. But I didn't get as far as fast. Of course, you find more enemies in war and politics than you do in music. Why *did* you choose music?" Andrés asked. "You'd have made a good politician. Your father was."

"Sometimes a person's not like his father."

"You say that with pride."

"Just the opposite, General. But everyone has his own battle to fight."

"You think you have a battle? You're a strange kid. Your father was right."

They sat and talked about the past, about how as a boy the conductor used to steal the metal fringe from Andrés's epaulets and shake it in a clay pot to hear the sound it made, about the day when Andrés and Carlos's father had taken him to see the hanged men and had made him stand at the foot of the posts and look at the purple faces and swollen tongues.

"Weren't you afraid?" I asked.

"Very much, but I wasn't going to show it to a couple of bastards like my father and your husband."

I couldn't eat my fish or my dessert. I ordered a cognac and gulped it down in two swallows.

"What's with you?" asked Andrés. "Since when are you a big drinker?"

"I think I'm coming down with a cold."

"What do you think of this crazy wife of mine?"

"I think she's pretty," Vives answered.

Then they talked some more about themselves. About the difference between music and the bulls. About how Carlos's father loved my general, and how he fought with his son who had done nothing but disillusion him with his insistence on becoming a musician instead of a soldier.

"Your father was never wrong," Andrés concluded.

"Salud, General," said Carlos. "Salud, curious one." He winked at me and patted the hand that was resting on the table.

"Salud," I said, and knocked back another cognac with one swallow, then for the rest of the evening concentrated on smiling.

When we left, a brilliant yellow moon was shining overhead. In a doorway, as if it were five in the afternoon and not three in the morning, a blind man sat playing a trumpet.

I HAD ALWAYS believed that the only thing I needed in order to live a tranquil life was to have Andrés with me every day. But the next morning, when instead of rushing off he announced that he was planning to stay and was going to move his office to our library, I wished he would go away. It was like having an antique armoire in the middle of the room—there was no way to avoid him. His noisiness filled every corner of the house. To top things off, he became very affectionate. He wanted to fuck every morning, and never left the house without me. Out of the blue, he named me his private secretary and made me attend all the meetings he was organizing to plan how to wrest control of the labor federation from Cordera, and to all his sessions with politicians—even when he went to pee, he wanted me with him.

Had it happened two days earlier, I would have been happy. Not only to have his explosive company once again, but to be invited to everything I'd been shut out of, the meetings and the deals I'd had to guess at after the fact, harassing Andrés with endless questions in order to get an inkling of what was going on. Now I could attend them all, and had I an opinion, they would have listened. The problem was that I had walked up those marble stairs in the Bellas Artes, and was in love with another man.

I was unfaithful in my imagination long before I touched Carlos Vives. I had no patience for anything but him. I had never loved Andrés that way, never spent hours trying to remember the exact size of his hands or desiring with all my body merely to see him. I was ashamed to feel that way about a man, to be so unhappy, then suddenly happy, without having any control over it. I became unbearable, and the more irritating I was, the more Andrés pampered me. I had never been so free to do what I wanted as I was then, and never felt so strongly that everything I did was futile, stupid, unwelcome. Because with all the things I had, and all the things I had wanted, my only wish now was for afternoon to come so I could see Carlos Vives.

At breakfast Andrés noticed that my hair had grown and was more lustrous than it had been in years; he thought my feet were more beautiful than those of a geisha, my teeth like a young girl's, my lips like a film star's. I, on the other hand, had never so despised my hips, my mouth, my eyelashes; I had never felt more stupid, more deceitful, more ugly.

With all that to bear, I spent that morning listening to my general dream up a plan for a group of deputies that could be called on to screw over whomever most deserved it at any given time. All I wanted was for afternoon to come.

Andrés had to go to the Palacio Nacional, and I went with him.

"So now you're going shopping?" he asked as he got out of the car.

"Probably," I replied.

The minute Juan drove away, I told him to take me to the Bellas Artes. When we got there, I leaped from the car.

"What time shall I come back, señora?"

"Don't."

As if he hadn't heard me, he said, "Will eight be all right?"

I went running up the stairs. I didn't hear any music. I was sure he wasn't there.

I pushed the door.

I heard his voice. "Everyone, again from seventeen."

The music began. I slipped in like a cat and sat toward the back. My hands were on my legs and without realizing I began to finger the cloth of my skirt. I watched him, rows and rows away. Again the arms, and the voice, commanding:

"That sharp means sharp, Martínez. Marquelo, don't be afraid. That's how it sounds. Good afternoon, señora, how nice to have you in the audience," he yelled. "If you can stop playing with your skirt, we will appreciate it."

I'm trading one madman for another, I thought, but didn't run away. I liked watching him from afar. I couldn't imitate what he was doing, but I remember him as well as the sea and night at Punta Allen.

I went up to the boxes on the second floor. I liked how he moved his hands, how others obeyed him without pausing to question whether his instructions were correct. It didn't matter. He had the power, and you could feel its reach. It flowed through the hall, the musicians, my body, as I leaned over the railing of the box, my head propped on my arms, my eyes following his hands.

Eight o'clock came and the music continued, swelling and ebbing. Juan would be at the door and Andrés would be furious, but

I sat motionless in the red velvet seat until suddenly Carlos's arms fell to his sides.

"Better, gentlemen, much better. I'll see you tomorrow. Thank you for today."

He stepped down from the podium and disappeared into the wings. I was wondering where he might have gone when suddenly he was beside me.

"Who's taking whom to get ice cream?"

"You're taking me," I said.

"You're the one who likes ice cream. I prefer whiskey."

"How did you know I like ice cream?"

"Don't you have ice cream when you're nervous?"

"Yes, but I'm not nervous now, and who told you that?"

"My spies. They also told me that yesterday you wanted to get out of your car and come to my hotel."

"They told you wrong. Who do you think I am?"

"A woman married to a crazy man who's twenty years older than she is and treats her like a teenager."

We were walking downstairs.

Juan was at the entrance, pale as raw dough.

"Señora, the General will kill us," he said, opening the door of the car.

"Tell him we're walking, we won't be long," Carlos ordered.

"No," said Juan. "I'm not going back without the señora."

"Then wait here, because we're taking a walk."

Carlos took my arm and we crossed the street toward Madero.

"I like that building," I said when we reached Sanborn's Casa de Los Azulejos with the blue tile façade.

"I can't buy it for you. Why don't you ask your general?"

"Go to hell," I answered.

"Your wish is my command," he said, pushing the door to

Sanborn's and starting in just as Juan overtook us and held a pistol to my ribs.

"I'm sorry, señora, but I have a family, so you're coming with me to pick up the General."

"Let's go, then, Juan," I said, and we ran to the car. We picked up Andrés as he was saying good-bye to some buddies at the gate of the Palacio.

"Hey, Princess. Have a good time?" he asked.

I wasn't used to his new tone; it made me feel like an idiot.

"I went to see Vives," I said, as if I were taking off my clothes.

"That's good," he replied. "Where did you leave him? Why didn't he come have dinner with us?"

"I told him to go to hell."

"What did he do to you?"

"He treated me like an imbecile. He said if I liked Sanborn's so much, why didn't I ask you to buy it for me."

"You like Sanborn's?"

"It's Talavera tile," I replied, and we went to dinner, arms around each other.

The next day General Basilio Suárez had dinner at our house. I purposely served *mole* Puebla-style because I knew he hated it.

General Suárez was as uncomplicated as a beef tortilla. What mattered to him was making money, and that was why he'd joined forces with Andrés. They were looking for contracts to build roads, but weren't getting them because the secretary of transportation was one Jesús Garza, whom they hated for being an Aguirre supporter and who obviously hated them back.

They were trying to concoct some way to bring Garza down, and Suárez, who wasn't the brightest, said, "I think we ought to accuse him of being a communist. And that's no lie, because the guy *is* a communist. And we didn't fight the Revolution for the Russians to come take it away from us."

"You're right, General. Later today I'll talk to the people at the Catholic Family Union and ask them to broaden their attack against Cordera and add a few others who deserve our attention. It's time we began to name names. So, by God, tomorrow we'll take the CTM from Cordera, give it to Alfonso Maldonado, a guy who doesn't play with fire, and begin to lay the groundwork for screwing over those two beauties Aguirra left us."

I was about to object, when Vives walked in.

"You're late," said Andrés. "We're talking politics, do you mind?"

"I mind, but I'll manage. I knew that in this house everything is politics, but I accepted your invitation anyway."

"Which was for two. It's three-thirty," said Andrés.

"You invited him?" I asked.

"I didn't tell you because I wanted to surprise you," said Andrés.

"Well, you did. Lucina, set a place for the señor," I said, adopting the role of mistress of the house and motioning Vives to a seat beside General Suárez. Andrés was at the head of the table; I was at his left, and the general to his right.

"I prefer the other side, if it doesn't offend the general," Carlos said, looking at Suárez.

"The son of General Vives could never offend me," said Suárez. "Especially if he chooses to sit beside a beautiful lady instead of a decrepit old ex-president."

"So sit down and stop interrupting," said Andrés.

"Sorry, Chinti, I'll be the perfect guest from here on out."

"What did you call him?" I asked, laughing.

"Don't tell her, I won't be able to put up with her."

"Of course I won't tell her, General. Besides, your wife and I aren't speaking. She left me standing in the middle of the street yesterday, right in the middle of a sentence."

"You annoyed her," said Andrés, "and she's very sensitive."

"Have you two finished?" I asked. And to Suárez: "Do you want more beans, or shall we have dessert? If we're going to wait for Vives, dessert will be a while."

"As far as I'm concerned, we can have dessert," said Vives. "I'd just as soon skip the *mole*."

"What polite friends you have, Andrés. Your musician not only interrupts us, he's finicky besides."

"What can I do? He's the son of the only bastard who ever earned my respect. I can't have him shot because he turned up his nose at your dinner."

"For all I care," I said, "he can starve. And you, General, what can we offer you?"

"*I'd* like apple pie and goat cheese," said Carlos. "It's been years since I've had goat cheese."

"Poor fellow," said Andrés. "We'd forgotten that you're just back from self-imposed exile."

"There are worse things. Some can't come back at all," said Suárez.

"You're thinking about President Jiménez."

"Who else?"

"It won't be long before Jiménez is back," said Andrés. "In fact, I think we need a bastard with his balls."

"And because he wants to keep those balls, he's going to come back, lock himself in his house, and keep his mouth shut," said Carlos, spreading cheese on a roll.

"You think so?" asked Andrés, in a tone he seldom used when he talked politics, especially with neophytes.

"I can promise you, Chinti," said Carlos. "Trust me." And he began to hum "The Boat of *Guaymas*" between bites of cheese and apple pie, as Andrés roared with laughter.

"Salud, Vives, I'm glad to see you again. Salud, General Suárez. This is your house."

A small, hunchbacked man appeared at our door carrying a large record book and a mountainous pile of papers in his arms.

"With your permission, General," said Andrés, inviting him in. "We've been expecting you. Come on in. Stand over here. No, better there between the señora and the señor," he said, pointing to me and Vives. "Please read it."

The man stood between us, opened his book, and began to read. "As dated March first, 1941, in regard to said property . . ." In short, Andrés had bought the Sanborn's Casa de Los Azulejos for me.

"Please sign here, señora," said the man, and handed me a pen. Andrés was watching us, amused.

"What did you do to get them to sell you that building?" asked Carlos.

"They sold it to my wife. She's the buyer."

"Your wife, on her own, couldn't buy a stick of gum," he said.

"Everything that's mine is hers," Andrés replied.

"Then she must be a millionaire."

"Nothing she doesn't deserve. Sign it, Catín, and do whatever you want with your Sanborn's."

"I'll never have coffee there again," said Carlos.

"Don't be bitter, Vives. What does it matter to you who owns it? It's a nice place."

"It was. Now it's been bought with money from who knows where."

"Don't you come here and tell me what you think of my money. Where do you think the English got the money to pay for your scholarship? You're telling me it was clean money? All money's the same. I take it wherever I find it, because if I don't take it, someone else will. If I don't give that Sanborn's to Catalina, Espinosa will give it to Olguita, or Peñafiel to Lourdes. It had five mortgages, and the woman who owned it was going to lose it no matter what; either I take it or the bank takes it. Better I get it and make my wife happy, because before you butted into things she had the happiest face I'd seen on her in ten years. You're a wet blanket."

I was amazed to hear Andrés explaining himself to anyone, allowing his honesty to be questioned, even admitting that his money wasn't clean. Why wasn't he yelling at Carlos? Who knows. I've never ever understood what went on between them.

"Go ahead, señora, sign," said Vives.

I picked up the pen and signed my name the way I had signed it ever since I married Andrés.

"Now you have your plaything," said Carlos. "So now what? Are you going to sleep under your Talavera tiles? Will you feel it's yours? I warn you that in this city there aren't many people who don't feel that they own that building. You may hold the papers, but as long as everyone is free to go in there and have a cup of coffee, the Casa de Los Azulejos belongs to everyone."

"That's the way I like it," I said.

"Great, and be the great Lady Do-gooder so everyone will love and admire you. How this woman wants to be loved!" he said.

O F COURSE I wanted to be loved. I've spent a lifetime wanting to be loved. More than ever the night of the concert.

Bellas Artes was filled by the time we arrived. Rodolfo and Chofi went in first, as the newspapers would report, accompanied by us. We went up to the presidential box. Right in the center of the theater. Everyone was watching.

In adjacent boxes were several of Rodolfo's cabinet members and their families. Down below were special guests and the kind of people that from a distance you think look happy. God knows why.

Down below, too, were the seats where I'd first sat and watched Carlos. Down there, he would have been close, he could have seen me.

The orchestra was noisily tuning up. The musicians were all in black suits, their shoes polished and their hair slicked back. Different from the way they dressed during rehearsals: colored shirts, wild hair, run-down shoes, and threadbare pants. Spruced up, they looked unreal. They looked identical, when individually they were as different as their instruments. Finally Carlos appeared, in tails and black tie, baton in hand, hair neatly combed. People applauded as he walked toward the podium. He stepped up on it, turned, and made an exaggerated bow.

"What a clown that Vives is," said Andrés.

I had goose bumps. We sat down, and Carlos signaled the orchestra with outstretched arms.

At the end of the first half of the program, the audience applauded as if he were God. I sat quietly, looking down.

"What is it, Catín? Didn't you like it?" asked Andrés. "Why do you look like you're about to have a baby?"

"I liked it," I said, getting to my feet like everyone else. "Vives is good."

"How do you know he's good? I don't know whether he is or not. This is the first time we've come to one of these things. To me it seemed too theatrical. The bands in the plazas are more lively, less likely to put you to sleep."

We left the box to go have a drink and talk. Chofi was proud of her husband's discovery.

"He's a genius," she said to the wives of the secretaries, who had gathered around her like chicks about a hen. She was wearing one of those horrible fox pieces that have the little heads on them. A bad choice with her broad shoulders, fat arms, and enormous breasts. As she talked, the heads bounced on her tits like ball fringe as she raved about Vives.

Her euphoria reached such a fever pitch that she got overheated. She took out her fan and fanned the furs. Anything short of taking them off. The other women nodded and added their own praise.

"He's so handsome!" said the wife of the secretary of the interior.

"That's something I think we all agree on," replied the wife of the secretary of the treasury, laughing aloud. "Who cares whether he knows anything about music."

They all laughed with her.

"But he is a great musician as well," put in the wife of the secretary of the exterior, transported, her eyes rolling back in her head. She was the daughter of Porfirio Díaz supporters who had held on to their fortune and had always looked down on us as latecomers to the world of international culture. Her father had been an ambassador, and she had "lived in France all my childhood."

"Yes, a great musician," said Chofi, smoothing her foxes.

Fortunately, the intermission was over. I don't know how everyone in Rodolfo's cabinet managed to marry such an absolute bitch.

The second half of the concert was especially sad and especially long; it seemed always about to end but, like a curse, came back just when you thought it was over. That was the music I had climbed the stairs to hear, that had lingered in my ears, that I couldn't hum without feeling afraid.

The first twenty minutes, I watched Andrés try not to fall asleep, then he began talking with Fito.

I was watching Carlos. I studied his back and his arms, rising and falling. I studied his legs. I studied him as if he were the music, as if he weren't the same man who could talk and make fun of me and joke with Andrés during a meal. He was different, someone totally absorbed in things that had nothing to do with us, things that had borne him from a different place and were taking him I didn't know where.

"This Señor Mahler needed a good fuck," Andrés muttered into my neck.

Several times people started to applaud, thinking that a booming kettledrum signaled the finale, but the music would begin again from a nearly inaudible pitch, a thin thread of a flute joined by a violin, and then a cello, and then all the instruments, rising in a deafening crescendo. Which was why when it was over, only I, who had heard it so many times, knew that it was the end, and began to clap. Alone.

I interrupted Fito's conversation with Andrés, and Chofi jerked awake. They stood to applaud, and with them, everyone in the theater.

Carlos, who had dropped his arms and was standing stock-still before the orchestra, turned, and finally I could see his face, his hair covering his forehead. He made that sweeping bow, stepped down from the podium, and exited.

As the applause continued I was wishing he would materialize and ask, "Who's taking whom to get ice cream?" When he did appear, he didn't go to the podium but directed attention to the orchestra, then again bowed, his head touching his knees.

Those bitches are right, I thought, he is handsome. And they've never heard his voice, they haven't walked with him along Madero, haven't wanted to insult him in the middle of the street.

I continued to applaud, like everyone else, like Andrés, who was yelling as if it were a patriotic rally on September 15.

"Something good had to come from General Vives. This boy's a real politician. Only a politician could wring that much applause out of an audience. Look at him, you'd think he'd just made the speech of a lifetime. You didn't get this much response at your inauguration," he said to Fito, guffawing.

"Vives, Vives, Vives," people chanted, while the seated orchestra members applauded or rapped on their music stands with their bows.

Vives entered from the wings, hair combed neatly back.

Again the applause swelled. He stepped up on the podium, lifted his arms to bring his musicians to their feet, turned toward us, and bowed nearly to the floor.

"Yes, he'd make a great politician," said Andrés. "He's an excellent actor, a ham. Too bad we don't do that business of the bow, it would make a great effect. Why don't you try it, Fat Man?" he said to Fito. "Just look at our wives, they're out of their minds. I'll try the bow if you promise me you'll give women the vote. The House has a bill before it that Aguirre never signed. I promise that with them voting and me bowing, I'll be elected president, and no one will say anything about the question of me being your buddy. I'll appoint Vives head of the party the day after I've been chosen, and we'll be off, touring the country with the whole damn orchestra. How does that sound, Catín?"

Five times Vives returned to acknowledge the applause, five times the orchestra rose to its feet and sat back down, but no one had stopped applauding. Least of all, the women. Every one of them in the surrounding boxes, Chofi's claque, was clapping as if Vives had just laid her.

"Let's go," I said to Andrés. "We can congratulate him at dinner, but this is too much, no matter how good it was."

"That's what I say, even if he was a toreador. You'd think he'd risked his life."

"Don't go," Rodolfo pleaded. He was incapable of giving an order. "It would look bad if I left."

"But we're not you," I told him.

"But you're *with* him," said Chofi, who took her cronyism very seriously.

Meanwhile, Vives strode briskly onto the stage, again took the podium, and almost overlapping the applause, cued the orchestra to begin playing. As if saying, "Everyone, again, from twenty-four." Except that the music was something hummable, the song my papa would have requested. I don't know how many mornings I heard him get up humming that tune. Sometimes he stood in the doorway of our room and whistled it until we poked our heads from beneath the sheets and grumbled at the sun and the early-bird father fate had given us.

Why wasn't my papa here, so I could talk to him? Why wasn't he here so I could complain about the mistakes we make in our lives? Or ask him what to do about this inappropriate feeling growing inside me.

The orchestra was my papa whistling in the early morning, and as always when he was there without being there, when something brought home to me the reality that his words and his hugs were gone and would never be anything but a memory, nothing more than the tenacity of my nostalgia, I burst into tears, sobbing and hiccuping until I was making almost as much noise as the orchestra.

I slipped from my chair to the floor, so no one could see what a scene I was making. Andrés, who never knew what to do at times like these, put his hand on my head and stroked me as if I were a cat, so that when the orchestra stopped playing I had a streaked face, swollen eyes, and tousled hair.

"There, there," said Andrés. "That was a bad idea, telling Vives that all you knew about music was that tune your father was always humming."

People had sprung to their feet and were wildly clapping and yelling, this time for real, as if they were at a bullfight. I was still on the floor. Through the bronze railing of the box I saw Carlos, after his last bow, throw back his head and laugh. My papa used to laugh like that sometimes. I stopped crying.

People were still applauding, but this time Vives did not return. Before the routine of the national anthem and honors to the flag that accompanied Rodolfo's entrances and exits, I ran to the powder room to try to repair the damage.

The party was in Los Pinos, the presidential palace. In a paneled room with huge chandeliers. Carlos was already there when Andrés and I entered with Rodolfo, Chofi, and the national anthem.

"Excellent, Vives," said Fito, gripping Carlos's hand.

"Maestro, I'm speechless," Chofi exhaled, massaging her foxes.

"Vives, you have natural political talent. Don't waste it," said Andrés.

"Thank you," I said.

"My thanks to all of you," Carlos replied. He was still laughing.

I began to tremble. What was happening to me was terrifying. I thought everyone could see it.

I took Andrés's arm and said we should go.

"But we just got here. We haven't eaten. And I'm starving, aren't you? Besides, look, Poncho Peña's here, and I need to talk to him." He left me in the middle of the room, within inches of Vives and his fans. They stole him away. Even Cordera had come over to congratulate him. As Vives embraced him he saw me over Cordera's shoulder, watching him. He took Cordera's arm and led him to where I was standing.

"You know each other?" he asked, without giving us time to answer.

"A pleasure," we both said, preferring to forget where we'd met.

"Why don't we go out to the garden?" said Carlos. "There are too many people in here."

He seized my hand and hurried toward the door. Cordera came with us. As we passed Andrés, Carlos said, "I'm taking your wife outside because we're suffocating in here."

"See if you can wake her up, she was ready to leave. Good evening, Alvaro," he said when he saw who was with us, then put his arms around me. "Listen to everything they say," he whispered before he kissed me. "See you in a little while," he said aloud, winking at Carlos.

"How's it going in the Congress?" Carlos asked Cordera when we were alone, strolling among the trees in the garden.

"Fine," said Cordera, looking at me.

"Are you going to be reelected?"

"That's not up to me, the Assembly decides that."

"Since when does the Assembly have anything to say about it? Don't tell me they're letting the Assembly do it?"

"Why not? That's the process."

"Don't play games with me, *mano*."

"What do you want me to tell you?" asked Cordera, spreading his arms wide.

We had walked deep into the garden. Carlos had slipped his arm around my waist, and before he answered, he pulled me to him.

"The señora knows her husband is a national disgrace. Don't let him get into it, he'll fuck you over. It's crystal clear, you're in his way. If you're reelected and can organize the workers the way you did the last term, you may even get to be president."

"Ascencio is already in it. The deputies in the House have been battling him, but who do you think wrote the speech the president will give in the morning? Who do you think thought up that part about how a road keeps going though the scenery changes? All to say that his politics are no different from Aguirre's but that he wants the masses to revise their methods by becoming more self-critical. Revise methods, that means revise people and positions. They want to screw us, *mano*, they want to shut us up. They're willing to sell off all our resources. They're with Suárez, who's into politics to make deals."

"But you have to fight them. Are you too tired?"

"No, that isn't it. It's more complicated than that. Can we talk tomorrow?" he said, again glancing at me distrustfully.

"You're afraid to die? You weren't once."

"Afraid, no. But I'm in no hurry, either. Besides, it's not up to me. I'll see you tomorrow. Good-bye, señora. Thanks for your discretion."

"How do you know I'll be discreet?" I asked.

"I know," he replied, and walked off in the other direction.

"What a country!" said Carlos. "Anyone who's not afraid is bored. Are you afraid?"

"I was bored."

"Not now?"

"Not now."

"What do you want to do?" he asked.

"When?"

"Now."

"Whatever you want. What do you want to do?"

"Me? Fuck."

"With me?" I asked.

"No, with Chofi."

When I woke up, Carlos was sleeping beside me, his lips in a little pout.

The apartment had a living room with a piano taking up half the space, a kitchen the size of a closet, and a bedroom with photographs covering the walls and a large window from which you could see the Bellas Artes. I wanted to stay. Carlos opened his eyes and smiled.

"Where are we going?" I whispered in his ear, as if someone might hear us.

"To the beach," he said, still half asleep.

"Then let's go."

"What time is it?" He yawned and stretched his arms.

"I don't know. Why don't we die right this minute?" I asked.

"Because I still have a lot to do. I've never conducted in Vienna."

"Will you take me to Vienna?"

"When they invite me."

"They haven't invited you?"

"First the war has to end, and I have to conduct better."

"You won't love me when all that happens," I said.

"I love you now," he said and began kissing me. Then he reached across me for his watch, which was on the table at my side of the bed. "It's four o'clock, I think maybe we will die today. Juan forgot."

"Forgot what?"

"That he was supposed to call us when Andrés was ready to leave Los Pinos."

"Why?"

"So you could get home before he did."

"But I don't want to go home."

"You have to. No way you can stay here."

"What a fool I am," I said, jumping up to gather the clothes I had strewn about the room. I was so furious I caught the zipper of my dress and yanked on it so hard I broke it. I looked for my shoes—what the hell, with my coat on no one would notice that the back of my dress was open.

"You and Alvaro are both assholes," I said.

"For a Puebla girl you have pretty hair."

"What do you know about anyone from Puebla?" I shouted.

The bell rang. It was Juan.

"Señora, the General doesn't want to leave Los Pinos. He says you told him you'd be in the garden and you must be out there and we can't leave you."

"Who's he with? Isn't the party over?"

"He's with Don Alfonso Peña."

"Still? He must be really drunk if he's put up with Peña all this time."

"Come on, love," said Carlos, already dressed and at the door. Juan drove us to Los Pinos. He went to park the car and we got out near the place where we'd been talking with Cordera. We started walking. Carlos had his arm around my waist, hurrying me. We went inside. Almost no one was there. Andrés and Peña were sitting on the far side of the room with a waiter on each side and a bottle of cognac before them. We went toward them.

"So, d'you get a breath of air?" asked Andrés, slurring his words.

"We weren't long. How did you get drunk so fast? You're drunker than I've ever seen you, Andrés. Why?" I was surprised. I was used to seeing him drink for hours on end without even getting tipsy.

" 'Cause to live in this country you either have to be crazy or crocked. I'm crazy mos' of the time, but t'night sanity wanted to take over and I did'n wanna let it. Right, *mano*?" he asked Peña, who was drunker than Andrés. Peña's eyes were crossed and he was staring at the floor.

"What I tried'a warn you 'bout is that they're lousy, dang'rous, fuckin' communis', an' you should'na lef' your wife with 'em."

"This guy's already having halluc'nations," said Andrés. "He thinks Vives is a communist. What comes nex' is a purple elephant and Greta Garbo in her underwear. Take 'im home, Juan, we're gonna sit here a while 'n talk."

"We'd better all go home," I said. "It doesn't look right to stay any longer."

"Oh, right, jus' look at *her,* worried 'bout what looks right," said Andrés, getting to his feet. "Fine, then, le's go home, but I want Juan t'go by and pick up some singers from Ciro's."

"Ciro's is closed by now," I said.

"I's not even three o'clock, he can still catch 'em. Juan, bring me a trio that knows 'Temor.' "

"But take us home first," I said.

"Don' we have another car? Where's your car, Vives?" Andrés asked.

My stomach lurched. Vives had left his car at his house.

"I let Cordera take it. He didn't have any way to get home," Vives replied, cool as you please.

"Fuckin' Cordera, he even gets away with my frien's cars. You're goin' to fall for that poor li'l Alvarito story, too? Lend him your car. Hah! If he doesn' have one, let 'im walk. Why should he take yours? Les not waste any more time. If we don't get our singers, I'll kill 'im for sure, never mind 'bout politics. He'll die for spoilin' our fun, and I'll be doin' the country a favor 'na bargain."

We drove home.

"Tel Juan t'let us out here at the gate. We'll walk to the house," said Andrés. "By the time I'm sittin' down in the sala, I wan' you to be back with musicians, Juan. And be sure they know 'Temor'!"

I jumped out and ran around to Juan's window.

"His watch stopped," I told him. "You won't find anyone at Ciro's. Better go to Maestro Lara's house, there'll still be a party going on there. Tell Toña to come fast. I need her."

CHAPTER

I HAD MET Toña Peregrino when Andrés was
governor. She and Lara came to Puebla. I invited them to sing at the Guerrero Theater for
one of those benefits that I used to have such fun organizing. They came for two days, but stayed five. I put them
up in our guest rooms, took them out to the ranch in
Atlixco, took them sightseeing all over, and they enjoyed
it, but no more than I did. Every night, Agustín would
play the piano and Toña would sing, just for fun.

We became friends. I took her to Lupe, my dressmaker,
who was a genius. In two days she made her three dresses
with trains and capes that disguised her weight. She was
divine the minute she opened her mouth, but the dresses
helped her get to the center of the stage without envying
the svelte Ninón Sevilla. As for me, I envied them both.
Once Lupe made her those dresses, Toña never went on
stage in anyone else's designs. Since I couldn't convince
Lupe to go into Mexico City, Toña often came to Puebla.
She always stayed with us. All kinds of things happened.
Once a man with a knife burst into the room where she

was sleeping, yelling, "Death to Andrés Ascencio." Those days, Andrés didn't sleep in the same room two nights in a row. Sometimes he stayed in mine, sometimes in Checo's, sometimes somewhere else. The night before the incident with Toña, he'd slept in that guest room. The man with the knife leaped on Toña, and all she could think to do was sing at the top of her lungs: "I see in your eyes an emerald glow."

The attacker had run out and she'd let him go. Years passed before she told me about it.

"What on earth made you think to sing?" I asked.

"What else could I do? All evening you'd been making me sing that chorus about the green that shines from the sea and the coral's blood-red mouth. I fell asleep thinking of it, and by then I couldn't tell the difference between palm trees and sultry women swaying in the breeze."

Since we loved each other, I was sure that when Juan told her it was urgent, she'd come, even in her nightgown.

I had scarcely gotten ice for the whiskey glasses when I heard the car pull up. I went to the door. Toña blew in like a gift from God, dressed in bright blue, her arms bare. She gave me a kiss.

"Good evening, good evening," she said with the voice of a goddess. "Anyone here want to have a little fun?"

"Toña!" cried Andrés. "Sing 'Temor' for me."

"I will, General, but first introduce me to these gentlemen," she said, staring at Vives as if trying to place him. "I know, you're the symphony conductor. I saw your picture. I never forget a face, do I, Cati?"

"And this is Deputy Alfonso Peña," I said, pointing to Poncho, who had fallen asleep with his head on the arm of a velvet chair. "You can see we've bored him stiff."

"Glad to meet you," said Toña, taking his hand and letting it drop. " 'Temor,' General? I'm sorry I didn't bring a piano player, I'll just have to get along as best I can."

"With your voice, Toña, is's always good."

"Do you need a piano player?" Carlos asked, sitting down at the piano.

"Don't tell me you know this kind of music?"

Carlos replied by playing the first chords of "Temor."

"Take a look at that," said Toña.

"From here?" asked Carlos.

Toña followed Carlos's lead.

"No, Toña," said Andrés. "From the beginning. 'Temor, afraid to be happy with you . . .' " he sang.

"Don't ruin it," I said. By now I was in a large chair, listening with fascination.

"Here we go, General," said Vives, and started from the beginning. Carlos followed Toña as if they'd been rehearsing for months.

He not only followed, but segued from one song into another. Toña never missed a beat. They were playing, cueing one another with their eyes.

> *"Not for nothing is the sky so high above us,*
> *Not for nothing is the sea so deeply blue,*
> *But high or deep, there's really nothing*
> *That can keep my love from reaching you."*

" 'This obsession is a madness, and the world is witness to my passion,' " I sang in my mousy little voice, unable to squelch my desire to sing.

Toña nodded, and waved me over to join them.

I sat on the piano bench beside Carlos, as with a few chords he moved from that song I'd always thought had been written for me to the opening of "The Night of Last Night."

" 'O, last night, that night of wonder,' " Toña began. " 'So much happened it all ran together, and now I can't seem to remember. . . .' "

" 'I am so bewildered, I who had at last found the peace that comes from love long passed,' " I sang with all my strength, and leaned against Carlos, who for a moment took one hand from the keyboard and stroked my leg.

"Now the one who's ruining everything's you, Catalina," said Andrés. "Shut up, and let the stars go at it."

I paid no attention. I continued: " 'But what are you doing to me, that I'm feeling what I never felt?' " My voice was reedy compared with Toña's, but I couldn't stop. " 'I swear to you that everything is new to me.' "

I even felt that Toña's voice had blended into mine, that I was the one singing.

" 'For you made me understand I've lived my life waiting for you,' " we sang, and with that I let my head plop down on the keys. *Boom!* was the finale to "The Night of Last Night."

"Catalina, stop fucking ever'thin' up," said Andrés. "I'm the one who's drunk. '*Ashes*,' Vives," he requested.

"Yes, '*Ashes*,' " I seconded.

"But you shut up, Catín."

"Yes, my love," I said.

" 'After bearing all the pain of knowing you'd forgotten,' " sang Toña.

" 'And after all the passion from a heart that's broken.' " I was with her word for word. She was behind me with her hands on my shoulders.

"Catalina. Shut the fuck up!"

"If anyone's fucking things up, it's you. You keep interrupting," I said, and caught up with Toña at "all the bitterness of a love like that you gave me."

"Pa . . . pa . . . pa . . . *pa*!" I stopped long enough to beat time on the piano.

" 'I could never forgive you, or give you what you gave me,' " we continued.

" 'You must know that in a dead love there can be no bitterness.' " From his armchair, Andrés slowly shook his finger, at whom, God knows.

" 'And if you try to stir the ruins that you yourself created, you will find only ashes of what was once my love,' " we ended.

"Drunker'n hell," said Andrés.

" 'Sing, if your heart wants to forget.' " Toña was following Carlos in a new song.

" 'Sing, if your pain is with you yet, " sang Carlos, accompanying himself with staccato chords.

> *"Sing, if today your love is fading,*
> *Sing, so a new love comes to you."*

"Para*ra* . . . para*ra* . . . para*ra*!" I hummed, and jumped up to whirl around the room.

Vives was laughing and Andrés had fallen asleep.

" 'Tear this heart out!' " I pleaded, still dancing around the room.

" 'Take it, take my heart,' " Toña followed Carlos's melody line.

" 'Tear this heart out, and if you should feel the pain . . .' " I was back with them again, beside Carlos on the bench. Andrés was right, I spoiled their voices, but at that moment that was the last thing on my mind.

" 'It will be because you can't see me, for if I leave my heart, I'll take away your eyes.' " I leaned against Carlos's shoulder, who struck the last three chords as Toña held the final "e-e-eyes."

"Stupendous, Toña," said Carlos. "I applaud you."

"And what about you two?" she asked. "Are you in love, or about to be?"

We left Andrés sleeping, and went out to the garden to watch the sun come up.

"Señora, shall I take the deputy home?" asked Juan, who was standing in the door to the entry hall.

"Please, Juan. And put the general to bed. You're a saint."

"Then come back for me," said Toña. "I don't want to stay for breakfast."

About an hour after the sun rose orangely through the trees, Checo wandered out to the garden, barefoot and in his pajamas.

"Why are you wearing what you had on yesterday, Mama?" he asked. "Put on your riding pants. Aren't you going?"

"Let's go, Maestro," said Toña, slapping Carlos's back, who by then looked bleary-eyed but handsome. "Good-bye, my dearest Catalina, have a good ride. The fresh air will be good for you."

Carlos took me by the shoulders and kissed my cheek.

"Tomorrow?" he asked.

"Tomorrow," I replied, and we moved apart.

Toña and he walked to the car, Checo and I toward the house.

"Hey," Carlos yelled from the gate. "It's already tomorrow."

When Checo and I came back from riding, I was feeling nauseated. I got off my horse craving orange juice. Lucina brought some to the garden gate, where I'd sat down to massage my legs while answering something or other Checo had asked me.

"The general said for you to come up as soon as you got back," Lucina told me.

I raced up the stairs three at a time, trailing mud into Andrés's bedroom. I sat on the edge of the bed and began tugging at my boots.

"Can I open the curtains? I can't see anything."

"Have mercy on a blinding headache," Andrés answered, moving across the bed until he could put his arm around my waist. "Tell me what Cordera and Vives were talking about last night," he said, rubbing my back.

"About the concert."

"And what else?"

"Vives asked Cordera about the Congress, but Cordera didn't say anything important."

"How long did they talk? What did he say?"

"All he said was that it was going well and that the party faithful would decide the election of the leader."

"Don't make things up. What did he say that was important?"

"Nothing. He left after five minutes."

"Then what did you and Vives do the rest of the time? Don't make it up. Vives and Cordera talked longer than that. You were gone a couple of hours."

"We were walking," I told him. "The gardens at Los Pinos are fabulous!"

"You sound like you just discovered them. You want to live there? Tell me what Vives and Cordera were saying."

"General, if I hear anything, I promise I'll tell you, but yesterday they said about four words."

"Tell me. Remember exactly what they said, because they use codes."

"You're either hung over or still drunk. What do you mean, codes?"

"They didn't make an appointment?" he asked.

"Just sometime."

"That means Thursday," he said.

"You're crazy." I was struggling with the boot that always gave me trouble.

"Did you get any sleep?" he asked.

"A little."

"So why are you so wound up? Every time you're up late you sleep three days, and can't get enough. How come you went riding?"

"Checo asked me to."

"Checo asks you every day."

"Today I wanted to go," I said, pulling off the boot and wiggling my toes.

"You're very strange today."

"I had a good time yesterday, didn't you?"

"I don't remember. Were you singing, or did I dream it?"

"I sang 'Tear This Heart Out.' " I started to sing it again.

"Shut up. You sound like an echo chamber."

"Go back to sleep. Why get up? It's Sunday."

"That's why I'm getting up. Garza is on today at the Plaza de Toros."

"It's a long time till four o'clock. Go to sleep. I'll wake you at two."

"That's not enough time. I invited people for one. To eat. Are you coming this afternoon?"

"You never invite me."

"I'm inviting you."

"I don't like bullfights."

"Crazy girl! You're coming."

"Whatever you say," I said, kissing the top of his head and pulling up the sheet as if he were dead. Then I tiptoed to the door and left him, already asleep.

In Las Lomas I had a bathroom three times larger than my bedroom. The walls were covered with mirrors and a skylight let the noon sun into the room with as much force as outdoors in the garden. Around the tub, which was large enough for five, were all kinds of plants. The bath was my favorite place, where I went to be alone.

That morning I ran into the bathroom, turned on the water, and threw off my clothes. I remember the feeling of my body in the warm water, surrounded by plants, lying full length, with my head wet and face upturned, watching the clouds float across the piece of sky framed by the skylight.

And what do I do now? I said, as if some friend were there with me. I can run away. Leave the General, everything, the children, the bathtub, the violets, the inexhaustible checkbook. I want to go away with Carlos, I said, soaping my head. I'll go today. Lorenzo Garza or no Lorenzo Garza. Not one more day of witnessing crimes and listening to lies. I'll move today, sleep in a different bed, even change my name. And if he won't have me? He'll have me. He said, "Tomorrow?" Then he said, "It's already tomorrow." But he didn't want to go to the sea with me, he brought me home. He never meant to stay with me. He doesn't love me. What if I knock and he doesn't let me in? What if he has a sweetheart on her way from England? Oh, fuck.

I got out of the tub, wrapped a towel around my head, walked to the mirror, and smiled.

I NEVER SAW Andrés kill anyone. Many times, behind a closed door, I heard him talking about death. I knew that he killed easily, but not with his own hands or his own pistol; for that, he had people eager to work their way up from the bottom.

Until I was with Vives, it never occurred to me to fear Andrés. My way of standing up to him had been through little games I could end as soon as they became dangerous. But not with Carlos. That's why I feared Andrés's pistol.

Sometimes at night I woke up trembling, drenched with sweat. If we slept in the same bed, I wouldn't be able to sleep. I would watch Andrés, his mouth half open, snoring, secure that beside him slept the same stupid kid he had married, the same innocent, a little older and less docile, but still the same. His Catalina, someone to laugh at and make his accomplice, the one who guessed what he was thinking but never wanted to know about his business deals. During that period, all the things I had seen since we were married accumulated in my body until one afternoon I felt a knot at the nape of my neck. I was stiff from there to my shoulder, one long shooting pain, like a raw nerve.

When I told Bibi, she prescribed exercise and massages that would, she said, have the added bonus of reducing my hips. Her masseuse came to the house, because there was no way that Gómez was going to let her take off her clothes away from home, even for a rubdown by another woman. But I chose to go to the center in the Colonia Cuauhtémoc, where they gave massages and exercise classes. It was managed by a smiling woman with gorgeous legs, whom I never saw in anything but incredibly high heels.

That's where I became friends with Andrea Palma. She was very amusing, always complaining that she had no bottom, poor thing. One day when we were lying side by side getting our massages, we ended up talking about the size of our bellies and concluding that a compromise between her ass and mine would make the perfect woman.

"If only you weren't so envious, and God wanted to do us the favor," she told me one day.

"You want God to do you another favor, Andrea? Isn't it enough, all the boys he puts at your disposal?"

"You are envious. That's because they keep you penned up. How does it feel to be faithful?"

"Terrible."

"It feels terrible to be unfaithful, too."

"Not *as* terrible."

"You're blushing," she cried. "Even your belly button is blushing. What are you up to? Don't tell me about it! Your husband is quite capable of cutting out my tongue if I don't cough up the truth."

"I wish I had your breasts," I said, as if I hadn't heard her.

"Don't play dumb with me, Catalina. Tell me."

"Tell you what? Nothing's going on. If you were me, would you dare deceive General Andrés Ascencio?"

"I wouldn't, but you would. If you're brave enough to sleep with him, you're brave enough to sleep with someone else."

"But for that he'd kill me."

"Like that poor woman he killed in Morelos?" put in Raquel, the masseuse.

"Who did he kill in Morelos?" Andrea asked.

"Some girl who was his lover and one day told him, enough is enough."

"That's a lie! My husband doesn't go around killing women just because they say no."

"That's what I was told."

"Well, don't believe everything you hear," I said, jumping off the massage table to escape the hands still working on my body.

"Catina, don't be silly," said Andrea. "I thought you were more sophisticated."

"Sophisticated? Sophisticated! How do you want me to act? You two are telling me that for twelve years I've been living with Jack the Ripper, and you want me to lie there like a lamb? You want me to smile like the Mona Lisa? What do you want of me?"

"I want you to think."

"To think what? To think *what*?" I screamed.

Our private conversation had become very public, and women on the other beds, along with their masseuses, had stopped whatever they were doing to stare at me, stark naked, my eyes streaming tears and my face aflame, shouting at Andrea.

"First, calm down," she said in a low voice. "And get back on the table; relax, smile at me, finish your massage . . . and then as soon as you leave here, find out exactly who Andrés Ascencio is."

I did what she said. The flow of her words and her dark eyes were soothing. For a while I lay silent, facedown, feeling that Raquel was pummeling my buttocks harder than ever.

"Find out what, for example? What?" I asked.

"For example, whether or not what Raquel told you is true."

"But how could that be true, Andrea? That's absolute crap. My husband kills for business purposes, he doesn't go around killing women who won't let him play with their pussies."

"Now you sound a little more intelligent. But why couldn't he be doing both?"

"Because he doesn't."

"That makes a lot of sense. 'Because he doesn't.' Because you don't want it to be so. So all right, he doesn't, and that's that."

"Right. But not 'and that's that,' " I said.

"Whatever you say," she replied, with her evil little chortle. "Are you still dieting?"

"Don't change the subject. Do you think I'm stupid?"

"You're the one who put an end to the discussion. Don't blame me because you're afraid," she said, getting up to follow Marta, who told her the steam room was ready.

"Are you going to the *temazcal*, too?" Raquel asked.

"Where did you hear about the woman murdered in Morelos?" I asked her.

"I heard it around, señora, but you're right, it must be a lie."

Raquel dyed her hair a reddish blond; she had bright little eyes and thin lips. She gave massages with small, strong hands. She had very little to say. She seemed made to listen and keep her mouth closed. That was why it surprised me so that she had butted into my conversation with Andrea.

What if he really did kill her? I mused as I was sweating in the *temazcal*.

"I don't want to die," I said to Andrea, who was opposite me, only her head protruding from the brick oven they put you into with a rubberized sheet around your neck. We looked like freaks with square bodies and tiny, sweaty heads.

"Especially now that you're getting so good-looking," she answered.

"Andrea, this isn't a game. I don't want to die."

"You're not going to die, Cati, don't be silly. You know your husband better than we do, no matter what we've heard about him. According to you, he's not a monster, so why are you worried? He wouldn't shoot you, even if you were running around on him. And why else would he do it?"

"He wouldn't. He's not some cheap thug."

"You've convinced me, darling. Now do you want me to convince you of what you've just convinced me? Why else do you come blubbering to me about how you don't want to die?"

We kept getting closer and closer as we spoke. We were out of the *temazcales* and toweling off, our faces and mouths so close that at times they brushed. Andrea was beautiful. Just as she was, no makeup, dripping sweat, drinking in what I was saying, sharing the fear I conveyed to her as I told her everything, from the stairway of the Bellas Artes and dinner at the Prendes, to the day I went to his house and started making it mine. Everything: the walks through the *zócalo*, the picnics, the afternoons at the movies, nights at the concerts, early mornings rushing home to my bed, euphoric and terrified.

"What shall I do, Andrea?" I asked.

"Right now?" she said. "Exercise." And gave me a kiss.

THAT YEAR ALL Saints' Day fell on a Wednesday, and Andrés decided we would cross the
bridge of the dead in the Puebla house. He
said he would be inviting some friends and for me to
organize everything. I was furious just thinking about
having to look after Andrés's guests and leave Carlos behind. If only they were interesting people, but he would
invite the undersecretary of taxes and revenues with that
idiot wife of his, always dolled up as if she were going to
be photographed for a fashion magazine, the secretary of
agriculture, who was so dumb he couldn't get two words
out, and the latest hotshot politician. Politicians were either in or out of fashion, and as soon as one was in vogue,
Andrés would invite him to spend the weekend with us.
He'd become the king of the house, the center of all
conversation. Andrés would let him win at handball, and
I had to oblige his dear wife with whatever she could
dream up.

I knew all about these vacations with fifteen guests and
three meals a day, plus appetizers and tea biscuits and

coffee at all hours. I'd be in the kitchen the whole time, coping with Matilde's bad humor.

I walked around muttering all day Thursday. Andrés informed me we'd leave Friday the twenty-eighth at noon and come back the evening of Wednesday the second.

"Aren't you afraid Fito will lose his grip on the country if you're gone that long? What will he do without his chief adviser and buddy?" I asked, wondering how I would get along in a dull, unbearable world without Carlos.

We spent Wednesday afternoon together, walking through the *zócalo* and up and down Juárez.

We had dinner at El Palace, overlooking the plaza. I had eels and he oysters; I ordered cake and ice cream and he an espresso.

"I have a room downstairs," he told me.

"I can stay until one," I answered, and we ran from the restaurant to a room with a balcony; I opened it to feel the cold air and see the government palace and the cathedral.

"We always have to hide when we fuck," I said.

"So why when you were sixteen did you marry a general who's the president's best friend?"

"How should I know why you do what you do at sixteen. I'm thirty now, I want to do what I want. I want to live with you. I want that gaggle of old women who come in their panties when they watch you conduct to know that I'm the one who gets that privilege. I want you to take me to New York and introduce me to your friends. I want you to bring me out in the daylight and tell General Ascencio everything."

"But for the moment, wouldn't you like to come to bed?"

"Yes," I said, and forgot my grievances.

★　　★　　★

But as we said good-bye I remembered again. I almost enjoyed telling him that for four days I would be isolated in Puebla without him but with my husband, my children, and my servants in my house—half refuge, half convent—a warren of corridors and flowerpots and odd nooks and fountains.

"How you suffer," he said coolly.

"You don't care, you don't care at all," I screamed. "You've got yourself laid, now you're sending me off with another man. Faggot!" I screamed, slamming the car door and ordering Juan to drive away.

I was livid all Friday morning. Lilia noticed right away.

"Don't you want to go? You used to like to go back. It's pretty in Puebla."

"So tell me what you think about that sweetheart your father drummed up for you," I said.

"He's nice," she answered.

She was sixteen, with perfect breasts, long, firm legs, brilliant eyes, and a laugh filled with self-confidence.

"He's a lousy bastard. He's been stringing Georgina Letona along for seven years, and now he's leaving her to court you because you're very pretty and very young—and, incidentally, the daughter of Andrés Ascencio. Don't you realize you're a business deal?"

"Don't complicate things, Mama. You're acting this way because you don't want to leave Carlos for four days."

"What do I care about Carlos?"

"From the looks of things, nothing, I guess." She laughed. "Shall we go for a ride?"

"I can't. I haven't organized the meals yet. I don't even know how many we'll be."

"So complicated," she said, and walked away, boot heels clicking.

Fifteen years ago, I had been like Lilia. At what moment did other people's meals begin to be more important than galloping off on my horse?

I called Puebla to talk with Matilde. For dinner, I asked her to prepare a pork loin with *pasilla* chiles.

"Won't that be too heavy for the evening, señora?" She liked to contradict me, and I heard that tone in her voice. I almost always yielded, to avoid an argument, but that morning I insisted on the pork.

"You don't think chicken with herbs would be better? The General likes that a lot."

"Make the pork, Matilde."

"Whatever you say, señora."

She was half in love with Andrés. She was my age and had a son who lived with her mother in San Pedro. She looked old. She had two teeth missing and never dieted or went to the gym or bought expensive creams. She could have been twenty years older than I was. She didn't like me and she had good reason. I sat thinking how I'd have to spar with her the whole time we were there.

I was still by the telephone table, staring at the tips of my moccasins, when Carlos walked into the hall, suitcase in hand.

"We leave at twelve?" he asked.

I didn't answer. I ran to take out my hair curlers. I put on pants, perfume, and lipstick. I went back to the sala, but he wasn't there.

"They went to the bar in the game room," Lucina informed me.

"Are you ready?" I asked. "And what about the children?"

"All ready."

The game room was at the back of the garden. All our houses were so enormous, it would have helped to get around in them by car. I walked through the garden and into the large room where Andrés and Carlos were playing billiards.

"How soon will you be ready, señora?" asked Andrés. "I'll give you till one."

"I'm ready now. But Lili hasn't come back from riding. Who else did you invite?"

"Just Puente and his wife. I want to see people in Puebla and rest," Andrés said, lining up his ball. He shot and missed the pocket. "What a lousy shot. What are you doing standing there? Round up your kids. We'll need three cars. Have Juan and Benito come with us. Who else is here?"

"I can drive," Carlos offered.

"Perfect. You, Catalina, go with him; take Lilia, the young ones, and their nanny. I'm not up to family chatter. Carlos will enjoy it because he's a free man. The older girls and Octavio can go with Benito. But everyone's leaving by two. All at the same time. We'll follow each other. Be sure Lilia brings something besides bathing suits and slacks. She'll need something dressy because the Alatristes are going to have her over one evening."

"Did you arrange that?" I asked.

"Yes, I arranged it. And don't ask in that tone. She's my daughter and I'm looking out for her future. You stay out of it."

"She's your daughter when it suits your purposes, but when it doesn't, she's our daughter. When she was ten, you handed her over to me with a big speech about how I would have to be a mother to her. Now she's your daughter."

"Because now she needs someone to ensure her future, not someone to wipe her nose and help with her homework."

"I'm not going to let you marry her off against her will," I said.

"Don't worry, she'll marry who she chooses."

"Why don't you offer him one of the older girls?"

"Because it so happens that she's prettier."

"Well, Emilito is no prize. He could just as easily marry Marta."

"Because you don't love her as much."

"That's right, I don't love her as much, and she's older. Lili is still a silly little girl."

"She's exactly as old as you when we were married."

"But the Alatriste boy is a fool. You are who you are, but not because any papa organized your life for you."

"How could my papa organize my life if I never knew him? My poor mother worked like a slave; let's not go over that story again. It's good Milito has a secure future, all the better for my Lili. Are you going to play or not, Vives?"

"I'm waiting for you two to stop arguing."

"Don't wait, fuckup, play. I'm arguing because I'm waiting for you. Otherwise, I wouldn't be wasting my time on this hard-headed woman. She should have been a lawyer. 'My honeybun,' her papa called her. Can you believe that, *mano*? Poor Don Marcos had no idea who his daughter was."

"Even less his son-in-law."

"All right, I've played," said Carlos. While Andrés concentrated on chalking his cue I winked at Carlos. Then I left.

We left at five. Andrés's face was fiery red; from anger, he said, but it was really the brandy. We still had to pick up Deputy Puente. One car following another. First Carlos, with us, then the car Benito was driving, carrying Lucina and the older girls with their two boyfriends, and last, Andrés, driven by Juan.

It was a pleasant drive. Verania and Checo first sang school songs, then fought over a storybook, and finally fell asleep. Lilia sat in back with them. We chatted awhile.

"I wrote to Loli," she said.

"Who's that?"

"Don't you know? The one who has the advice column in *Maruca*."

"And what did you ask her?"

"You know."

"And what did she say?"

"Shall I read it? I signed it Carmina from Puebla. Here's the reply. 'Simple fondness can lead to love; it all comes down to whether you see in him the qualities you prize in the prince of your dreams. But if there is a discrepancy between dream and reality, which often happens, love will not come. You can be sure.'"

"And do you feel fondness for Milito?" Carlos asked her.

"A little," she said.

"But he's not at all like the prince of your dreams," I said.

"Not really."

"Then love won't come," I pronounced. "What you have to do is send the little squirt packing. Tomorrow. Gently, nothing unpleasant, but go straight to the fucking heart of the matter. You tell him you're not sure, that your mama says you're too young, that you want to meet other boys, that you just want to be friends for now."

"And what will I tell Pa?" she asked.

"I'll take care of your pa."

"Promise? He says this is the best thing for me. You won't change his mind."

"What does your papa know about what's best for you? This is what's best for him. That way he cements his ties with Don Emilio."

"It's best that you tell him, Ma," she said, and soon she was asleep, too.

It was a clear evening and the volcanoes looked close enough to touch, enormous. In Río Frío, Andrés passed us, motioning us to stop. We parked in front of the cantina–general store. It was growing dark; the trees looked like ghosts behind us. The children jumped out, making a lot of noise.

"Anyone who wants something to drink, speak up; anyone who wants to pee, pee. Go while the going's good, because we're not going to stop again till we get to Puebla," said Andrés.

We arrived about nine. Carlos pointed out that you couldn't see the house from a distance, it was hidden, and yet from the terrace you could see the city settling in for the night. People in Puebla locked up early, went inside their houses with the big doors, and didn't wander around the streets after eight.

Andrés showed the guests to their rooms while I went to see about dinner.

"Set ten places," I told Lucina. I stuck my finger in the pot with the pork loin. "We'll eat in twenty minutes. Send in warm tortillas as soon as you have them."

I went upstairs to see which room was Carlos's. I asked Juan to carry up a large potted fern to set in his room. Then I went to change. I had new clothes in the closet. I never packed a bag when going from one house to the other.

I wore one of the dresses from my days as wife of the governor.

A heavy red cloth, tight across the bust, with pleats falling to the floor.

"Will you let me take it off?" Carlos said, coming up as soon as I entered the room.

I began plotting how I could sneak up to the third floor at midnight. Andrés made it easy, because as soon as we had dinner, he went off to bed.

Deputy Puente and his wife weren't sleepy, nor were the older girls and their boyfriends, so we sat around the fire talking.

I spent four nights in Carlos's room, slipping away as soon as Andrés was asleep, using the excuse that Checo had a cold or I'd been talking with Lili till early morning.

Andrés played handball every day. Carlos lost the first game to him, then came swimming with the children and me. Sunday we went to the *zócalo* in Atlixco to have ice cream. There he introduced me to Medina, the head of the CTM, a close friend of Cordera's.

"You'll forgive me, señora, although Carlos says you can be trusted, but Andrés Ascencio is a bastard. He wants to screw us just to show Alvaro that he's still in charge here. The men in CROM are on the payroll of the presidency. They're his flunkies. They have been for years, not just now. These are the people he put in at La Guadalupe after that strike that ended at gunpoint."

"How did that happen?" asked Carlos.

"I don't want to tell it in front of the señora. Although everyone around here knows about it."

"I don't," I said. "What happened?"

Slowly, little by little, Medina told the story.

The men at La Guadalupe had been on strike for a month. The workers wanted raises and fair pay for part-time work. They were confident; it was during General Aguirre's term, and since there were strikes everywhere, they forgot that in Puebla, Andrés Ascencio ruled the roost. They had their flags up for a month. Until the day the governor showed up.

"Start up those machines," he said to one man, who refused. "Then step aside." He took out his pistol and shot him. "You there, start up those machines," he said to a second man. He, too, refused. "Step aside," he said, and fired again. "Are we going to keep this up all day?" he asked the hundred workers watching in silence. "Let's see. You." He pointed to a young boy. "Do all of you want to die? There are plenty to take your place tomorrow morning."

The boy started up his machine, and the others followed suit, until the factory was roaring again, shift after shift, without a centavo in raises.

He'd done the same thing with the strike at La Candelaria: twenty dead. The newspapers had reported it as an accident.

Medina had many stories to tell. I began by wanting to hear them, but in the end got up to race the children around the *zócalo* while he and Carlos talked. When we came back to the kiosk, hot and red-cheeked, to get another ice cream, Medina got up, offered me his hand, and thanked me in advance for my silence. I didn't tell him that I believed half his stories but that I thought the part about Andrés personally killing worker after worker was an exaggeration. I didn't say that to Carlos, either. Instead, I talked about the countryside, and the children, and I sang the ballad about Rosita Alvírez. We got back to Puebla very late. Andrés had already told Lucina to serve dinner and was at his place at the head of the table.

"Where did you come from, filthy dirty like that?" he asked.

"We went to Atlixco to have ice cream," said Verania, who adored her father.

★   ★   ★

On Monday I stayed home. I hadn't played with my children in years. I found out they were very bright and decided that the best way to entertain myself while Carlos went to see Medina again was to be with them.

We spent the morning playing cards. I giggled and fussed like a girl, and before I knew it, it was two o'clock.

On Tuesday I had everything organized by early morning, and by ten had nothing to do but go somewhere with Carlos. I figured that no one would see me in his enormous Chrysler, hiding on the floor until we were out of the city, with its streets filled with busybodies. Then it was all open country, and no one to bother us.

I talked him into taking the Cholula highway to Tonanzintla, where the *cempazúchilis,* the flowers for the Day of the Dead, were in full bloom. November is the month for them and for alfalfa, and the fields were solid orange and green. We went into the village church, which was filled with big-eyed, frightened-looking little angels.

"Let's pretend I'm the bride," I said to Carlos. "Pretend I'm marching down the aisle to marry you. With your orchestra playing the 'Wedding March.' "

"I can't conduct and be the groom."

"Pretend you can." I ran to the door to make my entrance. Slowly, one step, another. "Ta-ta-ta-ta, ta-ta-ta-ta," I sang as I walked toward Carlos, who was standing at the altar beside the worn velvet kneeling pads.

"You're mad, Catina," he said, but lifted his arms toward the choir, pretending to direct. I maintained my unhurried pace until I was standing beside him. I reached out to hold his arms.

"Now you have to take your bride. Come on, we'll kneel here.

Everyone is watching. You promise to love me for richer for poorer, in sickness and in health, till death do us part. I take you for my husband, and promise to be faithful to you in sickness and in health, for richer for poorer, to love and respect you, till death do us part."

"You have that down to a tee. You've practiced. But why are you crying? Don't cry, Catalina. I promise to be faithful to you with a husband or without, through laughter and fear, to love and respect your divine ass all the days of my life."

We kissed each other, still kneeling there beneath the gilded ceiling and walls, facing the Virgin Mary tucked in her niche. We kept kissing until an old woman in a rebozo came up to us, her face wrinkled and warty, so tiny she was at eye level as we knelt.

"Have you no respect for God?" she asked. "If you want to do what you're doing, go do it in a stable, don't come here to dirty the house of the Virgin."

"We were just married," I said. "God likes love."

"Love! That's not love! It's pure lust. Go on outside," she said, lifting the tip of her scapulary to cover her face from chin to eyes. She began praying. Then very quickly, while we stared at her as if seeing a ghost, she whipped out a bottle of holy water and sprinkled it over us, saying more prayers in her shrill voice.

"Where's that stable?" Carlos asked her, getting up and pulling me to my feet.

"Spirits from purgatory! May God have mercy on your souls, because your bodies are going to burn in hell."

We looked for a spot among the sown fields. We lay down on orange flowers, we rolled in them as we took off our clothes. At times I saw flowers, at times the sky. I made more noise than I ever had. I wanted to be wanton. I was wanton. I was Catalina, with no memory of my father, of my children, of my house, of my husband, of my love for the sea.

We laughed. We laughed like two idiots who had no future, no house, not a fucking thing. I don't know what we were laughing about. Maybe about how much we wanted each other.

"You're all orange from the flower of death," Carlos said. "It must be nice to have a tomb that smells like this, where people come and cover you with orange flowers on the Day of the Dead. When I die, I want you to bury me here."

"You're going to die in New York, on a trip like that one you made last month. Or in Paris. You're too international to die around here. Besides, you're going to be so old that it won't matter to you what your tomb smells like."

"When I do die, I want my tomb to smell the way you smell right now. And now we'd better be going because it's two o'clock. If you aren't there when your husband sits down, he'll kill us both."

"I'm tired of my husband. Every day he's going to kill us about something. Let him do it and get it over with. We can be buried here and fuck all we want to underground, no one will bother us there."

"Great idea, but while you're killing us let's get going."

We got up and walked to the car. On the way, I cut flowers, and when we got home arranged them in a clay jug I placed in the center of the table.

"Who put that crap there?" Andrés asked when he came to the table.

"I did," I said.

"You get nuttier every day. This isn't a tomb. Take them away, they're bad luck and they stink. Forgive my wife," he said to our guests. "Sometimes she's a misdirected romantic," and then indicated where he wanted everyone to sit.

"Where do you want to sit, Carlangas?" he asked Carlos when there was only one place left, the one beside me. "Next to my wife?"

"Delighted," Carlos replied.

"That goes without saying. What's the soup today, Catalina?"

"Mushroom, with squash blossoms."

"How about that. You have flowers on the brain. But this is a good soup, and good for you. I recommend it, Deputy," he told Puente, the deputy from CROM who was our current guest.

"Were you up very late last night?" Carlos asked.

"No more than usual. We had a lot to talk about, didn't we, Deputy?"

"And still more to come, General," was the reply.

"Oh, not again," begged his wife. "It's late when you come upstairs, a woman could freeze from the cold."

She was a short woman with large eyes and black, black eyelashes. She had an impressive bustline and a waist she always cinched in with scarves or belts. She liked her husband. Who knows why, because he was dreadful, but the fact was that every chance she got she was petting him, and when he voiced his opinions she listened as if he were a genius, constantly nodding her head. Which probably was why when the deputy ended his most eloquent observations with, "Isn't that right, Susy?" she responded, "Absolu-*tive*-ly, my love." And made a final emphatic nod. They were a team. I could never be part of a team like that. I lacked the dedication.

"How was your game?" I asked.

"Fine," said Andrés. "I won't ask how it went with you two, because I can guess. I don't know what you see in the country.

You can tell you never had to work in the fields. Did you visit your friend Medina?" he asked Carlos.

"We didn't have time. We stayed in Tonanzintla. The church is impressive, I'd like to give a concert there."

"Do it. Tomorrow we'll go arrange that instead of wasting your time visiting Medina."

"Medina is my friend, and he has his problems."

"Bullshit. The only problem he has is letting himself be led around by Cordera and insisting on being head of CTM in Atlixco. Because in Atlixco, CTM is going to hell in a handbasket, and Medina along with it—or my name isn't Andrés Ascencio."

"Why do you have to get into it, Chinti? Let the workers decide who they want," said Carlos, with that big-brotherly air that so irritated the General.

"The one who ought to stay out of it is you. Stick to your music and your intellectual world, and if you want to, devote yourself to difficult women, but don't get mixed up in politics, because in that business you have to know what you're doing. It would never occur to me to direct an orchestra, but I promise you it's a lot easier to move your hands in front of some mariachi band than to govern sons-of-bitches with the bit in their teeth."

"Cordera and Medina are my friends."

"And me? I'm not your friend? You see, Deputy Puente? That's the thanks I get." He looked at me, and continued. "What do you think, Catalina? Has the artist convinced you that 'the left, united, will never be divided'? Women are bad news. You spend a lifetime educating them, explaining things to them, and the minute some damn parrot flies by they believe everything he says. This woman here, sitting right here before you, Deputy, is convinced that that bastard Alvaro Cordera is a saint ready to throw in his lot with the downtrodden of the world. She's seen him three times, mind you, but she believes him. Just to oppose her husband. Because that's the new Catalina. You should have known her at sixteen. Such a pretty thing, a sponge soaking up everything you said, incapable of a bad thought about her husband or of not being in his bed at three in the morning. Ah, women. They're sure not the same anymore. Something has stirred them up. I hope yours stays the way she is, Deputy, you don't find them like her anymore. Now even the ones that seemed the most docile are acting up. Take a look at mine."

Andrés knew me so well that he smiled before taking another mouthful of *mole,* and then, with his mouth still full, he said, "When I say 'mine,' I am referring to you, Señora de Ascenio. Anything else is just hearsay, necessary but not indispensable."

"The General is always so plainspoken," said Deputy Puente.

Beneath the table, Carlos put his hand on my leg.

The meal went on forever. When finally the Santa Clara pastries and coffee were served, I relaxed. In a few minutes, everyone would go off for a siesta. Andres never cared where I was during that time. After the second or third cognac he would get up, go to the kitchen, thank the girls, and then, no matter who the guest might be, say, "Excuse me, please. I have some urgent personal matters to attend to."

Then he would go to a room in the back of the house where it was always dark by mid-afternoon. He would sleep exactly an hour and a half and wake up ready for dominoes. Again my presence was not required, as long as I made sure there was enough coffee, plenty of brandy, and a dish of chocolates; then I could peacefully disappear until suppertime.

"Shall we go to the *zócalo*?" I asked Carlos.

"Which room is the *zócalo*?"

We were laughing when Andrés returned from his demagogic

thanks to the servants and stopped behind me. He put his hands on my shoulders and pressed hard.

"Excuse us, please. We have urgent business," he said.

"I told the children I'd take them to the *zócalo* to get balloons, and then to the forts to climb trees," I said.

"You're a model mother. Tell them you'll take them when I start my domino game."

"Oh, Mama," said Verania. "How could you?"

"Andrés, I promised," I said.

"That's fine. Promises don't cost anything. Haven't you ever noticed all the promises I've made? Promise them you'll take them at six. You can't go right now."

"We'll wait for you here, señora," said Carlos.

"Will you tell us about your papa?" Checo asked him.

"Whatever you want," Carlos said.

"Don't be long, Ma."

"I won't, darling," I answered.

Andrés led me into our bedroom and closed the door. He sat down on the edge of the bed and motioned me to sit beside him.

"Where did you go?" he asked.

"You know that already. You have me followed and then ask me questions."

"I sent that idiot Benito, and he lost you after you left the church. What message did the woman in the rebozo pass to you?"

I laughed. "She said she would drive out the devil, and sprinkled us with holy water."

"And gave you a message from Medina."

"No, no message from Medina. Nothing."

"Benito said she said something about a stable."

"I didn't hear her."

"And you didn't hear that about the spirits from purgatory?"

"That I heard. She said that in a prayer."

"What was the prayer?"

"I don't remember, Andrés. I thought she was crazy. She wanted to throw us out of the 'house of the Virgin,' and I don't know what else."

"Well, try to remember."

"I can't remember. Now may I go? Who's going to follow us this afternoon?"

"This afternoon you're going to stay here in bed with your husband. Because as a spy you're worthless and you're enjoying the role of girlfriend too much."

I took off my shoes and pulled my feet up on the bed. I put my arms around my legs, with my head between my knees. I sighed.

"Why do you want me to stay? So you can do me the favor of your company? It's been months since we've been together."

"Distance becomes you. You're beautiful."

"And Conchita?" I asked.

"Don't ask tasteless questions, Catalina."

"I'm asking out of courtesy. I'd like to know how the women you sleep with are faring."

"How vulgar you've become," he said.

"Since when are we so refined? That must be something you learned from José Ibarra's niece. The Ibarras have always been very distinguished. Do you still have her out at the Martínez de la Torres's ranch? I know you bought her velvet drapes and Louis XV furniture so she wouldn't feel lost among all those Indians. What does she do while you're not there? Doesn't she get bored? I guess she does her petit point. Poor baby. I'll bet when she takes her walk among all those peons and bulls, she pulls her little net veil over her face."

"She had a little girl."

"Are you going to bring her here?"

"She doesn't want that."

"The others didn't want it, either."

"But the others weren't good mothers, and this one is. She loves the child and asked me to leave her there to keep her company."

"All the better for me. I have enough children underfoot, to say nothing of teenagers."

"Don't complain. My Lilia'll be going soon."

"Your Lilia. Now sugar's too sweet, she's your Lilia. You've been at each other's throat as long as I've known her. She loves me more than you, and I'm just her stepmother."

"So she doesn't fight with you. That doesn't mean she loves you."

"It must mean something. You brought her to me when she was ten. She's nearly sixteen now."

"And she's your handiwork?"

"None of them's my handiwork. I feed them and listen to them, the rest is your doing. In this house you grow up any which way you can: your children, our children. You think I 'educate' Checo?"

"Badly, but don't go all serious on me. Take off that sweater and lie down here by me," he said, pulling me toward him. "Your waist is smaller, what did you do?"

"It must be love," I replied.

"Dammit, woman. Don't think you can provoke me. I know you're more faithful than an Arabian mare. Come here, I've neglected you. Since September, is it?"

"I don't remember."

"You used to count the days."

I yawned and stretched my legs and moved up against him. I was wearing velveteen slacks and I let him caress me through them.

"Unbelievable how good you still look. No wonder you have Carlos panting after you."

"Carlos is my friend."

"Like Conchita, Pilar, and Victorina are mine."

"And the mothers of your children."

"That's how women are. They get pregnant the minute you wave a cock at them. Don't you want Carlos's kids?"

"I have more than enough with yours. And Carlos hasn't waved his cock at me."

"Come here, damn you. Repeat what you just said." He stuck his face right against mine, holding my chin so I had to meet his gaze.

"I'm not fucking Carlos," I said, looking him straight in the eye.

"It's good to know that," he replied, and kissed me. "Take off those clothes. What a job it is to get you out of your clothes," he said, tugging at the slacks. I didn't resist. I thought about Pepa, who'd said: "In marriage there comes a moment when you have to close your eyes and say a Hail Mary." I closed my eyes and thought about the fields.

"Carlos doesn't fuck you? So what were you doing when you got that yellow all over you?" he asked.

"Rolling on the flowers."

"That's all?"

"That's all," I said, without opening my eyes. He entered me. I lay beneath him, imagining the beach, thinking about what to have for dinner the next day, going over what was left in the refrigerator.

"You're my wife. Don't forget it," he said afterward, lying close to me, stroking my tummy.

Still on my back, looking at my lifeless body, I said to him, "I'm not afraid anymore."

"Of what?"

"Of you. Sometimes you frighten me. I don't know what you're thinking. You look at me, without a word, and go out at dawn carrying your riding crop and your pistol without making any plans with me. I begin to believe you're going to kill me like all the others."

"Kill you? What makes you think that? I don't kill what I love."

"Then why do you wear your pistol every day?"

"So people who want to kill me will see it. I don't kill, I'm too old for that now."

"But you order killings."

"It depends."

"On what?"

"Lots of things. Don't ask about things you don't understand. I'm not going to kill you. No one is going to kill you."

"And Carlos?"

"Why would anyone kill Carlos? He doesn't fuck you, he didn't visit Medina, he's my friend—almost my little brother. If someone kills Carlos, he'll have to answer to me. I swear it by Checo, who loves him very much."

Later he fell asleep with his hands across his belly, chin sagging, one boot on and the other off, no trousers, shirt unbuttoned. For a while, I lay beside him watching him sleep. He looked awful. I reviewed the list of his other women. How could they love him? Because he had charisma? I'd thought so. I had loved him, I'd even believed that no man was as handsome, as clever, as appealing, as brave as he. There were days I couldn't sleep unless he was beside me, months I missed him, all too many evenings spent wondering where he might be. Not anymore. That day I wanted to go with Carlos to New York, to the Avenida Juarez, wherever I could just be a dumb thirty-year-old woman with two children and a man she loved more than them, more than herself, more than anything, waiting to take her to the *zócalo*.

I leaped out of bed and dressed in seconds. Carlos was waiting, and I'd lain there like an idiot watching the grizzly bear sleep.

"Bye," I said in a low voice, and pretended to take a dagger from my belt and plunge it into him as I left.

I ran out to the patio, calling, "Children, Carlos, let's go. I'm ready."

It was getting dark. No one was in the inside patio. I went to the back garden. I went upstairs, calling them. I didn't find them. All their rooms were dark. I knocked at Lilia's door, the only one with a light.

"What is it, Mama? The way you're yelling, you'd think the sky was falling."

She was beautiful. Wearing a tightly belted robe, her face clean and childlike. One after another, she was rapidly taking out curlers. Her hair waved below her ears.

"Where are you going?" I asked.

"To dinner with Emilio," she said in the same tone her father used to say, "To the office."

"What a waste, *mi amor*. Sixteen years old, and that body, that head with still so much to learn, those shining eyes, and all the rest, is going to end up in Milito's bed. Asshole Milito, opportunist Milito, moronic Milito, his father's true son, a man who's as much a thug as your father but puts on airs besides! It's a shame, *mi amor*. We'll regret this forever."

"Don't exaggerate, Mama. Emilio plays a good game of tennis. He's not handsome, but he's not ugly either. He's very pleasant, he dresses like a dream, and it suits my papa for me to marry him."

"That's true enough," I said.

"He likes music. He takes us to Carlos's concerts."

"Because they're fashionable, and because it gives him a chance to sit still for two hours without anyone noticing he's not thinking."

The bedrooms opened onto an outside corridor with a wrought-iron railing lined with flowerpots.

"It's cold. Can we finish inside?" she asked, stepping back into her room. I followed her. She stopped before the dressing table to brush her hair.

"Where is everyone?" I asked. "Why did they leave without me?"

"Because they don't love you anymore," she said, and her laugh was still a child's laugh. "Not even a note?" she asked. Then I remembered the fern in Carlos's room.

"Be beautiful, *mi amor*. I'll be in the sewing room. Stop by and show me," I told her, and went to check the potted fern. I burrowed among the leaves and found a note.

My dearest.

I expected you to come soon, dressed or not. I had to leave because Medina sent me a message asking me to meet him at six at the door to San Francisco. I took the kids and a precise memory of your plump ass with me.

Kisses, if only on the lips.

ME

I ran down the stairs and across the patio, where I met a just-awakened Andrés.

"Who's ready for dominoes?" he asked me.

"I don't know. Carlos and the children went down to San Francisco. I'm going to look for them. I didn't go by the game room, but I'm sure there'll be some takers there. I'll tell Lucina to bring the coffee and chocolates." All of which I said as I hurried past him.

"Carlos took the kids? Who gave him permission?" Andrés yelled.

"He always takes them," I called back as I ran down the steps to the garage. The car nearest the door was a convertible. I climbed in and skidded down the hill toward San Francisco. When I got to the park, I drove more slowly. I reasoned that the conversation with Medina wouldn't have taken place at the door to the church, and that Carlos would need a place for the children to play while he was talking. I didn't see them through the trees, or walking the rims of the fountains, or drinking the filthy water spouting from the mouths of the Talavera frogs. They weren't on the swings or the slides—not in any of the places they usually played. Neither did I see Carlos on any of the benches, or drinking coffee at one of the *chalupa* stands. I was suddenly furious with him. Why did he have to get mixed up in politics? Why didn't he stick to conducting his orchestra, composing his strange music, talking with friends and poets, and fucking me? Why this idiotic rage for politics? Why couldn't he be friends with someone less complicated than Alvaro? Where were they? It was cold. I was sure they'd gone out without sweaters. All three of them will catch a cold, I thought, and I'll have pneumonia from driving around in this damned open car. Where *are* they? Did they go to the *zócalo*?

I parked at the foot of the stairs of the church, got out, and ran up them to see if they were still inside. Maybe they were waiting for me there.

A long atrium leads to the church of San Francisco with its blue tile façade and slim towers. At the end of the atrium, right against the closed door of the church, were the children, huddled on the ground.

"What happened?" I asked as soon as I saw them alone, so strangely quiet.

"Uncle Carlos left with some friends and told us to wait here." It was Checo who answered.

"How long ago was that? And who were these stupid *friends*, Verania?"

"I don't know," she said.

"It wasn't Medina? Remember, that man we had ice cream with in the *zócalo* in Atlixco?"

"No, it wasn't him, Mama," said Verania, who was then about ten.

"You're sure?"

"Yes. Checo told you they were his friends because the one who took his arm said, 'Come along, friend,' but he didn't want to go. It was because they had pistols, and that's why he said for us to stay here, that you'd come if he wasn't back soon."

"Why didn't you call the priests? Where are the priests?" I asked.

"They closed the door," said Verania.

"Good-for-nothing priests. Priests! Priests! Priests!" I screamed, pounding on the church door.

A monk opened.

"May I do something for you, sister?" he asked.

"An hour ago a man who was here with my children was taken away by armed men, by force, and you had the door closed at six in the evening. All that shit about getting your churches open after the Cristeros uprising and now you keep them closed?" I lunged toward the monk. "Who told you to close that door?"

"I don't know what you're talking about, sister. Be calm. We close the door because it's getting dark earlier."

"You never know anything unless it's to your advantage. Come on, children, let's get in the car. Hurry."

I BURST INTO the house shouting, with the children, shocked into silence, hanging on to my coat. I bounded up the three flights of stairs to the game room, and when we reached the top they were still clinging to me, infected by my panic.

Andrés opened the door. "What's the matter?" he asked. He was chewing on a cigar and had a glass of brandy in one hand and a domino in the other.

"Someone took Carlos. The children were all alone at the door of the church," I said slowly, deliberately, as if reporting information he already knew.

"Who'd want to take him? He must have gone somewhere I warned him not to. And he left the kids alone? Not very responsible."

"The children said he was taken against his will," I said, and again feigned composure.

"Your children have a vivid imagination. Get them into something warm and put them to bed. That's what they need."

"What are you going to do?" I asked.

"Start the game, I have a double six."

"And your friend?"

"He'll be back. If not, in a little while I'll have Benitez get the police to look for him. Are you going to get the kids' pajamas?"

"Yes, I'm going to get their pajamas," I said, as if someone else were in control, as if someone had muzzled me. I put my arms around the children and walked back down to the second floor.

Lilia was just coming out of her room. She was wearing a black dress with red trim, stiletto heels, and dark stockings. Her lipstick was bright red and she had caught her hair back with two silver combs. She looked very grown up, and she didn't call me Mama.

"Cati, can I borrow your Persian lamb? I got ice cream on mine yesterday. Did you find Carlos?" she asked.

"No," I said, biting my lower lip.

"Poor Mama." She hugged me.

I wanted to scream, to rush out and look for him, tear my hair, go mad. Lilia stroked my hair.

"Poor Cati." Slowly, I pulled away from her perfumed embrace.

"You look beautiful," I told her. "Are you leaving now? Let me see. Walk away, I want to check your seams. They're always crooked."

I made her walk down the corridor.

"Let me straighten the left one," I said. "Get whatever coat you want from my room, and don't kiss Emilio. Don't give away anything too soon."

She kissed me again, and ran down the stairs.

I took the children to their room. When they fell asleep, I turned out the light and lay down on my stomach beside Verania with my head resting on my crossed arms. I began to cry, slow, enormous tears.

Don't let him suffer, I said to myself. Don't let him die slowly. Don't let him be in pain. Oh, don't let them touch his face or break his hands. I hope someone has the heart to shoot him.

"Señora," said Lucina, coming into the room. "The señor wants to have dinner."

"Please go ahead and serve," I said hoarsely.

"He wants you to come down. He said to tell you that the governor is here."

"And Señor Carlos?" I asked.

"No, señora, he isn't here." She came to the bed and sat on the edge.

"I'm so sorry, señora. You know how much I love you. It made me happy to see you so happy. . . ."

"Did they kill him? What did Juan tell you?"

"I don't know, señora. Juan told them he was sick when they sent for him. Benito drove. We wanted to tell you, but how could we, you were in there with the General."

Again I buried face in my arms. No tears now.

"And Benito?" I asked.

"He hasn't come back."

I got up.

"Tell the General I won't be long. And ask Juan to come up."

I put on a black dress. I wore the earrings and medallion Carlos had given me. They were Italian. The medallion had a blue flower; on one side it said *mamma* and on the other *February 13*.

I came into the dining room as Andrés was seating the guests.

"At your service, señora," said Benítez.

"She doesn't deserve it, Governor. She's late."

"My apologies. I fell asleep with the children." There were more people than I'd expected.

"Do you know our Prosecutor?" Andrés asked.

"Of course. How nice to have you," I answered, without offering my hand.

"And the chief of police?"

"My pleasure," I said, consciously pretending not to know him.

"The governor was good enough to come with these gentlemen when I advised him of our friend Carlos Vives's disappearance."

"Wouldn't it be better to be out looking for him?" I asked.

"They need more information." This from Deputy Puente.

"Is it true he just left your children in the street?" Susi Díaz de Puente asked me. "I think he must have been 'kidnapped' by some girlfriend."

"I hope that's the case," I replied.

"Señoras, this is serious business," said Andrés. "Carlos was Medina's friend, and Medina was killed this morning. Do you know what happened, Governor?"

"More or less. It seems he was killed by his own people. There are lots of radicals inside the CTM, and Medina had convinced his followers to go over to CROM. A sane enough plan, but some lunatic must have killed him for what they considered a betrayal."

"I don't believe Medina would have wanted to switch to CROM," I said.

"Why not?" asked Andrés.

"Because I knew Medina. Carlos loved him."

"Well, I hope he didn't love him enough to try to defend him," said Andrés. "He's always been foolish that way. Just today I told him he should stick to his music and stop taking risks. But he can't stay out of trouble."

"I think he's a good man," said the prosecutor. "And an excellent musician."

"Let's hope nothing has happened to him," said the police chief, who was a horrible man. He'd been a lieutenant when Andrés was governor. He was known as Pineapple Face because of his terrible skin. Whatever had happened, he knew all about it.

The food was served. Andrés began praising my skills as a housewife and after that I stopped following the conversation. Lucina was serving.

"More beans, señora?" she asked, leaning down. And then, very low: "Juan says they have him at Ninety House."

"Thank you, only a few," I replied.

"Truly, but truly, everything is delicious, señora," said Benítez.

"Thank you, Governor," I said, turning to look at him. I met the eyes of the man sitting next to him, Tirso Santillana, the prosecutor, a respected lawyer who had never agreed to work for Andrés.

I found it strange that he wanted to work for Benítez. He was an unusual man. As he looked at me, I had the sensation he saw something interesting.

"You're worried, aren't you?" he asked.

"I respect Carlos a great deal," I replied.

"I promise I will do everything I can to find him."

"I will always be grateful," I said, and then to everyone: "Shall we go to the sala for coffee?"

"Yes, let's," said my husband, rising. Everyone followed his example, like performing monkeys. We went to the sala, where I made a point of seeking out Tirso.

"You trust the governor, then?" I asked him.

"Of course, señora," he answered. He smiled as if we were talking about the weather.

"They're holding Carlos in Ninety House. Save him," I said.

"What are you talking about?"

"Ninety House is a prison for political enemies. My husband set it up when he was governor, and it's still used. Carlos is there."

"How do you know that?"

"What does it matter? Will you go? Say you got a tip. You go ahead and I'll send someone to notify your office. But hurry, please," I said, laughing again. He echoed my laughter, to continue the sham.

"Governor Benítez," he said. "I must leave now. I want to see if they've learned anything in my office."

"This Santillana, so efficient. I always wanted him to work for me, but he wouldn't do it. How did you manage it, Felipe?" Andrés asked.

"I got lucky," Benítez answered. "Go ahead, Santillana."

Pellico, the chief of police, was irritated. If the prosecutor left, he would have to go, too, and he didn't want to leave. He was happy with his brandy, his coffee, and his easy chair.

"You'll stay for a while, won't you, Pellico?" I asked.

"If you ask me to, I have no choice," he said. He settled back in his chair and began helping himself to chocolate mints.

"I'll walk you to the door, Señor Santillana," I said, taking his arm as we walked downstairs to the entrance. Andrés had decorated the entry hall with coats of arms and war memorabilia.

Juan was hiding outside the door.

"What happened, Juan?" I asked.

"Benito left them at Ninety House. That's all he knows."

"Take me there," Tirso ordered.

"I'm going with you," I said.

"Do you want to blow everything?" he asked.

I let them go, and returned to the sala, trembling.

"Why are you talking to yourself, Catalina?" Andrés wanted to know when I returned.

"I'm saying the multiplication tables so I can help Checo."

"If this woman had been a man, she'd be a politician. She's more pig-headed than all the rest of us put together."

"Your wife is a woman of many qualities, General," said Benítez.

"I'll go ask them to bring wood for the fire. It's really cold," I murmured.

The singer Andrés had invited to play that night was called El Charro Blanco, the white cowboy. He was an albino. He sang in a sad voice, whether someone was listening or he was being drowned out by conversation.

He sat down beside me in front of the fireplace and began to sing. "On a distant mountain, a horseman is riding; he's alone in the world, and riding toward death."

"Charro! Play 'Relámpago,' and stop all that depressing stuff. Can't you see we have a lot on our minds?" said Andrés.

El Charro simply changed key, and began, "It's all because I love her so, because I'm afraid to let her go. Blinding fury from the sky, lightning bolt to kill my hope . . ."

"That is one fucking wonderful song. Again, from the beginning," Andrés ordered.

El Charro began from the beginning, joined by everyone in the room, because when Andrés sang, no one dared talk. Now El Charro was the center of attention. Andrés began calling him "brother" and asking for one song after another.

"You sing, Catalina. Don't sit so close to the fire, it isn't good for you. Sing 'With You in the Distance.' "

"Let's hear Catita," said El Charro, but he sang alone. He was just ending the song when Tirso rushed into the sala.

"I found Vives," he said. "He's dead."

"Where did you find him? Governor! I demand justice!" Andrés cried.

"How did it happen, Tirso?" Benítez asked.

"I would like to speak with you in private, Governor, but first I want to tender my resignation. I found Vives in a clandestine prison. The men there receive their orders from Chief Pellico."

All hell broke loose. Pellico looked at Andrés.

"Ask for his resignation," Andrés shouted at Benítez. "What house are you talking about? Where is Carlos? Who took him there?"

"Tirso, justify that accusation," said the governor.

"I don't know what anyone's talking about," Pellico yelled.

Puentes's wife fainted. Puente launched into a speech worthy of the Chamber. I left.

Near Tirso's car, Juan had his arms around Lucina.

"Where is he?" I asked.

"In there, but don't look," Juan begged.

I opened the door. The first thing I saw was his head. I stroked his hair. It was bloody. I closed his eyes. There was blood on his collar and his jacket. A hole in his neck.

"Help me get him inside," I asked.

Between us—Juan, Tirso's chauffeur, Lucina, and me—we carried him to the room with the fern. We laid him on the bed. I asked them to leave. I don't know how long I knelt there beside him, looking at him. It ended when Andrés came in with Benítez.

"I told you!" he said as he approached the bed. "Why didn't you listen to me?"

"We'll bury him in Tonanzintla," I said, getting up and walking to the door.

Outside, the corridor was dark. Enough light filtered up from below to allow me to walk past the flowerpots without stumbling. The guest rooms were on the third floor, near the handball court and swimming pool. There should have been a light, but Carlos and I had removed it two nights before so I could sneak up without being seen. The children slept on the second floor. Only Andrés and I had a bedroom on the first. Between our room and the room with the fern lay five minutes of stairways and corridors. I walked through the darkness with the experience learned from previous nights, out through the garden, then to my room. I combed my hair, put on a black coat, and went to look for Juan in the kitchen. He drove me to the Gayosso Mortuary.

"You should have called, señora," said a sleepy-faced man attempting to be pleasant.

"I want a plain wooden box, no iron trim, no black bows, and no cross," I said.

The coffin arrived about nine. At eleven we were in Tonanzintla. There was sunshine and a large crowd. Benítez had brought teachers and students from the conservatory, and party activists. Cordera had come from Mexico City and walked with me behind the coffin.

The cemetery in Tonanzintla isn't walled. It sits beside the church at the foot of a hill. It was the second of November, and people were visiting the other tombs, covering them with flowers and offerings of *mole,* bread, and sweets. I had someone cut all the flowers from the field where Carlos and I had lain the day before, some five hundred bunches. I had them distributed among the people Benítez had brought and the workers who'd come with Cordera. Everyone had flowers to leave at Carlos's grave.

The gravediggers set the wooden coffin beside the hole they'd dug in the earth. Then Andrés took his place beside it and began:

"Compañeros, workers, friends. Carlos Vives died a victim of those who do not want our society to continue along the rewarding paths of peace and harmony. We do not know who cut short his life, that beautiful life that was so threatening to them, but we can be sure they will pay for their crime. The loss of a man like Carlos Vives is not only a sorrow for people like myself and my family and the many friends who had the privilege of knowing him, it is an irreparable loss to society. It was my desire to speak of his qualities, of the many ways in which he served his nation, of the many works with which he enriched our Revolution, but I cannot, I am too stricken with grief . . ." et cetera, et cetera.

Then Cordera spoke. It was as if I were watching a movie. I felt nothing.

"Carlos," he said. "We shall always draw strength from the memory of your honesty, your intelligence, and your courage. We do not have to ask for justice, that is a path we are already following. Helping us find it, you lost your life. We know who killed you: the powerful killed you, they who have weapons and prisons. It wasn't the poor, the workers, the students, the intellectuals. The political bosses murdered you, the despots, the oppressors, the tyrants, the exploiters."

When he finished, the peons lifted the coffin and lowered it into the ground. I threw my handful of flowers into the hole.

"Now you have your flowery grave, imbecile," and walked quickly to the car before the tears began.

The following week came all the official statements. I was so numb that they all sounded alike, the ones from CROM and CTM, the governor's and Rodolfo's, Cordera's and Andrés's. All agreed that Carlos had been a great man, that his death must be avenged, his killers found, the country saved from traitors and the threat of violence. His friends published a letter in the newspaper demanding justice, acclaiming Vives's virtues and the irreparable loss to art. I read the names of people with whom I'd heard Carlos talking on the telephone, that he had mentioned in conversations with Efraín and Renato. I didn't know them; he had said it was better if I didn't, that no one would understand, that they wouldn't trust me, that Efraín and Renato did because they were his closest friends and because they had done so many crazy things in their lives they had no trouble understanding craziness in others. I cut out everything I could find about Carlos and kept it in a silver box like the locked one in the very back of my closet, the one in which I kept all his notes, a photograph we'd had taken in the park, and all the clippings about his concerts. I saved even the unfavorable reviews and articles. I had a picture of him conducting with his hair falling over his forehead and arms lifted high. I sat and stroked it.

Tirso denounced the Ninety House and the governor dismissed Pellico and declared his sadness and amazement. Pellico came to the house looking for Andrés. I was leaning over the second-floor railing and saw him go into Andrés's office.

For a few days there was a great uproar in all the newspapers, with Benítez issuing statements against corruption and Andrés restating his faith in justice and government institutions. Pellico was arrested.

A few months later, seven men escaped from San Juan de Dios. Pellico among them. Until very recently, we would receive Christmas cards from him with Los Angeles postmarks.

I STAYED IN Puebla. I was afraid to go back to Mexico City. In the house on the hill I was protected by walls and familiar memories. I no longer wanted challenges or surprises. Better to grow old watching others in love, sitting in the garden or by the fire, closeted in the little house I had bought across from the cemetery in Tonanzintla, where I went when I wanted to scream and hide. It was nothing more than a brick room where I'd brought a rocking chair and a table for my boxes of photos and clippings. The sun never shone in because an enormous tree in the patio was covered with bougainvillea that spread across the roof, rooting in the tiles and creeping in through the windows. There I could howl at the top of my lungs, until I fell asleep on the floor. I would wake up with swollen eyes and return to Puebla ready for another period of calm.

After Carlos's death, Lilia rebelled against her father. She didn't trust him and wanted to be with me all the time. We went together to buy fruit in La Victoria and she took me with her to the department store to help her choose the dresses and shoes she bought every few days. She adopted the current style of gold bracelets heavy with huge medallions. You could hear her coming, like a belled cow.

I didn't like shopping at El Puerto because that's where Andrés's women shopped. He had an arrangement with the management for both his daughters and his most recent paramour. Not me. I went only because of Lilia. I liked her. She was as curious and nosy as I was. Ready for anything. Andrés's other daughters weren't like that.

After a period of obeying her father and having dinner with the Alatristes every time they invited her, she decided to fall in love with the young Javier Uriarte. He had an India motorcycle, and she liked to sneak out and race up and down the Veracruz highway with him. I covered for her, and even became friends with the boy, whom I liked and who saved me from the Alatristes.

Emilito went back to Georgina Letona, who forgave him all his sins, after already having tolerated a courtship of eight years. She was extremely beautiful and wildly in love with him. I've never seen such eyes as hers. Thick black eyelashes, eyebrows that seemed to have been drawn on, and perfectly centered eyes identical in color to the honeyed mane that fell to her shoulders. I never heard her snort with laughter; she'd smile, revealing small, even teeth between lips that parted with a spontaneity anyone would envy.

Lilia and I ran into them once walking down Reforma, holding hands. When he was with her, Emilito lost that idiot look I most remember.

"Can you imagine how ridiculous it would have been for me to marry this man? He'd have cheated on me before we were married," Lilia said after that meeting.

I put my arm around her shoulder and told her she was right, and lucky that Uriarte had shown up to save her from ridicule.

Four days after that chance encounter on Reforma, Emilito came with a piano to serenade Lilia. They blocked the whole street, but the piano was the least of it. He'd brought Agustín Lara to play and Pedro Vargas to sing. A star-studded review right outside our house in Puebla.

Lilia, barefoot and in her pink robe, ran downstairs to our room.

"What shall I do, Mama?"

Her father had gotten out of bed to see what was going on.

"Turn on the light, silly. What do you mean, what shall I do?"

"If I turn on the light, he's going to think—"

"Turn it on," yelled Andrés.

"If she doesn't want to, she shouldn't turn it on," I said. "Then she'd have to put up with his thinking she's accepted him."

"I'll put up with him. I'm going to be his father-in-law."

"But Lilia doesn't want to," I said, as the strains of "Little Lantern" continued outside, and Lilia peered through the curtains.

"He's so ugly," she said. "He always looks like he's suffering."

"Of course he's suffering," Andrés said. "You've taken up with that idiot on the motorcycle."

"That isn't why. You know perfectly well that the boy's in love with Georgina Letona."

"You shut up, Catalina. Don't go putting ideas in my girl's head. Turn on the light, Lilia."

"I want you to know I don't agree with this," I said, getting out of bed.

"Go on, daughter," said Andrés. "Pay her no mind. She's bitter."

Lilia climbed into the bed I'd just vacated. They lay there, listening to the music with the lights blazing. I went down to the servants' quarters to wake Juan. I told him to slip out back and go tell Uriarte about the serenade.

I knew the boy would be there in fifteen minutes with ten friends, a guitar, and a shotgun.

We heard shouting and yelling.

"Lilia! Come outside and tell this jackass which one of us you want," Javier Uriarte called, while his friends swarmed over the piano. They put Agustín Lara in a car and pushed Pedro Vargas into the seat beside him. His bodyguard locked Emilito in a protective bear hug as Javier rushed at him, fists swinging. His friends fired shots in the air, yelling, "Fair fight! Let them slug it out!" Emilito broke away from the bodyguard and faced Uriarte. In seconds they were locked together, stumbling around in circles.

Andrés forgot he had an interest in the outcome and watched as if he was at a boxing match. Emilio defended himself, but had little skill. Lilia watched, huddled at the window beside her father, biting her nails.

"Why are you crying? Enjoy it," said Andrés. But she couldn't stand it. She left the window, belted her robe, and suddenly appeared below, approaching the boys. With no hesitation, she pushed between them.

Emilito was panting, his tie yanked up to his nose. Uriarte pulled Lilia to him and put his arms around her. A second later, Andrés was at the door, calling her.

She left Javier and came back to the house. She hurried past her father and came upstairs, where I was watching.

"He's going to kill him," she said, no longer crying. "Like your Carlos, he's going to kill him."

We went back to her room with our arms around each other. Her sisters and the younger children were looking out the windows.

They applauded when they saw her. We watched Andrés pat Emilito on the back. Javier and his friends walked back toward the fountain, and within minutes the street was quiet again.

The next week Uriarte called Lilia. I heard her on the telephone in her room.

"I can't. My papa's here."

After a while we heard the motorcycle. Javier circled around the house, blowing his horn until Lilia threw down a note that fell into his open jacket. It said, *I love you.*

For six months she refused to talk to Emilio. Six months in which she walked around on a cloud that dissipated when Javier drove off a cliff, motorcycle and all. No one knew how, but he did not survive it.

His parents recovered the body and buried him in the French cemetery. And that was the end of it. I went with Lilia to the cemetery and left her to weep and ask forgiveness for God knows what.

Soon after, Emilito came to speak with General Ascencio.

Andrés received him in his office. A strange room, long as a corridor, with saddles along one side and torero, charro, and Andalusian riding costumes along the other. At the rear, an enormous rolltop desk was covered with humidors and lighters. Andrés had at least four hundred lighters, and as he listened to whoever was talking business, he lit them, one after another, to entertain himself.

When he and Emilio finished talking, he called me and said: "Lili is going to marry Emilio Alatriste in a few months. Tell her, and make the arrangements."

I smiled and took Emilito's arm. We walked out to Lilia in the garden.

THEY WERE MARRIED a year later at our ranch in Atlixco. *Le tout* Mexico attended. From the president, who gave the bride away, and all his cabinet, to commanders of the military zones, fifteen governors, every wealthy *poblano,* and Lucina and Juan, who ended up, arms around each other, in the middle of the dance floor, undisturbed by anyone.

I will never forget the picture of Lili dancing with her father, resting against him as if she enjoyed his protection, letting his hand at her waist lead her around the center of the enormous garden: ancient trees and a river into which flowers had been thrown in Matamoros early enough that at three in the afternoon they would drift by the ranch in San Lucas where the eldest daughter of General Ascencio was being married.

I helped Lilia choose her dress. She looked beautiful in layers of misty organza. I watched her dancing with her father, her head thrown back, her feet flashing as she followed him in the two step.

Then the orchestra struck up "Over the Waves," and

Andrés handed her to Emilito so she would be in his arms as "their song" was played. I don't know when that bit about their song was hatched, although it was all the same to Lilia. Like a true actress, she sank her teeth into the role she had to play.

The bride and groom circled the dance floor as the guests applauded.

"Kiss! Kiss! Kiss!" And after a moment of looking at each other, then staring at the ground, their lips came together for a second, and they resumed their dance in silence.

Andrés came back to the table we were sharing with our new in-laws. He asked for a cognac, pulled out a cigar, and began puffing away.

"My dear Alatriste, welcome to the family," he said. "Are we moving along on the business of the radio stations?"

"But of course, General. Welcome to ours," Don Emilio answered with a long laugh.

"Everything turned out beautifully, Catalina. Congratulations," said Emilio's mother.

"You're too kind, Doña Concha," I replied, as my eyes were drawn to the extremely handsome face of a man sitting at a table with Bibi and General Gómez Soto.

"Not at all," said Doña Concha. "To go to all this effort for a girl who isn't even your own daughter. Who *is* Lili's mother?"

"As far as I'm concerned, Doña Concha, I am."

Bibi noticed my curiosity as I looked toward her table, and came over to rescue me from Concha. I walked back with her to meet the heavenly Clark Gable look-alike who stood and held out his hand.

"Quijano, at your service," he said.

"How kind," I replied.

"You haven't met Quijano, Catalina?" General Gómez Soto asked. "He's a fellow *poblano,* and a famous movie director."

We began talking about movies and movie actors. He invited me to the opening of *La dama de las camelais,* his first film, and I accepted, telling him how much my mother had liked that novel, and the strong influence it had on our household. They laughed.

"Really, it was our Bible. In my house no one could cough without my mother thinking we were on our way to an early death. She kept a horrible iodine syrup in every room in the house. One cough and out came the tablespoon to save us from Marguerite Gautier's terrible death."

We danced. Under the watchful eye of Andrés, who nonetheless never stopped talking, I whirled by in the arms of that perfect man. I couldn't tell if it bothered him, but I wished I could have danced that way with Carlos.

"Trade?" asked Lilia when we passed her and Emilito.

I relinquished Quijano and tried to follow the bumbling steps of Emilito. I thought about Javier Uriarte, about what fun we would have had with him, and felt enraged. Lilia returned. "Trade?" and she turned from Quijano and began to dance with me, leaving the two men standing in the middle of the dance floor.

"He's really handsome. Where did you find him?"

"Lili, you're crazy. I love you so much," I told her.

"Whatever you say, Mama,' she replied.

I kissed her and again we went back to our partners. Quijano danced me around the floor and I enjoyed how good we were together. We never missed a step, as if we'd been rehearsing all our lives.

It began to get cool, and Lilia came over to say, "I'm leaving. Emilio doesn't want to stay for the *pozole.* Will you come with me to change?"

"I'll be waiting," said Quijano, walking me to the edge of the floor.

I thanked him and went with Lilia to the main house.

In her bedroom were four half-packed suitcases, all in a disarray that seemed irreparable. I took the hairpins from her veil and coronet. As soon as she felt them gone, she shook her head, and tulle and flowers flew. Her black hair fell halfway down her back, and she breathed as if she'd been holding her breath for hours. She stepped out of her high heels and tugged at her dress. Before I could help with the fastenings, she was standing in the middle of the room in her slip. She pulled it over her head. Pale stockings sheathed her long dark legs. An old-fashioned garter ringed one thigh, elastic with white satin and lace. I told her how in my grandmother's day they used to slip off the garter and another girl would hold out her foot and try to catch it before it fell. That meant the bride's good luck was passed on to another, and she would soon find a sweetheart to marry.

"Come over here, I'll give it to you," she said, hopping around in her bra and panties.

"I have a husband," I said.

"So you'll find another."

She let the garter drop just as I slipped my toes beneath it. For one moment our feet were joined by shirred satin and lace, then she pulled her foot free and hopped away. I lifted my skirt to slide the garter above my knee.

"I've always loved your legs," Lilia said, stepping into the skirt of her suit. It was a French fabric and fit her perfectly. She added a red silk blouse and then the navy-blue jacket that matched the skirt. She had lost a shoe. We found it underneath a suitcase.

"Your seams are crooked," I said.

"You always say I have crooked seams." She turned her back to me so I could straighten them as I did on any other day. I knelt behind her.

"Then what? I get there and that's it?" she asked.

"You get where?"

"Under him."

"Under him, and hope that's enough," I said, and kissed her.

"Give me your blessing, then. The way you did when I was little and you were leaving on a trip," she asked, as she heard Emilio calling her.

She was curious and bossy, like her father. And, like him, arbitrary.

I touched my fingertips to her forehead, then her chest, then one and the other shoulder, watching her choke back laughter and nerves, her eyes moist and cheeks flushed.

"In the name of the Father, the Son, and the Holy Ghost, may all go well with you, and especially with the Holy Ghost."

I sat there on the floor until a servant came to ask if he could take down the suitcases. Then I got up to straighten the mess Lili had left behind. I left the room with the suitcases.

Below, in the garden, I heard shouting around the bride and groom, who were about to leave in the Ferrari Andrés had given Lilia as a wedding present. It sported a "Just Married" sprayed in shaving cream and boots tied to the bumper to clatter as they drove away. Lilia climbed in and waved like a movie star. Her brothers and sisters came to kiss her good-bye. The only one who seemed out of place was Emilito, who stood looking back as if waiting for something.

"Bye," said Lilia, holding up her face to kiss her father, who was overseeing the bedlam of the farewell. Emilito pointed to a black Plymouth parked behind the Ferrari.

"We're going in that one, darling. The suitcases are already inside."

The elder Alatristes came to tell the couple good-bye. They kissed their son, and Doña Concha began to cry. Lili hadn't budged.

"Get out, Lilia," said Emilito.

"I want to go in this one," she replied.

"We're going in that one."

"If that's how you feel, we'll each go in our own."

She slid behind the wheel of the Ferrari and started the motor. The boots made a terrible racket and the Ferrari disappeared with a roar through the main gate.

"Now, that's a woman, not a pushover," said Andrés, fueling the anger of Milito, who set off after her in his car. Then Andrés offered me his arm, asked where I'd been, and led me to the dance floor. When we returned to the head table, Doña Concha and her husband were no longer there.

"We'll thank everyone now," Andrés directed, picking up a bottle of champagne and two glasses. We went from table to table to toast our guests. With a special speech for each one, we thanked them for coming and for their gifts. Andrés was a genius at such things.

As Andrés solemnly embraced his compadre, Rodolfo told us he had to be getting back to Mexico City. Martín Cienfuegos was with him, and they would go together. As he toasted the secretary of the treasury Andrés cranked up his cordiality another notch. They despised one another. Each was sure the other was his greatest rival on the road to the presidency—recently, Andrés was more convinced of that than Cienfuegos. We walked with them to the gate.

"That ass-kisser Martín is winning over the Fat Man. It doesn't take much—that house he gave him alone is enough to buy the presidency, and Fito's ass," said Andrés, after we had made the rounds of the tables. He said it with anger but, for the first time, also with sadness.

At Bibi's table, Gómez Soto was dead drunk, muttering nasty remarks. Quijano got up as he saw us.

"Has your daughter gone?" he asked.

"Yes, she left."

"D'ya see how well these two dance?" Gómez said to my general, pointing to Quijano and me. "You 'n me, we're too ol' t'dance like that."

"You may be too old," said Andrés. "I can still hold my own. Right, Catín?"

I attempted an elegant smile.

"Right, Catalina?" he repeated.

"Of course," I answered, gulping champagne as if it were water.

"Will you be in Mexico City?" asked Quijano, as he kissed my hand.

"Sometime soon," I replied, as Andrés argued with Gómez Soto over who was younger and who had more children.

Bibi gave me a shrug that said, "You play the hand you're dealt," and I decided to hurry along the *pozole* before everyone was as drunk as Gómez Soto.

The *pozole* was accompanied by fireworks and a new orchestra. It was nearly five A.M. when Natalia Velasco and María Bautista, who had snubbed me in cooking class, came half dragging their husbands to thank me for inviting them.

I told them good-bye with a smile and the queenly airs I had mastered after years of being on the receiving end. The best revenge at moments like this.

I went inside to see if the *chilaquiles,* dried beef, coffee, and bread were ready. There were forty women in the kitchen, making tortillas and helping with the cooking. I went over to check the sauce for the *chilaquiles.*

"I don't want it too spicy," I said, not stopping to look at the woman tending the pot.

"It's a little spicy," she answered. "You don't remember me, do you, señora?"

Now I looked. I said yes, hoping to convey that I'd seen her before, but she must have known that I didn't know when or where.

"I'm the widow of Fidel Velázquez, the one they killed in Atencingo. Do you remember the day you took me to your house? That's where I met Doña Lucina and she asked me to come today. I see her often, and she tells me about you."

"And your children, how are they?" I asked, to show I remembered something at least.

"Big. Before long there'll only be three. I work in the factory here in Atlixco. And anything extra I can find. I came here today; next week I'll be cooking figs to sell in Puebla."

"I'll buy them. Come to the house and bring what you have," I said, tasting the *jitomate* and asking Lucina to bring me tea and aspirin because I had a headache.

I went to the sala to drink my tea. People were beginning to come inside to escape the cold. I asked the servants to bring cognac for them. I took a glass myself, and drank it in rapid swallows. Then I fell asleep in a big chair, until someone came to tell me the guests wanted breakfast.

"Shall we have a siesta?" asked Andrés after he dunked a final croissant in his coffee.

"Let's do," I said. And I went to sleep beside him for the first time since Carlos's death.

I WANTED TO dispel the ghosts of my memories, but without Lili's lively company it was more difficult than ever. I went from Puebla to Tonanzintla, from Carlos's grave to the garden of my house, with nothing better to do than bite my fingernails, be grateful for my friends' compassion, and spend afternoons with Verania and Checo after they got home from school.

With the children, it was all giving and pretending to be happy. I took them to the fair, to climb a hill, or to look for salamanders in ponds near Mayorazgo, anything to rid my mind of everything but games or easily resolved problems. Sometimes I thought I was having fun, and put all my energy into being tender and high-spirited, but my children had learned not to need me, and after a period of being together, it was hard to tell who was being patient with whom.

When I sat on the ground in the garden, chewing on blades of grass, my head buried between my knees, they felt bad about coming up to me; they would leave me alone and go off to look for an excuse to call me.

The woman from Atencingo gave them one. One afternoon they came running to tell me that there was a lady selling figs, and that I had told her I would buy them all.

They brought her, with her basket, to my corner of the garden. It was about five o'clock one bright afternoon, and standing there in the light, with her basket on her arm, a toothy smile on her freshly scrubbed face, she radiated assurance and charm.

She sat down beside me, set her basket on the ground, and began chatting as if we were old friends and I'd been waiting for her to come. Not once did she apologize for interrupting, ask if it was a convenient time, or stop talking long enough to see if I wanted to listen.

Her name was Carmela, in case I didn't remember. Her children were such and such an age, and her husband, as she had told me, was the one murdered at the mill in Atencingo. She had saved enough money to put a marble cross on his grave and she visited him to tell him how things were at work or in the fields. I didn't know it, but she and Fidel had always fought for justice, and that was why they had helped Lola, that was why she joined the union at the factory in Atlixco. Her hatred was renewed when they killed Medina and Carlos, and she couldn't understand why I was still living with General Ascencio. Because she knew, because surely I knew, because everyone knew, who my general was. Not that I'd asked, not that I'd thought about it, but she had brought me these black *limón* leaves for my headache . . . and other ills. Tea from those leaves gave you energy, but you came to depend on them and you had to be careful because taking them every day made you feel better for the moment but would kill you over time. She knew a señora in her village who died after drinking the tea only a month, although the doctors had never believed that was the reason. Her heart just stopped, they said, and didn't know why, but she was sure it was the leaves, because that's how they were, good, but risky. She had brought them to me because she heard me say at the wedding I had a headache, and because I might have other uses for them. She would leave the figs to see if I liked them, and now she had to go because it was late and she might miss the bus home.

I listened without answering, sometimes nodding, crying when she spoke of Carlos as if she'd known him, eating fig after fig while she recounted the virtues of her leaves. She didn't seem to expect a reply. She said what she had to say, got up, and left.

Lucina was entertaining the children. I could hear them yelling above Carmela's words, but they stayed out of sight until she left. Then they came running to eat figs and ask questions. I answered every one, the words tumbling out, possessed of a sudden, strange euphoria. Afterward, we rolled in the grass and ended the day by jumping on the beds and having a pillow fight. I didn't recognize myself.

Andrés's other daughters listened to our shenanigans in amazement. The two still living in the Puebla house were virtual strangers. Marta was twenty and had a boyfriend for whom she was embroidering sheets and towels, tablecloths and napkins. They would marry as soon as he finished school and could support her without asking Andrés for so much as his blessing. They spent evenings in the study. He was planning to be an engineer, but for the moment she was the one drawing plans in India ink. Marta and I never fought, but neither did we have much to do with each other. When she came to live with us, she was too old to need me to comb her ponytail, and she had always known how to live without making a fuss or letting anyone make a fuss over her. To this day I never see her. She moved to the ranch she inherited near Orizaba. Her husband gave up engineering for agriculture and they rarely leave home.

I also had little in common with Adriana, Lilia's twin. She never got along with her sister, whom she thought offensively frivolous, and even less with me. She joined the Catholic Union behind her father's back. The only act of defiance I ever witnessed was the night she announced her defection at dinner like someone reporting she'd been working in a brothel while everyone thought she was at mass. Her militancy had little effect on anyone. Andrés even thought it might be helpful to have a connection with the church, should he need it. We let her attend mass and dress like a nun without a word of criticism.

Marta and Adriana weren't any company, and as I wasn't company for Checo and Verania, I went back to Mexico City.

Andrés was living in the Las Lomas house, at least officially, along with Octavio and his sweet Marcela. My arrival didn't disturb them. In their eyes, I was the matron of honor for the wedding they would never have.

I looked up Bibi. Two years earlier, Gómez Soto's wife had had the decency to die and allow Bibi to move from clandestine lover to honored wife. The day of the wedding, the general had put all his houses in her name and written a will making her his sole heir.

Everything was smooth as silk in that new union. The newlyweds went to New York and then on to Venice, so that finally Bibi sunbathed outside her garden. They traveled across the country in a train the general had bought for the convenience of visiting his newspapers. At last Bibi could show off the international élan she had cultivated for so long within her four walls.

One early morning she came to my house. I was in the garden, in my robe, my face bare of makeup. A woman had come to give me a pedicure, and my feet were soaking in a basin.

Bibi burst in dressed almost like a man, in low-heeled shoes and slacks and a checked shirt. She looked pretty but strange. I don't remember if she said hello; I think her first words were a question.

"Catalina, how did you manage to love one man and live in another man's house?"

"I don't remember."

"Come on, it wasn't twenty years ago," she said.

"It seems longer than that. What is it? You seem different?"

"I'm in love," she said. "I'm in love, I'm in love." She repeated it in different tones, as if saying it to herself. "I'm in love and I can't bear that disgusting old man I'm living with. Disgusting, horny, boring, and filthy. Can you imagine, he conducts business in the bathroom. He brings people into that little toilet on the train and makes them state their business. So now what do I do? Kill him? I'll kill him, Cati, because I'm not sleeping with him one more night."

She was transformed. She had taken off her shoes and was sitting in the grass with the soles of her feet together, clapping her knees every three words.

"So who are you in love with?"

"A bullfighter from Colombia. He'll be here tomorrow. He's coming to see me, and doing a few fights while he's here. We met in Madrid one afternoon when Odilón was talking with one of General Franco's ministers. I was waiting in a café, and he came up: 'May I sit here,' you know. We made love twice."

"Two times and you're in love?"

"He has a divine body. Like a teenager."

"How old is he?"

"Twenty-five."

"You're ten years older than he is."

"Seven."

"Same difference."

"Cati, if you're going to act like my mother, I'm leaving."

"Sorry. Does he have a nice ass?"

"A nice everything."

"That's enough. You want to trade your general for a 'nice' prick? Does he have enough money to fill your swimming pool with flowers?"

"Of course he doesn't, but I'm fed up with swimming pools. He's going to be a famous bullfighter. He's sensational."

"At twenty-five, if he were going to be famous, he'd already be there."

"He got a late start because of his parents. He had to study law before his first fights, and, of course, leave Colombia. I think Colombia must be something like Puebla."

"Does he know who your husband is?"

"He knows he owns newspapers."

"Now what?" I asked. "What are you going to do about Odilón?"

"I don't know. I didn't know what I could do to kiss him off without ending up in the street, but yesterday Odi went to one of those orgies where you get measured. You know, they bring in whores and the men strip to see who has the biggest cock. The masseuse told me that one of her clients told her. I went disguised as a whore and saw him there, making a fool of himself. Well, what else would he do? They were all old goats like him. Of course they wouldn't measure up to teenagers, but it was pitiful."

"How did you get in?"

"The owner took me, she's a client of Raquel's, too."

"Bibi. I'm beginning to see the old you. I thought you'd turned into a babbling fool."

"What should I do? Can you think of something?"

"Act offended. Hurt to the point of tears."

"I'm not you. I can't pull that off."

"Write him a letter breaking it off for reasons he is well aware of and which are an affront to your honor."

"Will you write it for me?"

"If you'll wait till Trini finishes amputating my feet. She's a savage. She finds a little hangnail on your big toe, and before you know it she's going at your shinbone with her scissors."

"Be careful, señora, or I won't tell you the latest gossip about Doña Chofi," said Trini, who also did Chofi and had her confidence.

"It better be good. My poor friend Chofi is deadly dull. We've been trying to get a good story out of her for fifteen years, but can't get anything but her quarrels with the chauffeur and the cook."

"Lately there've been a few about Don Rodolfo," said Trini.

"Those are the most boring of all. They fight because Chofi doesn't hang the paintings where Fito tells her to, or because he leaves the gold coins he's been given lying around the house. Stupid things ike that."

"Wrong. I was about to tell you that the gold coin turned up. The chauffeur had it, and when they asked him about it, he said the señora had given it to him in exchange for a special favor, but as he was a man of his word, he couldn't say what the favor was."

"No, Trinita. I don't believe you."

"It's the truth. Don Rodolfo was furious. He threatened to get out his pistol."

"But he didn't."

"He was about to, but the chauffeur said he would confess."

"What about that Chofi! An old cow with a roving eye."

"You should have seen her. All her brassiness came out. She put her hands on her hips, walked over to Don Rodolfo, took away the gun, and said, 'If someone has to tell you, it will be me. René did me the favor of taking Zodiac to the poodle parlor to be shampooed and trimmed, something you object to because you say only little pansy pooches have that done.' "

"Now there's a true drama," I said. "Not like your situation, Bibi. Big deal, falling in love with a bullfighter. Come on, I'll help you write your letter."

"Just a draft," said Bibi, "because I want to give it to him on the paper I bought in Switzerland, and I only have one sheet and one envelope left."

"What difference does it make what paper it's on?"

"I know my husband. When what I say doesn't suit him, he returns the letter sealed in an envelope like the one I sent him, as if he hadn't opened it. 'Scribbles, Bibi, scribbles,' he says to me. 'That's all I see all day. Anything you want to say to me, say it in person, I'm at your service. Just ask, my love,' and makes like he hasn't read it. That's why I want this envelope, since I only have the one and there aren't any in all of Mexico. If he opens it—and he will—he'll have to admit it."

"What shall we say, then?" I asked.

"Well, all about the orgy I saw."

"Tell me exactly what it was like. And how did you get in?"

"Raquel helped me. When I got back from Spain, I'd gained a lot of weight and the first thing I did was call her, and as soon as she came, she wanted to know everything, so I told her about Tirsillo and how I wanted to get away from Odi and all that. Then it turned out that Raquel gives massages to a woman who runs one of those 'measuring' parlors and she had told Raquel that my husband booked it for the bachelor party of one of Governor Benítez's brothers. You know about that, don't you?"

"Of course. Did you see him in the buff, too?"

"I saw everything they had, all of them. Brusca was a doll. She dressed me up as a whore who'd been badly burned. She says they always want some expensive novelty. She bandaged me all over, from my legs to my face, and sat me right in the middle like a mummy. I had to sit there the whole time. I could hardly breathe."

"You're making it up."

"I swear it. They all arrived together. It was a man's party. There were women, but they didn't pay much attention to them. They were just there, alongside the bottles and the glasses. I was the one they were most interested in. 'Poor little whore, what will you do now?' they'd ask. I didn't open my mouth, just lowered my eyes. Odilón didn't focus on me much. He was mad I was in the middle of everything."

" 'Take that pitiful creature out of here, she puts a damper on things.' He said that at the same time he was madly grabbing one girl's ass. 'Let's see the groom. Let's see that tool of his,' he ordered. 'Make him show you,' he said, pulling a blonde over to the guest of honor. 'What do you think, my girl, is he scared?'

" 'Show me, good-looking,' she said.

"And right there, the guy took off his pants. They all cheered. 'Let's see more, get it up, get it up,' they yelled.

"And the blonde, just as naturally as if she were polishing a candlestick, started working on his prick.

" 'All *right*! Now, there's a stud for you,' said Victoriano Valázquez. He's the bride's brother.

" 'Fan-tas-dick, fan-tas-dick,' they chanted. Like kids at recess time."

"And you say they *all* stripped?"

"Every last one. Even my poor husband, pathetic as he is."

"And you were watching? What a thrill!"

"Hardly. Too many cocks. You can get excited over one, but not a roomful. They were ridiculous. They were all playing with themselves. They stood hip to hip to see whose thing was the longest. Really stupid, the whole bit. I didn't see how it all ended, because Odilón insisted I cast a pall over everything and made Brusca take me out."

"Took you out? But what else did you see? Did they fuck the girls in front of each other?"

"Not while I was there. They just have them there to liven things up. It's really a boys' party. They just want to see each other's cock. They have the girls there so no one will say they're queers. That's how Brusca explained it. Now, write the letter."

"All right. What is it you want from Gómez?"

"The house, the servants, the chauffeurs, and money. Lots of money," she said, and began to dance around, singing, "The moment I saw him, I said to myself: He's my man."

"Then don't elaborate. I think you should be brief, precise, and to the point. 'Odilón: I was the whore with the burns the other day. I want a divorce and a lot of money. Bibi.' "

"No. I want him to feel bad and think I'm hurt. But I'm so happy I can't drag myself around looking pitiful. That's why I came to you; you're an expert in high drama, so don't tell me all you can do is write something I could write myself."

"That's the best way. Let's be practical for once, Bibi. Why waste words?"

"You've become practical?"

"It was about time."

"Don't start in with how you want Carlos back, because that can't happen, Catín. Accept it."

"I do accept it," I said, turning somber.

"Please, don't start sobbing. This is urgent."

We spent the morning wadding up drafts. *Odi: my heart is crushed. Odi: what I saw has so upset me that I no longer know if what I feel is hatred or pity. Odi: how can you seek happiness elsewhere and wound me with behavior so unworthy of you?* Et cetera, et cetera.

Finally, at two in the afternoon, we pulled off a sober, injured letter. Bibi copied it and went away delighted.

I didn't see her for three days. On the fourth she came to the house, once again Señora Gómez Soto. She was wearing a hat with the veil over her face, a tailored gray suit, dark stockings, and high heels.

We went to the sala to talk; it seemed appropriate for her attire. She turned up the veil, crossed her legs, lit a cigarette, and said, very solemmly, "This face you see was very nearly the face of a damned fool."

I laughed. She laughed, too, and began her story.

Her bullfighter arrived the same afternoon she sent the letter to her husband. She went to pick him up at the airport and installed him in the Hotel Del Prado. She wasn't overly pleased that he had a woman with him, a gypsy type he said was his agent, but she was so wild to be laid that she booked a room for each of them and pushed the matador into one of them.

Later, she was so delirious and grateful that she started gushing about the future, describing the steps she had taken to get a quick divorce. The bullfighter couldn't believe it. The woman of the world looking for an occasional lover, happy to reward his courtesies with brief notices scattered throughout the sports sections of her husband's newspapers, had turned into a lovesick adolescent asking for matrimony and martyrdom.

Quarrel with the general? How could Bibi be so naive as to believe that he could fight in the bullrings of Mexico without the support of her husband's chain of newspapers? Besides, she might want a divorce, but he didn't. His agent was his wife.

With all the dignity she could muster, Bibi dressed and fled the hotel. Despite her haste, she took time at the front desk to remove her signature guaranteeing the matador's expenses.

As soon as she walked in the door, she desperately called for the maid she had asked to deliver the letter to her husband's room. Unfortunately, the woman was so efficient that she'd gone to the extreme of putting the letter into the general's hands.

Bibi locked herself in her bedroom to berate herself for the fit of irresponsibility and lust that had led to this moment. She hated me for not stopping her and for being an accomplice to her suicide. She didn't know what to do. She couldn't even cry. Her tragedy didn't lend itself to anything as glamorous and comforting as tears.

The next morning she went downstairs at the hour her husband usually ate breakfast.

She found a congenial general swilling orange juice between huge mouthfuls of scrambled eggs and sausage. When he saw her, he rose to his feet, held her chair, suggested that she order the same breakfast and for once forget about diets and her poached egg. She agreed to sausage for breakfast . . . she would have agreed to anything. She didn't know whether to be grateful the general was playing innocent or tremble when she imagined what he might be plotting behind the pleasant demeanor.

She opted for gratitude. Never had she been sweeter or prettier, never more suggestive. Breakfast ended with the cancellation of a very important meeting at the general's office and their repairing to bed.

That night they attended a dinner at the United States embassy, and when they returned Bibi found the unopened envelope on her dressing table. Had her husband not seen it? Where had he found an envelope when there weren't any in the country? She fell asleep with her questions unanswered, clutching the unopened Swiss envelope with her initials imprinted on the blue seal.

She awakened in time to set up a romantic breakfast in the garden beside the pool. When the general came down, she was wearing a white organdy apron and the smile—half-wifely, half-angelic—that had served her so well in life and which she never hoped to lose. She personally cooked and served breakfast. Later, as modestly as if removing her clothes, she untied her apron and sat beside her satisfied general.

Their last cup of coffee coincided with the arrival of the small, nervous assistant who always trailed after her husband reminding him of appointments and taking notes. Bibi poured him coffee while Gómez Soto visited the bathroom before leaving the house. Bibi and the assistant were friends, often joking about the general's obsessions.

"You've got bags under your eyes," Bibi said.

"I haven't recovered from my whirlwind trip. I went to Switzerland and back in thirty hours. Just to buy some envelopes, can you believe it?"

"A good lesson not to mess with your meal ticket," I said when Bibi finished her account.

"It was delicious, even so," she answered. "If you're in the mood to play, Alonso Quijano is previewing his film on Tuesday. He asked me to invite you."

I called Palmita, who had always seemed like a sensible woman, and ended up going with her. The movie was terrible. But I still found Quijano attractive. So much so that first I went to the cocktail party and then to his house and from there to his bed without a thought for Andrés. Until near dawn, when I awoke, half-afraid. I dashed off a note, *Thanks for the warm welcome,* and left.

I got home as the sun was peering through the trees in the garden. Just as it had the morning I watched it come up with Carlos.

It seemed so long ago, yet I remembered it as if time hadn't passed. Afraid of Andrés? Afraid of what?

I barged into our room, wanting him to notice. But he hadn't come home either.

WITHOUT BEING AWARE of it, I changed.

I asked Andrés for a Ferrari like Lilia's. He gave it to me. I wanted him to deposit money in a personal checking account, enough to cover my expenses, the children's, and the house. I had a door cut into the wall between our bedroom and the adjoining room and moved into it, claiming I needed more space. Sometimes I slept with the door closed. Andrés never asked me to open it. When it was open, he came to my bed. In time, we seemed like friends again.

I observed him as if he were a stranger. I studied his way of talking, the deals he made, how he went about them. He no longer seemed unpredictable and arbitrary. I nearly always knew what he would decide about certain matters, whom he would send to which meeting, how he would answer the secretary of such and such, what he would say in any given speech.

I slept with Quijano often. He moved to a house with two entrances, two façades, two streetside gardens. One entrance on one street and the other on the street behind it. He came in one way and I the other. We would meet in the middle, a room filled with sunshine and plants. Quijano was a very solemn man. He tried to analyze what he called "our relationship" in long commentaries that sounded like drafts of screenplays of upcoming films. He talked about my freshness, my spontaneity, my charm. I would drift off to sleep listening and feel relaxed for hours after.

Andrés bought a house in Acapulco but never went because he thought the beach was a waste of time. I appropriated it. Quijano and I often spent weekends there. I invited other friends as a cover and took the children. Lilia came when she wanted to get away from Emilito, and of course Marcela and Octavio were there. My affair with Quijano was more or less obvious to everyone, even Verania, who never said anything to her father but instead kicked Alonso's shins and told on me to Checo every time she could.

The house was between Caleta and Caletilla, surrounded by the sea, and the late afternoons were a dream. I could have done nothing but sit on the terrace, gazing toward infinity like an old woman lost in her memories. To me the sea had meant Carlos Vives ever since we'd stolen three days on a deserted beach in Cozumel. I watched it, trying to recover something. What would I choose? We had so much. Why not death? I asked myself, since even the days we spent by the ocean evoked those thoughts.

"I'm going to die of love," I said one afternoon, laughing as we walked barefoot in the warm water.

In my imagination, I was always the one who died; it even seemed romantic to think of Carlos mourning my loss, inventing my virtues, feeling an emptiness inside, looking for me in things we'd shared.

I often imagined Carlos crying after I was gone, mad with grief, killing Andrés. Never dead.

I spent hours in Acapulco staring at the sea, with Alonso's hand on my leg, remembering Vives.

"No one dies of love, Catalina, not even if we'd like to," he had told me.

I would have stayed there, but in order to keep the house I had to earn the privilege in Mexico City and listen to Andrés rail against his compadre Rodolfo, hear how his plans to be president were thwarted every time he turned around, listen to the hero-of-the-nation speeches he was called on to make in Puebla.

And then there was Fito, with his frequent calls for my presence at strange gatherings. One day I had to go with him to lay the first stone at what was to be the Monument to Mothers. He made a long speech about the enormous joys of motherhood and things like that. Then he invited me to Los Pinos for lunch.

Chofi, who had pleaded a headache and escaped the sun and crowds at the dedication, asked me how I had liked Fito's speech. Instead of answering that it was beautifully done and shutting my mouth, I launched into a disastrous diatribe about the annoyances, the hassles, the horrendous responsibilities of motherhood. I was a real harpy. So, Chofi said, my love for Andrés's children was all show, and how could I say I loved them if I wasn't even proud of being the mother of the ones I'd given birth to? I didn't apologize or say anything in my own defense. I didn't care if they thought I was a bitch. I had sometimes despised being the mother of my own and other women's children, and it was within my rights to say so.

I left right after coffee, and for quite a while had no word or invitation from them. Chofi did call at the death of Doña Carmen

Romero Rubio, the wife of the former dictator Porfirio Díaz, to ask if I was going to the funeral and to complain that her husband had forbidden her to go. She had always believed that poor Carmelita was a victim. For once, I was on her side.

"You're right," I said. " 'Poor Carmelita' indeed. But where would you and I be if life hadn't come down on her so hard?" Chofi hung up with the conviction that her husband had been absolutely right to forbid her to go to the funeral.

On the other hand, Alonso went. He was strange that way. I never knew what was going on in his head. Carmelita Romero Rubio's funeral, a nightlong celebration of the liberation of Paris, weeks spent with the anthropologists who discovered Toltec sculptures in the center of the city—they were all the same to him. Everything was potential material for a film director.

At that point, Andrés was up to his neck in problems. A journalist had accused his friend the secretary of the treasury of collusion with black marketeers and of profiteering at the expense of a public suffering major shortages. The newspaperman was a friend of Fito's, and my husband was convinced the article was his compadre's idea and was aimed directly at him. I tried to convince him that his theory was a little too byzantine, but he was so sure he wouldn't listen to me.

A few days later, the CTM organized a march of eighty thousand people to protest the shortages, again implicating Andrés's friend. To top it off, privatization had necessitated removal of controls once in the hands of the secretary of the treasury. Andrés was more convinced than ever that Fito planned to betray his friend—among other reasons, because he was Andrés's candidate to replace Fito. This time I didn't say anything, because Fito signed a decree abrogating the secretary's control over the production of cement, reinforcing rods, and who knows what else. Stripped of that authority, my general's candidate chose to withdraw.

Andrés went around for days cursing Fito, the left, and Maldonado, the union leader he had installed to oust Cordera. He was so furious that he didn't want to go to the state of the union address on September 1. That morning I had to beg him to get dressed and urge him to remember that if he had a fight with Rodolfo to keep it private.

We thought we were going to just another of Andrés's compadre's tedious speeches, but to our surprise we had a good time because the deputy who gave the rebuttal pontificated about its being a government leader's God-given responsibility to defend the nation, criticized the way the elections were being held, and, in passing, accused the right of demeaning the Revolution and the left of encouraging immorality and anarchy. It didn't go down well with anyone. After Fito left the Chamber, the deputies savaged the man who delivered the rebuttal and unseated him. Andrés nearly died laughing. He was overjoyed that his compadre was running into difficulties and was sure Fito would call him because he couldn't handle them on his own. That was why Fito had appointed him his adviser, to handle things. But this time, Fito didn't need him.

Following the congratulations in the Palacio, the entire cabinet met for dinner. To his astonishment, Andrés was not seated at his compadre's left. His place card was toward the foot of the table, at the end of a string of ministers. Not at the head, as it had always been. On Fito's right was the aged general who was secretary of defense, and Martín Cienfuegos was ensconced on his left.

Andrés despised Cienfuegos as never before, and as never before bemoaned having helped him when he was nothing but a shyster; and as never before he was infuriated with his mother, who had been so enchanted with Cienfuegos that she treated him like an adopted son.

He couldn't remember at what moment Martín Cienfuegos had ceased to be his ally and subordinate and taken his first independent steps. Perhaps the morning years earlier that Andrés had introduced him to Rodolfo, perhaps not until as governor of Tabasco he was the first to declare his support for General Campos, and from there became his campaign manager. Andrés kept going over all that, pausing only to call Cienfuegos a bastard opportunist.

On Rodolfo's left, more neatly combed and with a wider smile than ever, Cienfuegos was in Andrés's line of vision throughout the meal. He came home bad-mouthing his compadre for being so goddamn stupid that he would end up handing over the presidency to that fucking clown Martín Cienfuegos. Because that's how his compadre was, he got taken in by fancy manners: the less aura of military the better; the more elegance the more dazzled the old idiot was.

Andrés began drinking and ranting, still expecting Fito to call. But Fito didn't call. After a few days, he managed to get the leader of the Chamber to revoke the accords reached on September 1 and reinstated the man who replied to his address.

Andrés couldn't control his urge to see Fito. He returned from Los Pinos vomiting bile, with a screaming headache. Every ray of light was torture. He locked himself in a dark room to tell me over and over how the Fat Man had praised Cienfuegos's role in resolving the conflict. What angered him most of all was that his compadre said he hadn't consulted Andrés because he didn't want to bother him. He couldn't believe it, although every day it was more clear that Fito could set matters straight on his own without having to call on Andrés or even ask his opinion. Rodolfo seemed inclined to make up his own mind about who would succeed him, and it was clear that Andrés was simply in the way.

The headache Andrés brought back from Los Pinos lingered. One day I offered him some of Carmela's tea. He drank it, grumbling about campesino superstitions, but when the pain turned into a desire to go out and confront Rodolfo, he sat staring at the empty cup.

"I'm sure it's a coincidence, but what harm can it do to drink it?" he said.

"None," I said, drinking a cup myself.

The dark green liquid smelled of mint and *epazote*. After I drank mine, I went out to dinner with Alonso and stayed with him till early morning. I laughed a lot and never felt sleepy. Carmela's tea did wonders for me, too, but the next morning I didn't have any. Andrés, though, wanted more—that morning and many after— until the day came that tea was all he wanted for breakfast.

He got up every day cursing his ties to Fito, all the time he had devoted to pleasing that fat-ass, and lay about chewing over the defeats of the previous day and planning some new offensive against Martín Cienfuegos, until I came and sweetened his green tea.

One day, after his tea, he asked his assistant to bring the newspapers because, he said, he had a premonition. He must have had some inkling beforehand, but he feigned surprise when he showed me what was spread over all the front pages. The office of the attorney general of the Republic, under the direction of a man named Rocha, one of Cienfuegos's loyal followers, had dug up the case of the disappearance and death of a Señor Maynes in Puebla. According to the articles, he was acting at the request of Maynes's daughter Magdalena, who asserted that the author of the crime was the then-governor of the state, General Andrés Ascencio.

All the witnesses who years earlier had been content to say their rosaries now sprang up to testify about the car that had kidnapped the gentleman near the theater, about the tone of his voice as he called for help, about all the cases he had won in suits against the governor's interests. Magda told about the morning we had run into them in Cuernavaca, saying she had seen her father arguing with Andrés Ascencio and had asked him about it. Her father had told her about the governor's plans to cheat the owners of the Agua Clara resort out of their property, and had forbidden Maynes to defend them. Magda said that her father not only did not back down, he also refused the thirty percent of the deal the governor had offered him to bury the complaint. That, she concluded, was when he threatened to kill him.

Andrés was getting up from the table, cursing, and I still had my nose in the newspapers, when the assistant came in with a summons from the attorney general's office.

"These guys are even more stupid than fucked up," said Andrés. "You'd think I had nothing on them."

He poured himself another cup of tea and went off to bathe, whistling. He emerged from the shower euphoric and rosy. Naturally, he did not honor the summons but went to look for Fito instead.

Who knows what they discussed. The result was that the next day the newspapers published an interview with the attorney general himself, in which he exonerated Andrés of any charge and referred to him several times as the respected principal adviser to the president of the Republic.

Except for Magdalena, who was never asked any further questions, all the witnesses said they were mistaken in their judgment,

moved into Andrés's room. We had never su~
more than we did that new year with our reco~
and acting like sweethearts.

It was well into January when we returned to Mexico City. I
didn't call Quijano. Andrés's tantrums, his tirades against the Fat
Man, and helping him stomach the imminent candidacy of Cienfuegos were entertainment enough.

At the beginning of February, we went to Puebla, where Andrés's choice for governor was being installed. In Puebla, Andrés's
voice still carried authority, and he took endless pleasure in the
honors and obsequious treatment he was given. There he felt so
comfortable and secure he forgot his role as adviser to the president. Like Andrés, I had no desire to go back to Mexico City,
and the two of us shared an enormous house that was completely
empty after Lucina took the children off to school.

Andrés was growing old. One day a foot hurt and the next a
knee. He drank brandy from noon to night and black *limón* tea all
morning. I would have felt some sympathy for him if the garden
and the room with the fern didn't constantly remind me of Carlos.

Lilia came to visit me every day to tell me the latest gossip and
make me laugh. I sometimes saw women friends in the afternoon.
Mónica was working at such a pace that sometimes all she could
do was give us a kiss and disappear. In contrast, Pepa spent whole
afternoons in her garden, the serenity gained from her rendezvous
in the market evident in her face and words. I also had my sister
Barbara back, who was like a guardian angel—better than an angel
because she didn't judge me, she just laughed and cried and, like
me, slipped from wild laughter to torrential tears at the drop of a
hat. She was with me the afternoon Andrés came home feeling
ill. He'd been in Tehuacán, where he'd gone to be honored. One

and after a few days the guilty parties were revealed to be members
of a gang of hired thugs who unfortunately could not testify because they died in a shoot-out with police who had come to arrest
them.

At any rate, Andrés was hurt and did not see the Fat Man again,
but neither did he have to resign his post. He bought a cigar
factory and set out to make it the biggest and best in the country.
He repeated every hour on the hour that true power is in the
hands of the wealthy, and that he was going to become a banker
to ensure the subservience of every future horse's ass who would
ever sit in the symbolic Chair of the Eagle, the one in which
Zapata, in his wisdom, refused to be photographed.

Andrés's waning influence didn't concern me. I was going
around with Alonso as if we were a couple. We had dinner at
Ciro's almost every night. I went with him to galas and spent hours
with him on the set. One night after a bottle of wine, I even
kissed him in public.

I came home in the early hours and for weeks wouldn't open
our connecting door. Occasionally, like someone visiting her
grandfather, I had morning tea with Andrés.

I spent the entire month of December in Acapulco, with no
remorse. The children were on vacation, their father had always
said that Christmas was an idiot invention, so why should we
spend it together?

I didn't call him until a few days before New Year's to ask,
insincerely, why he didn't come join us. I couldn't have been
more surprised when he showed up on the morning of the thirty-
first. He had lost about twenty pounds and aged ten years, but he
was ramrod straight and still had the ironic smile he had put to
such good use. Verania called to him from the terrace and ran to
kiss him. Marta and Adriana and their boyfriends had come with

him. Lilia and her boring husband, and Octavio and Marcela, were already in the house. The General's entire family.

Alonso, of course, was with me. I also had Mónica and her children, Palma and Julia Guzmán. Bibi was scheduled to arrive that night with Gómez Soto, and Helen Heiss with her children. Octavio and Marcela had invited three couples and Lilia had brought Georgina Letona, her husband's ex-girlfriend, to see if she could marry her off to my brother Marcos. As if she didn't know that Milito was still fucking her . . . or maybe because she did know.

In all, we were more than fifty for dinner. I thought that in all that crowd no one would notice Alonso, and was as sweet with Andrés as I could be. I even apologized for having filled the house with people when he had expected a family reunion. We spent the afternoon on the terrace drinking gin and lemonade while Alonso walked on the beach with a happy Verania and a Checo bent on killing crabs.

Andrés was silent for a long while. Finally he said, "Armillita was gored by a bull in San Luis Potosí, and Briones got his in El Toreo. Where will I get mine?"

His voice was so serious that I nearly felt sorry for him. He said that a fortune-teller had told him that when in a calendar year two matadors fell within the same two-week period, his death would soon follow.

"Well, you're safe, because this year is over," I said, laughing. "As long as you don't die tonight, by the next time two bullfighters are gored within two weeks of each other you'll have buried us all."

"You are still my brightest light," he said in a strange voice.

I didn't know whether he was mocking me or if the gin had gone to his head more quickly than usual. In either case, I felt nervous, and gave him a kiss.

THAT YEAR DID not begin well for Alonso. [A]ndrés's presence in Acapulco became into[ler]able. Only logical. Despite Alonso's perf[ect] body and fashion-model clothes, despite his youthful fa[ce] and pleasant manner, Andrés was more impressive. All [he] had to do was walk into a room or approach a group [in] conversation and all attention would shift to him. He w[as] a hero to his children, a magnet to my female guests, th[e] owner of the house, and, in the bargain, my husband.

One afternoon when I dreamed up an outing to wat[ch] the sunset on Pie de la Cuesta, Quijano didn't want [to] come. When we got back, Lucina told us he had left [on] urgent business. In private, she handed me a brief n[ote] that said, *I'm leaving. I'm sure you understand the reas[ons.] Even so, I love you. Alonso.*

During dinner, Andrés cracked endless jokes abou[t the] "fop" who had done us the favor of leaving the fi[eld] to themselves. His children laughed at all of them, [I at a] few.

The first night I felt guilty about Alonso, the se[cond]

of those homages where he was surrounded by officials publicly acknowledging their debt to him and calling him their benefactor. That day the new governor of the state, the mayor of Puebla, and, of course, the mayor of Tehuacán, had gathered to declare him that city's favorite son.

It was about five when we heard the sound of the cars.

"What a bore, Barbara," I said. "He's back. He'll want me to listen to the account of his triumphs."

He had spent the breakfast hour reminding me how the workers had fought among themselves when he had become governor, how during his administration he had built roads and schools, and put an end to discontent.

"I am going to tell them," he said, giving me a preview, " 'I do not come as your governor, all that is behind me. I come as a son of the state of Puebla, as a citizen, and as a man who knows how to offer his heart.' How does that sound? You're not telling me how it sounds, Catalina, why else do you think I keep you around?"

In the madness of the recent months, Andrés had again named me his private secretary and I went along with it to pass the time. I handed him a draft of something I'd written and pointed to a paragraph at random. He read aloud:

"I shall always be at the service of each and every one of you, in Puebla and elsewhere, as an official and as a simple citizen. I ask that you settle your quarrels, overcome your difficulties, continue to work with enthusiasm, like brothers, like men who went to the Revolution with a well-defined social agenda, a Revolution for which, should it become necessary, I would again go with you into battle, without personal political ambitions—those have been fulfilled—but, yes, with the desire to safeguard the tranquillity and progress of our beloved state."

After he finished, he said, "I've been right about you all along. No one's as clever as you, you'd think you were a man. That's why I forgive your playing around. Yes, I met my fucking match in you. You're the best of my women, and the best of my men, my girl."

Before he left, he asked for his tea and offered me a cup. I drank it slowly, waiting to feel the strange euphoria it produced.

Matilde had not gone back to the kitchen. She had set the tea on the table and watched us drink it. She said to Andrés, "Please forgive me, General, but you're drinking a lot of those leaves, and too many aren't good for you."

"Not good, you say? If it wasn't for this tea, I'd be dead. It's the only thing that keeps me going."

"But it's bad in the long run. I see you fading away."

"Not because of the tea, Matilde. Don't tell me you still believe in those things?" Andrés replied before taking his last sip. "The señora looks great, and she drinks it, too."

THE MAYOR OF Puebla rushed into the room with the fern.

"Señora, I think the General got too excited," he said. "Please come quickly, he isn't feeling well."

I went down to what had been our bedroom. Andrés was on the bed, paler than usual and breathing with difficulty.

"What is it? Didn't it go well? Why didn't you stay for the dinner?" I asked.

"I got tired and didn't want to die away from home. Call Esparza and Téllez."

"Don't carry on so," I said. "Everyone gets tired, you've been just lazing about for months. You should go to Acapulco more often."

"Acapulco. Only you can put up with that place. And you do it to get away, to leave me behind, using the excuse that the sea is good for you. What's good for you is getting away from me."

"Liar."

"Don't play dumb. We both know what the Acapulco house is for."

"How would you know, you almost never want to come."

"I don't have time to go splashing around, and I can't rest there. The sea bothers me, it's never quiet. Like a damned woman. Where I want to go is to Zacatlán. I rest well up in the hills, and the days last so long you have time for everything."

"But there's nothing to do. What use is time there?" I asked.

"You're a rootless bitch and so you always have something bad to say about my part of the country," he said, trying to pull off his boot.

"I'll call Tulio to help you, don't try to do it yourself, you really *are* tired."

"I told you to call Téllez, but you want me to die without getting help."

"We call Téllez every time you sneeze. I'm embarrassed."

"Embarrassed is the last thing you'll ever be. Call him. Now I'm going to do this right for you. I'm going to die. Call Téllez to be a witness so no one can say you poisoned me."

I sat on the edge of the bed and patted his leg. He kept on speaking with a softness I had only seen flashes of. He was odd.

"Well, I fucked up your life, didn't I?" he said. "The others will get what they want. What do you want? I've never been able to figure out what you want. I haven't devoted a whole lot of thought to it, but don't think I'm stupid. I know there are many women inside you and that I've known only a few."

It came to me how he had aged. Through the last weeks I had watched him grow thin, shrink a little, but that afternoon he aged in minutes. Suddenly his jacket seemed much too large. His shoulders were thin and his neck bowed. His beard disappeared inside the hard collar of his military jacket, and the gold braid seemed stiffer than ever.

"Take that thing off," I said. "I'll help you."

I began unfastening the unyielding cloth, struggling with gold buttons too large for the buttonholes. I pulled off one sleeve and walked around behind him to pull off the other. I kissed his neck.

"Do you really want to die?" I asked.

"Want to die? I don't *want* to die, but I am. Can't you see?"

Esparza and Téllez, the best of the local doctors, who treated Andrés for his occasional colds and diarrhea, as well as the more serious maladies he invented every three or four days, made their usual calm entrance, certain they would do what they always did: prescribe aspirin in a new color. They knew the drill. The last month we had called them every time my husband found himself with nothing to do or no one to talk to. He had a need to have people around him, listening and admiring every word he said— when we moved to Mexico City, we'd taken most of his regular listeners with us; in Puebla we always ended up calling Esparza, Téllez, or both, along with Judge Cabañas, so that the group would be large enough for the "illness" to end with a game of poker.

"What are you dying of now, General?" Téllez asked, and with Esparza began the familiar ritual. They listened to his heart, took his pulse, and made him take deep, slow breaths. The only change in the routine came from Andrés. Usually, as they examined him, he ticked off the list of his symptoms, which were many and contradictory. It hurt here and here, and there where the doctor had his hand, it hurt there, too. That afternoon, he hadn't a single complaint.

"Go on and do your thing, you bastards," he said, "I'm going to die on you anyway. I hope you will shed a few tears, if just to remember what you've got out of me. I hope you'll cry, because this woman who calls herself my wife is already celebrating. Just look at her, she's getting ready to run off with anyone who'll have her. And plenty will be willing, because this woman is in her prime, better than when I found her God knows how many years ago. How many was it, Catalina? You were a little girl. You had a nice hard ass and a head to match. That hasn't gone a bit soft on you. The ass, maybe a little, but not the head. The good thing is that Rodolfo's going to be here to watch over her. My compadre Rodolfo, stupid idiot that he is."

"He needs rest," said Téllez. "Did he take some stimulant? Maybe he was affected by all the emotion of the homage. You rest now, General. We're going to give you some pills to help you relax. There's nothing the matter with you but exhaustion, you'll be a new man tomorrow."

"You bet I'll be a new man, a stiff and cold new man. Oh, and rested, of course. Everyone wants me to die. They don't realize what a hole I'll leave; they need men like me. But they'll know once they're in the hands of Fito and that idiot candidate of his. Me tired? Fat Man's the one who's tired, he can't even think straight. Picking Cienfuegos as his candidate!"

"So it is Cienfuegos? Who told you?" I asked.

"Nobody told me, I know. I know many things, and I know my compadre, he'll spread his cheeks to the first one who asks him. And Martín has asked him a thousand ways to Sunday, not the least of all by deceiving him. He's got him thinking he's intelligent."

Cienfuegos was Andrés's worst enemy because there was no way Andrés could touch him. Not because he had once been

don't you listen to Dr. Téllez? Take the pills and play some poker before you go to bed."

"I'm already in bed, and not to my liking. All I see is the ceiling, not someone on me."

"We're going now," said Esparza.

"None too soon, you bastards," Andrés replied.

"You rest, General. No coffee, no cognac, no stimulants. I'll be here early tomorrow to see how it went."

They left me alone with Andrés. I sat beside him.

"Want more tea?" I asked, pouring it for him.

He sat up to drink it and again asked, "What do you want, Catalina? Are you going to have a fling with Cienfuegos? And who's Efraín Huerta? And how does he know that one of your breasts weeps tears of tenderness?"

"Where did you find his poems?" I asked.

"Locks are no use in my house."

"What is?"

"He was one of Vives's friends, wasn't he? He doesn't know you very well, though. Your breasts can't weep. Nothing on you weeps. You couldn't weep if your life depended on it. And tenderness, Catalina? What an innocent. It's not for nothing he's in the Communist party."

I walked to the window. "Go on, die," I muttered, while he talked himself to sleep. Then I went and lay down beside him.

He woke up after a while, put his hand on my leg, and patted and stroked me. I opened my eyes, winked at him, wrinkled my nose.

"Why don't you get up and call Cabañas for me?" he said. "My leg hurts."

"You mean Téllez, don't you?"

"Cabañas, Catalina. I don't have time to waste."

By the time Cabañas came, both of Andrés's legs were swollen, and he was speaking with difficulty.

He struggled to ask, "Did you bring number two, Cabañas?"

"Yes, General, I brought them all."

"Give me two."

"What's 'two'?" I asked.

He didn't answer. He picked up his ever-present fountain pen with the green ink to sign.

A moment later, he died.

I CALLED HIS children. Someone notified Rodolfo, who was there by eleven. He came in with his belly, his ponderousness, and his custom of wanting to run things.

"We'll take him to Zacatlán."

"Whatever you want," I said.

"That was what he told me."

"I believe you, Señor Presidente, we'll take him to Zacatlán."

"Thank you for your cooperation. I know about the will."

"There's nothing to thank me for. I expect things to be done correctly."

"If you have problems, count on me."

"I hope I can count on you so I won't have problems."

"I don't understand. He was like a brother to me, you're his wife. What do you want me to do?"

"I want you to stay out of it, not help me, and don't make any deals with his other widows. They'll all get their part, but they will have to come to me to get it."

"What other widows?"

"Fito, my friend, this isn't your wife you're talking to. I know very well who his other widows are, and how many children there are besides the ones who've lived with us. I know which haciendas are for which women, which houses for others. I know what businesses, what money, even what watch and cuff links go to each person."

He said nothing more, nodded, and went to stand beside the gray coffin. He attempted a sorrowful face, but his usual look of boredom won out.

My house filled with people. They pushed their way toward Rodolfo. The men embraced him, clapping him on the back; the women pressed his hand.

I was standing at the opposite end of the coffin. I didn't want to sit down. I stood there the entire night, shaking hands and receiving embraces. I didn't cry. I never stopped talking. With every person who came through, I talked about Andrés, I recalled where they had met and the last time we'd seen them.

About two, Fito went to get some sleep. Lucina brought me tea. I sat down for a few minutes. Checo was in the chair beside me. He seemed so young.

"How are you, Mama?" he asked.

"Fine, my darling. And you?"

"I'm fine, too," and that was all we said.

Verania had gone to bed earlier. The doctor had to look after Marta because she was feeling dizzy.

"I see that your sweetheart hasn't come to offer his condolences," Adriana said at one point.

"Don't talk like that," I ordered.

"Don't try to teach me manners now," she replied. "It's a little late. Besides, everyone knows about Alonso. I'm sure half the people here came just to see him walk in wearing his 'I was a friend of the deceased' face."

She was right. And hateful. How solid that girl's hatred was. Lilia, Marcela, and Octavio stayed with me until dawn.

The line of the aggrieved and the grieving stretched through the night. I never moved from my place as widow.

"I admire your fortitude, señora," said Bermúdez, a man who when Andrés was governor had acted as his master of ceremonies in political proceedings.

"I congratulate you, Doña Catalina," said the mayor's wife.

Everyone was there. I think I enjoyed that night.

I was the center of attention and I liked it. The first thing everyone did was look toward me the minute they came in. Almost everyone had a hug for me or some kind words, but best of all was what Josefita Rojas told me. She marched in with the quick steps and proud bearing we knew so well from seeing her hurry about town as if she wanted to wear out the streets. She never got into a car. She lived on Loreto hill, and from her house walked to the city center, to Santiago church, wherever she was invited, clocking off the steps that kept her alive. Josefita gave me a strong hug, then put her hands on my shoulders and looked into my eyes.

"Well," she said. "I'm happy for you. Being a widow is the ideal state for a woman. She places the deceased on an altar, honors his memory every time she must, and devotes herself to doing all the things she couldn't do with him around. I tell you this from experience, there's no better state than widowhood. And at your age! As long as you don't make the mistake of tying yourself down to another man right off the bat, your life is going to change for the better. I don't want people to hear me say it, but it's the truth, and may your poor dead husband forgive me."

About six in the morning, I thought it time to go change my clothes and freshen up. At that hour there was almost no one left in the room. I stepped closer to the open casket and stared at the dead face of Andrés. I tried to find some trace of sweetness in those features, some wink of complicity, but saw only the stiff expression of his anger, the look I had known when he had something on his mind and went for days without speaking, too deep in his thoughts even to say good night.

Good-bye, Andrés, I told him. They're coming to take you to Zacatlán. You wanted to be put to rest there, and Fito is determined to please you. Now, of course, it's anything you want, just ask. He can't do enough for you. How ugly you look. I'm shocked by your face. Your face has always shocked me. Go show it to someone else, I already have enough trouble without having to remember that reproachful look. You don't want me to kill myself out of grief, do you? You heard what Josefita said, I'm going to be better off without you. I don't want to go to your funeral. I know they'll put me in the same car with Rodolfo and I'll have to endure his company all the way to Zacatlán. And you there in your coffin, removed from all the aggravation while I'm stuck with him. Is that how it's going to be? Will I never be rid of him? He'd be better off not coming on so strong. It worked for you because you were fun and caught me when I was young. How you made me laugh and how you frightened me! I'll never forget your face the day I made the scene about your killing Lola. What did it matter to me, you wanted to know. So, you've left everything for me to divide. What you really want is to screw everything up, as always. You want me to get a taste of how hard it'll be? Whose is whose, according to your wishes? You want me to

chat with Juan and have him sing to me. The first thing Rodolfo did was try to roll it up. It was stiff from lack of use, but his secretary pushed until the handle turned and the glass began to close. I felt embarrassed for Juan, he wasn't used to such rudeness. Checo noticed. Juan was his friend, and for long periods had been his father and mother. He said he wanted to ride up front so he could see. He didn't ask: in three seconds, he opened the door, got out and jumped in beside Juan. From there he turned to give me a look. Wretched boy, leaving me with Rodolfo and his secretary.

"Tell Regino to pull out and let us take his place. You go with him," Fito ordered, and then it was just the two of us. I put my head in my hands and bent forward, sighing. I really loathed El Señor Presidente.

The cars began to move forward, slowly, as if we were going no farther than the French cemetery in Puebla.

"At this rate, it will take us two days," I told Rodolfo when at last we were out of the city. He turned to look behind us. The end of the line of cars following us was out of sight.

"You're right," he replied, and lowered the window glass to order Juan to call out to the chauffeur of the hearse that was carrying Andrés to his last homage. Andrés would have been pleased at the number of people. The driver of the hearse led the cortege at a less funereal pace.

"Is that better?" Fito asked, patting my gloved hand.

We drove through towns gray with dust. All the towns along the highway before the road started up into the mountain are like that. Towns where it is nearly impossible to grow anything green. Nothing but dirt and dirt-covered campesinos. In some, the governor had organized contingents of party faithful to stand with flowers at the side of the road. When we came to such a group, we would stop while the more important members came to the car and shook hands. The others would place the flowers on the hearse and then step back, sombreros in hand.

I was incredibly sleepy. As much as I tried not to nod off, I couldn't keep my eyes open.

"Make yourself comfortable and take a little nap," said Fito.

At the mere suggestion, I was wide awake. Just the thought that he might see me when I was not in command of myself, even drooling as I slept. I couldn't conceive of such humiliation. It was easier to chat. About him, about Andrés, the children, the country, the war.

We had never had so long to talk. He wasn't as stupid as I'd believed. Or as boring. Or maybe he only seemed less boring because we got past talking about who would succeed him and about what he thought of each of the candidates. I had extracted from him that Cienfuegos was his choice. He talked about him until about five o'clock, when we reached Zacatlán.

The streets were filled. EVERYONE WHO LOOKS AT ME IS ALL EYES said a painted sign on a truck that passed us on the highway. That's how I felt. Assholes, Andrés would have said, all of them looking out their assholes to stare at me and criticize.

We went by the main plaza to pick up Doña Herminia. Fito embraced her.

There in the street, clinging to Rodolfo, she seemed older and frailer, but as soon as she was in the car, she was as strong and indifferent as ever. Not a tear, not a word. Ninety-four years old.

There were at least twenty speeches at the cemetery. I thought we would never be through. Verania and Sergio stood beside me the whole time. As if we were actors playing a family united in grief. Verania even let me put my arm around her, and Checo held my hand like a sweetheart.

When the gravediggers were ready to shovel the dirt over their father, I told the children to take a fistful and throw it in first.

I bent down at the same time they did and took a handful of earth and threw it upon the coffin in the depths of the dark hole. The other children did the same. I tried to remember Andrés's face. I couldn't. I wanted to feel sorry that I would never see him again. I couldn't. I felt free. I felt afraid.

I wanted to sit down there in the dirt. I wanted to be free of all the eyes staring at me. I wanted not to care if I broke down and cried like Lilia, whose face was streaked and who was sobbing loudly, like Marcela, leaning against Octavio, like Verania, hiccuping from her sense of surprise and abandonment.

I thought about Carlos, about how I wouldn't allow myself to cry at his funeral. Him I could remember, perfectly—the smile and the hands ripped from me so suddenly.

Then, as was fitting for a widow, I cried more than my children.

Checo did not let go of my hand, Verania patted me, it began to rain. That was Zacatlán for you, always raining. But I didn't care if it rained, this was my last visit here. I thought that, still weeping, and thinking it, I stopped. There were so many things I wouldn't have to do now. I was alone, with no one to give me orders. So many opportunities, I thought, and there beneath the rain I burst out laughing. Sitting on the ground, playing with the wet earth that ringed Andrés's grave. Enjoying my future. Almost happy.